First edition 2023

Copyright © 2023 Fleur Blüm
ISBN 978-0-6483654-6-4

Editor: Annie Seaton
Cover Design: Get Covers

Published by Fleur Blüm, Melbourne, Australia

I0586087

Fleur Blüm is a Melbourne-based writer, performer and musician.

Her blog can be found at https://fleurblum.com/blog

Novels also by Fleur Blüm:

Sophie's Path: A choose your own romance adventure

Discovering the Franklins

My Mother's Secret

Singular Focus

The Sins of the Father: a Barrett Women novel

The Mother's Fault: a Barrett Women novel

Poetry Collections:

My Body. No Apology

Consider the Watchmaker

Smells Like Teen Angst

Singular Purpose

By Fleur Blüm

This book is for all the women who have told me to believe in my own power. You know who you are.

Reader discretion is advised; this novel contains content that may be distressing for some readers, including coercive control, supernatural themes, and supernatural violence.

Chapter 1

Freya woke and turned to look at the love of her life, who lay gently snoring next to her, early morning falling on his salt and pepper hair. The late spring morning was neither too hot nor too chilly, and she felt out of sorts. Her belly was tight and fluttery, as though she had forgotten to do something very important.

Turning to the clock on her bedside table, the time was just before seven. Unusual for her to wake before her alarm on a weekend, and she wondered what had broken her sleep until the cry of a raven, throaty and raw, a sound somewhere between a shout and laughter, reached her.

She eased herself out of the bed, careful not to disturb Jacob. A couple of years ago, a raven's call would have meant nothing to her. But not now.

For more than a year after she had closed the hole between her world and Vanaheim, she waited for it to reopen. Waited for her life to be plunged into danger and magic once more, but as time went by, she started to believe they had stopped the end of the world, their task was done and she could go back to her ordinary life as a financial analyst.

Walking into the silent lounge room her toes scrunched the plush carpet as she moved to the front window. Then the raven called again; this time it was accompanied by a glimpse of something behind Freya's eyes. She'd had visions back then too; disturbing, hard to decipher, and usually predicted the future. They'd been gone for nearly two years.

In her vision a group of people in pale robes stood in a circle around a small bonfire. Their robes were flimsy, lightweight, whipped up around their knees and ankles by a strong wind. She couldn't see much in the deep night but there were no large shadows to indicate buildings or nearby trees only a black, empty paddock, and figures around the bonfire. She counted a dozen or so, women by their long hair and shape, their mouths moving rhythmically as though they chanted. Her visions never had sound.

Freya shuddered as the vision faded and pulled aside the curtain; two ravens sat on the balcony railing. She recognised them.

'Shit.' Dressed only in a long, faded, black T-shirt she wore to bed, she pulled open the front door and stepped out, not quite closing the door behind her.

'You're back,' she addressed the ravens. The concrete walkway was cold under her bare feet and the skin on her legs raised in goose bumps. Hugging her arms around her, more for comfort than from cold, she approached the birds.

'Did you show me the people in the field?'

The bird on the right bobbed its head and cawed softly, the other cocked its head, watching her. Freya pinched the bridge of her nose and closed her eyes for a moment.

She put out her hand to stroke the bird on the right, running the back of her forefinger down his sleek black breast. 'I have another job to do then. I've been waiting for this day, but I had hoped you wouldn't come back.' She turned to look back over her shoulder into the apartment where Jacob slept.

He had insisted they wouldn't be called on again, that their magic was gone, their duty done. Her right eye had been taken by one of these ravens three years ago, on her birthday; the day everything changed.

'Someone's trying to get magic from the other realms and use it here? In that circle you showed me.'

The ravens bobbed their heads. She'd never quite worked out which was Muninn, or Memory, and which was Huginn, or Thought, the raven familiars of Odin.

'And that's all I get, is it? People standing round a fire—and I have to stop whatever they're doing.' The bird she was stroking shuffled closer to his buddy. Freya dropped her hand to her side. 'Alright, I'll tell Jacob.'

As soon as she'd agreed, the two birds flapped their great black wings and took off over the quiet Melbourne rooftops.

Freya shivered and headed back inside. She'd first met Jacob when he was helping her learn to live without her right eye. They had moved in together after they had defeated the last person who threatened the natural order—Victor Mikkelsen—a disgruntled warlock who wanted more power than he had been given.

Freya stood by the bookshelf, her hand hovering over the books of magic she'd used to defeat him. Pulling out a large leather-bound volume she flipped through the pages without really seeing them.

Victor had punched a hole through reality to link the Earth to Vanaheim, land of the old gods: the Vanir. Magic flowed from Vanaheim to earth, and in return Vanaheim drained life human force, forcing hundreds of people into comas until they could close the rift.

'Freya?' Jacob's voice broke into her thoughts. She looked up to see him leaning against the bedroom doorframe. 'That's Hettie's book, isn't it?'

'I didn't know you were awake.' She returned the volume to the shelf and walked towards him. Jacob tied his burgundy towelling robe around his waist, one eyebrow raised in a question.

'I had weird dreams,' he said.

She hugged him, laying her head against his chest, warming herself against his body.

'Something's happening, isn't it?' he asked, wrapping his arms around her.

'The ravens were outside,' she said into his chest.

Jacob rested his chin on the top of her head. 'It was too much to think it was finished.' He sighed.

'Let's have some coffee and breakfast. I can't think about this on an empty stomach.'

'Shall we go out?'

Freya nodded her head, inhaling his musky, familiar scent, drawing strength from him.

*

The local café around the corner had mismatched furniture, lots of wood panelling, and a courtyard with a vine-covered canopy out the back. Unless the weather was wet or cold, they preferred to eat in the courtyard. This time, when they arrived about half an hour later, there were no tables left outside. Instead, they sat on the high stools in front of the plate glass window at the front of the café.

'I hadn't noticed anything, I mean until this morning,' Freya said.

'Same. Nothing until you told me the ravens had come to see you.'

'I had a vision; a circle of people doing a ritual, but it was unclear who they were or what they were trying to do.'

'Are you ready to order?' a young brunette woman said, having appeared to Freya's left.

'I'll have the big breakfast, with everything.' Freya wanted comfort food.

'I'll have the omelette, ham and cheese please.' Jacob was pale and quiet.

As they waited for their food to arrive, Freya gave him thinking space, leaning her elbows on the countertop and watched the goings on outside. People doing their normal Saturday morning business.

She cleared her mind, then imagined a shield of pink light around her, wrapping herself in it like fairy floss, and tried to tune into the thoughts of people around her. Dinah, Jacob's younger sister's talent was like a radio, picking up thoughts and feelings from people around her, while Freya's ability presented more like seeing through someone else's eyes. Sometimes she also knew things without any reason or evidence.

An image formed behind her closed eyelids; inside the café, a view from the kitchen including the back of Freya's head. She supressed the urge to touch her hair. Popping into other people's heads wasn't something she had been able to do since the portal closed. Things were certainly happening if she had enough power to do that.

Freya let go of the connection and imagined tendrils of her thoughts spreading out into the world. She was drawn to someone in the courtyard, bombarded by strong emotion as soon as she made the connection. The person's heart was breaking, the man sitting in the chair opposite gripped the mug of coffee in front of him so hard his fingertips turned white.

'Babe?' Jacob's voice broke through and she fluttered her eyes open. 'What were you doing?'

'Testing something out.' A prickling of guilt ran down her neck and across her collarbone.

'And?'

'I haven't been able to get into anyone's mind since— well, I jumped into one dude in the kitchen, and a woman in the courtyard who might have just been broken up with.'

'Mmm, you've tried it a few times and it's never worked.'

'Here we are, I hope you're hungry,' the young brunette waiter said as she laid their meals down on the deep-reddish-brown wooden counter.

Freya felt strange, and not just because she'd hopped into two other people's heads. She took a mouthful of hash brown and chewed.

'We'll have to tell Dinah.'

Jacob laughed. 'She'll be thrilled. She's heading into year eleven next year and needs to put all her energies into schoolwork and this shit comes up again.'

'She had some fun with us last time—'

'I kept most of this to myself, but she really struggled to go back to being normal again. When she had the mind-reading thing, she could pretend she wasn't deaf, was a regular kid, but when it was taken away it was worse than it had been before.'

'I thought she'd had been okay.' Freya loaded a fork with mushroom and spinach. *Perhaps I was wrong,* she thought.

'I didn't want to make a big deal of it, we were all still reeling from saving the world, but she hasn't got back to where she was before. I don't know how she'll react to having the ability back or to knowing that it comes with an obligation to fix the fucked-up stuff happening out there.'

Freya nodded. 'No doubt she already knows. If my ability is back, she's probably started to hear things. At least she'll know she's not going insane this time.'

Jacob's lips compressed into a line, but he said nothing. Freya made a mental note to text Dinah. No use pretending it wasn't happening. The ravens on the railing were all the proof she'd needed to know there was trouble ahead.

Halfway through his omelette, Jacob turned to her. 'We'll have to start prepping. We have no idea how long it will take to find them, whoever they are, what they're up to, or what we'll have to do to stop them . . . and we should train. That thing you did on the beach was amazing, but we'd never tried anything like that before, we should try to figure out what we can do.'

Freya made a noise of agreement. 'Why today though? There's nothing special about today.'

'You're not listening to me, are you?'

'Sorry.' She turned to look at Jacob and was reminded again how deeply she loved him. Replacing her fork on the plate, she cupped his stubbly cheek in her hand. 'I heard what you said but you're right, I wasn't really listening. We should practise. It was more luck than skill at the beach. Perhaps Odin acted through me, but it would make me more confident if I knew how to wield my power without having to rely on divine intervention.'

'You make sense sometimes,' he said, placing his hand over hers on his cheek.

'Gee, thanks.' She poked her tongue out, and her shoulders dropped, releasing tension she wasn't aware of holding.

Chapter 2

Freya and Jacob finished their meal without much more conversation, except to share the odd observation about a passer-by. After walking home hand in hand, Freya knew she needed to start working on the problem but didn't know where to begin.

Message boards and occult forums had been a good source of information last time, as well as news coverage of the coma-like condition. It had been a while since she'd looked for unusual magical happenings.

The people in her vision, all women as far as she could tell, were probably a coven or community of practitioners. Freya had to find out what they were doing, and perhaps knowing who they were would help. If they were like Victor and his cronies, they would have made some enemies along the way—pulling weak or vulnerable people into their sphere, showing arrogance and disregard for the finer nuances of practice or social etiquette, or being boastful enough to be seen as apart from the group.

Seidhr was not a popular branch of occultism, especially outside of Scandinavia, but it had power. Wicca and other branches could also tap into magical energy sources, although she had been narrow in her focus last time, sticking with *Seidhr*, it could be worth exploring other power she had access to.

Resting her laptop on crossed legs in the armchair she browsed forums, watchful for anything that pulled at her. The chair, one of the few objects she'd brought from her tiny apartment, was her thinking place. Jacob sat on the couch with his own computer, headphones on. She didn't ask what he was doing, if he was researching, they could compare notes later, and if he was listening to music or watching YouTube to distract himself, there would be plenty of time later to knuckle down.

The forums were unusually busy; it had been more than six months since she'd last checked for concerning activity. Most of the people she'd been familiar with from the last time were still there. Moderators tried to keep people on topic, and to maintain the peace, they also had more experience and were likely to guide newbies. Freya wondered how much power they really had if they spent their time in online forums instead of out in the world, perhaps they had enough power to know it was real, how it worked, but not enough to make them megalomaniacs or dangers to society.

It was too bad she never encountered Theo Halloway, occult bookshop owner and good source of magical gossip, in these forums. The older generations must have other networks offline, she made mental note to contact him about what he had heard on the grapevine.

Closing her laptop, Freya sighed.

'What's up, babe?' Jacob looked up from his screen.

'It feels like we're back where we were two years ago.'

Jacob nodded. 'In a way…but we didn't have each other then, or Dinah, or know about *Seidhr* or the ravens or anything else. It might seem daunting but we're in a better place than we were last time.'

'I guess so.' Freya put her laptop on the coffee table and moved to join him on the couch. 'It was too much to hope we were finished with magic, wasn't it?'

'Once your view of the world has been changed so completely, you can't go back. The things we know, we can never unknow. Most people don't even know it's happening. We were chosen for a reason.'

'Doesn't make me feel any better.'

Jacob put his arm around Freya and pulled her close. 'I know.'

*

The next morning Jacob and Freya visited Jacob's sister, Dinah, at her home in St Kilda where she lived with her father.

'Thankfully she hasn't got a boyfriend. We'd never get time with her if she did,' Jacob said, as they pulled into a parking spot near the house. Jacob sent a text to his sister to say they'd arrived; she didn't always hear them knock.

Dinah pulled open the front door a minute or so later, wearing black, skin-tight, ripped jeans slung low around her hips and a cropped T-shirt which showed off her flat belly. Freya didn't think of herself as old but when confronted with what teenage girls thought was fashionable, she felt it.

'Hey.' Dinah turned back into the house and didn't check whether they were following.

'What's going on? You don't usually text to make sure I'm home.' She plonked herself onto a couch.

'I'm not allowed to visit my sister?' Jacob asked.

'Nah, not like that, all formal.'

The three of them sat in the loungeroom; chemistry books and bits of paper were scattered all over the coffee table and next to Dinah on the couch.

I thought you might already know why we wanted to see you, Freya used her mind to send the thought to Dinah, if she received it, it would confirm that her abilities had returned.

'Oh shit,' Dinah said.

'You heard me?' Freya said aloud.

'Yeah.' Dinah's face had turned pale, and she looked down at the floor.

'I had a visit from the ravens yesterday.' Freya could have told Dinah the story with her mind, but it seemed rude to do so in front of Jacob, who couldn't hear the conversation. 'Your powers are back too.'

'I didn't know what it was. It's quieter than last time, but I can hear other people's thoughts, like low background noise in my head. If I don't listen, I don't really notice them, but when you just . . . you know . . . when you projected at me, it was like shouting in my mind.'

Freya and Jacob nodded.

'What did the ravens want?'

'I had a vision, let me show you.' Freya brought the image of the ritual in the field to her mind. Dinah would be able to see it in her own mind. They hadn't figured out how to broadcast the other way, from Dinah back to the other two, but Freya and Dinah could both experience the visions.

Perhaps that was something we should work on in the coming months, Freya thought.

'We think they're trying to get magic from another world. The more I think about it, the more I believe this must be their portal opening ceremony. I don't know whether it's in the past, present or future,' Freya continued.

'Have your powers come back?' Dinah asked Jacob.

'I haven't tested them,' he replied. 'We did some research yesterday, but I was avoiding it.'

'Typical.' Dinah smiled.

'So rude,' Jacob said, smiling.

'We thought we would do some more thorough testing of our skills this time. What happened on the beach worked out in the end, but—'

'Can you cast lightning bolts or smoke or whatever? That's super cool,' Dinah interrupted.

'It will be useful in a fight if my power can be used as a weapon, or to defend us while we reverse the damage this group causes.'

'Looks like a coven or something,' Dinah said.

'I thought the same, I only saw women, but I didn't see everyone. We should look for new groups, separatists who think they're too good to be in the regular forums or communities.'

'If they're doing something big enough for Odin to send the ravens to us, it must be extreme,' Jacob said, as both women turned to him. 'Last time Victor's plan put the whole human race at risk, and yes the sickness spread slowly but what if something had come through the portal? What if those in Vanaheim got greedy and wanted more life forces than Victor's cronies supplied? Once you've had a taste of power you only want more.'

Freya's eyebrows raised in surprise. 'You seem very sure about that.'

'It's like any other addiction. The first hit is so sweet, but you always need more to get the same feeling back. Magical energy is the same, especially if you're stealing it from people. Seems like Odin agrees with me, since we were sent to stop it.'

'How do you know so much about addiction?' Freya asked.

Jacob looked away and rubbed the back of his neck. 'What I'm about to tell you can never get back to Dad, okay, Deens?' He paused, waiting for his sister to nod agreement. 'Before I was with Rhonda, I dated a lady called Sasha, and she . . . liked drugs. Cocaine was her drug of choice, but she used others as well.'

Silence descended over the room.

'I got into it as well. I'm not proud of it. I enjoyed it way too much and had to end it with her. As far as I know she's still abusing herself with substances, but if

I'd stayed with her, I would have ended up in rehab, arrested, or dead.'

'Or all of the above.' Freya put her hand on his knee. 'I'm glad you didn't stay.'

'Me too. That's heavy.' Dinah fidgeted, picking at the ripped edges of her jeans. 'I have a chem test tomorrow and I haven't studied for it, so can I start on the magic stuff after that?'

'Of course, we don't want to get in the way of your schoolwork. You're doing VCE next year and that will be serious,' Jacob said.

'Over the holidays I'll have more time. I don't wanna be left out though.'

'We'll keep you in the loop, I'm sure you will be able to pick up some stuff here and there, particularly with your talent back,' Freya said. 'You want us to help with chemistry? I did pretty good at that when I was at school.'

'When was that, nineteen ninety?' Dinah laughed.

'She's so rude,' Freya commented to Jacob.

'I have nothing to do with that.' He smiled.

'I'm alright, I just, y'know, don't want to study.'

'I know that feeling. Trying to remember anatomy was such a pain at uni. Rote learning the names of things . . . where's Dad today?'

Dinah shrugged and looked out the window. Freya and Jacob exchanged glances, brows drawn together.

'Dinah? Where's Dad?'

'I dunno, he doesn't tell me anything. He went out last night, dressed up fancy, so I assumed he was seeing that slut he's been dating.'

'That's not a nice thing to say,' Freya said.

'You haven't seen her. She's gotta be like, twenty-five, total gold-digger, though Dad doesn't have as much money as she thinks he does, and she's always all over him. It's totally gross.'

'She's younger than me?' Jacob asked.

'Definitely, you're ancient.'

Freya was concerned at the way Dinah had described her father's new partner. Some allowances could be made for being an angry teen, but there was no reason to be so nasty to another woman, even if her motives were questionable.

'Are you right for food? Do you know when Dad'll be back?' Jacob's frown deepened. He must have shared Freya's concern that Dinah was left unsupervised for long periods while their father gadded about, thinking only of himself.

'I've memorised one of his credit cards, I can order whatever I want for delivery if I get hungry, plus there's some basics in the cupboard. He does a shop every week or so and never questions what I put on the list.' Dinah grinned, as though daring her brother to disapprove of her deception.

'I'll have a word to him. He shouldn't be leaving you on your own so much. I guess spending his money on takeaway is the price he pays for being a crap parent.'

25

'Let us know if you come across anything, but no pressure. We'll look into it, and speak to Theo, and tell you what we find,' Freya said.

She and Jacob said their goodbyes and made their way back to his car. He jumped into the driver's seat, although Freya was still allowed to drive, she'd avoided it since she'd lost her eye.

'Are you okay?' she asked, the only sounds were the engine and the radio playing soft rock.

'What the fuck is Dad thinking? She can't be left alone. I mean, I'm sure she can take care of herself, but it's not fair. He's still her father.'

'Can't she stay with her mother?'

'No, her mum lives in Perth. Plus, they don't get along. When Dinah was about eleven, her mother decided to become a bit of a hippy, wouldn't get her medications, or take her to the doctor, said her deafness was a punishment for something she'd done in a past life, that sort of shit, and Dad said he wouldn't make her see her mum if she didn't want to. Annie moved to WA just before the whole coma thing started.'

Freya made a noise of agreement, surprised neither of them had ever mentioned it before. If it was her family she wouldn't talk about it either. What a shame she didn't have a female role model, especially in the difficult puberty years. And to make out being deaf was not only Dinah's fault, but somehow deserved, was cruel.

'Dad, with all his faults, has been one thing that Dinah could count on. He's not very emotionally available, but he cares enough to get angry when she acts out . . . most of the time.'

A suspicion began to form in Freya's mind. 'Do you know how long ago this new person came into his life?'

Jacob glanced at her briefly before turning back to the road. 'What are you implying?'

'Nothing, but now we're dealing with another magical apocalypse—'

'That's a bit over the top don't you think,' Jacob interrupted.

'Maybe. Anyway, now we have another . . . thing to deal with it might pay to be suspicious of new people. We have no way of knowing who's linked to the circle, and until we work out who they are and what they're trying to do, we have to be super vigilant.'

Jacob was silent for a moment, a bland pop song burbled in the background. 'I'm not saying I disagree, but also, I don't want to be too paranoid. Dad's girlfriend bears some scrutiny but let's not get carried away.'

Freya crossed her arms over her chest. 'I'm not very trusting these days.'

Chapter 3

The next day at work Freya got an email from her best friend, Eva Chowdhury.

Hey gorgeous, let's have lunch this week. Let me know when's good. X

She read it and told herself she would reply later. Her mind was focussed on getting to the occult bookshop and speaking with Theo. Despite her distrust of him, he had connections to the community that would be vital to stopping whatever was coming. He was a weak, easily influenced coward, but as long as she kept that in mind, they should be able to use any information he had.

The bookshop was in a laneway off Little Bourke Street; a nondescript door and a set of stairs led to the maroon-coloured front door of the bookshop. The shop was all in one room, bookshelves and displays crammed together made the space seem even smaller. Other times she'd visited, Theo had stood behind the counter, flipping through some rare book or other, keeping an eye on patrons.

Freya pushed open the door to find Theo hovering in front of one of the rotating display bollards filled with angel cards, fairy cards, and twee tarot decks of various types.

'Right on time,' he said, spinning around to face her. He looked older than the last time she'd seen him. He must have been in his sixties, although his dyed black hair made him look a little younger. His hands were slim and claw-like, and he wore his usual over-the-top Victorian era costume, all black, with a maroon cravat. 'I'll put the kettle on.'

Behind the counter was a dark red crushed velvet curtain which hid the tiny kitchenette where he kept a couple of cups and a small teapot. While he dipped his head behind the curtain, Freya looked at the other patrons; three in business attire on their lunchbreak, perhaps looking for amusing gifts, and one young woman in her early twenties, with teal and black hair looking at the vampire section. None of them gave Freya the vibe of being involved in the current problem.

'You were expecting me.' Freya leaned her hip against the counter, her eye roaming around the kitsch nonsense covering the shelves.

'Of course. As soon as my talents started to—well as soon as I realised my second sight was strengthening, I knew it would be only a matter of time before you showed up. Something is happening again, isn't it?'

She sighed. 'I hoped you would have information for me.'

'Of course. I don't know how much help I can be.'

Always prevaricating and downplaying, she thought. 'I had a visit from the ravens. It seems the Gods, or whoever is in charge, have turned on my abilities again to sort out an emerging problem.'

'Yes, the ravens, I saw them in my mind. Do you have any idea who we are looking for?'

Freya was careful how much she gave to Theo, especially as his gift worked best with a physical connection. He placed her cup of tea in front of her and she waited until he'd withdrawn his hand before reaching for it. 'A new circle, perhaps a coven, has formed. They intend to perform a ritual, something I'm tasked to prevent.'

Theo nodded, wrapping his fingers around his cup as he sipped his tea. 'I've heard murmurs, mumblings. I'm not as well connected as I used to be, but I still dabble. People know my abilities are modest at best and tolerate me hanging about more powerful practitioners.'

Freya made a sound of agreement, hoping he would continue.

'From what I gather, my abilities have increased, but this is not a universal condition. Anyone I've spoken to since Saturday, when I first noticed the change, has not had a similar change. Which leads me to believe that I have been chosen specifically to assist you.'

'Interesting.' *Though perhaps they just aren't telling you,* she thought.

'I would know if they were lying to me. Not necessarily what the truth was, but I know when someone is keeping something from me.' He arched an eyebrow.

'It's not nice to poke about in someone's mind without permission. I need to work on my blocking,' she added.

'You're much more difficult than anyone else I've tried lately. But I agree, you should shield yourself as best as possible. Your plan to test your power is a good one, but only if it cannot be detected by this other circle.'

'Do you have any guidance for protecting or shielding? I can use all the trustworthy resources I can get my hands on.'

'I see you've decided to trust me for the moment—' he held up his hand to stop her as she opened her mouth to protest. 'I know you don't fully trust me; I haven't yet proven myself worthy. I have some books on magical protection and various other types of occult working. Your powers come from *Seidhr* but that doesn't mean it's the only style you can practice. Call me unfaithful, but I believe all forms of magic are valid and all can teach us something.'

Freya frowned.

'Magic that harms others is different, especially since what you put out comes back to you.' He set down his tea and looked to the bookshelves in the far corner of the shop, where he stored all the sources with real power. The only person left in the shop now was a frumpy twenty-something woman in an ill-fitting suit.

'She's not going to buy anything,' Theo said, following her eyes. 'Comes in here every week or so, reads the books she's interested in in the store and then leaves.'

'Tourist?'

'Some ability but no money. At least she knows where to get good information.' He winked and stroked his cravat before moving to the back corner as though gliding over ice.

Freya wondered if he thought of himself as a movie vampire, he had certainly styled himself on one. The books in this corner were older, dustier, without the flashy covers and glossy author photos on the back. If authenticity was directly opposite to marketing splash, these were the books to trust.

'People like Hettie and myself, we've had years to perfect our own practice. Of course, you know that, you have her spell book, but for those who don't have the luxury of a lifetime to train, I would try some of these. Crowley was as mad as a cut snake, but he had power. Ignore all the self-aggrandising and you'll find some useful spell-work. You'll probably get some value out of Skinner's tables, he's from Sydney though I think we can forgive him that. Yronwode did some good stuff on hoodoo, you can probably use too.' As he said each author's name, Theo handed her a volume. When he'd finished telling her the relative strengths and weaknesses of each author, and their practices, she had eight books of various sizes, thicknesses, and ages, and had started to wonder how she was going to pay for them all.

'I think that will do to get started,' she said with a small nervous laugh.

'I do get a little carried away, don't I?' He put his spindly hand to his collarbone. 'That will keep you going.'

The store was empty, and as Freya put her books on the counter to pay, she glanced at the time. 'I need to get going.'

'Some of these books are quite rare and expensive but given that I've been chosen to help you, we can call them a loan. The newer ones are normal prices, I'll put them through as marked, yes?'

'Alright,' she said. It was reassuring to pay for some of the books, Freya would have been more suspicious if he'd tried to give her the entire set free of charge.

Despite the loaners, Freya spent over a hundred dollars on books. Her concentration was flagging after so long trying to keep Theo out of her mind, and she was sure he'd spent a fair amount of energy probing her.

She texted Jacob when she was back to her desk.

Theo sold me half his library this afternoon. We'll have plenty of research to do offline as well as the online stuff.

Her manager, Graham, had narrowed his eyes when she returned to the office with a bulging bag of shopping after having been away for over an hour. *Perhaps I should have told him I had an appointment*, she thought.

*

That evening Jacob was already home when she walked in a little after six.

'You weren't kidding, that's a big bag,' he said.

'It covers all the main occult schools, last time we focused on *Seidhr* but Theo reckons we should learn what we can from other traditions too.'

'There could be something in that.' Jacob reclined on the couch; he'd paused the crime show he was watching. 'My last client today was a no show, so I got home a little earlier than usual. I've got potatoes, veggies and a chicken in the oven. Should be ready in about half an hour.'

Freya smiled, her day had been tiring and the visit to Theo hadn't helped. 'You know the way to my heart is through food.' She dropped her handbag and the books onto the floor by the front door and snuggled up to Jacob. As they watched the end of the episode he'd already started, she tried to enjoy the feeling of being in his arms. With everything that had happened last time, she focussed on learning to wind down, to be comforted and to lean on Jacob, and have him lean on her. The times they nearly failed were always when their cohesion as a team had been under threat.

'Oh shit—sex magic,' she blurted.

'What?' Jacob paused the show again.

'We'll have to get the protection pouches out, we don't want a repeat of the shooting shaft of light we had that one time.' It had been powerful enough for Dinah to feel from across the city.

'It would give us away.' He turned to her and smiled, his eyes glittering.

'That wasn't a proposition.' She batted his chest.

'If you say so.'

They ate dinner together; Freya had told herself to relax and start researching later but her mind kept returning to the books. They didn't know how urgent the mission was, the ravens had not been back since Saturday, but the feeling of impending doom wouldn't leave her.

'You're not listening to me, are you?' Jacob said.

'Hmm?' Freya's fork dangled from her hand.

'I asked if you have a plan, but you were off in your own world.'

'Sorry.' She put her fork down, her plate was half-cleared as her mind focussed on magic rather than food. 'I don't have a plan. Do you have any ideas?'

'With so many books, I reckon we have a scan through the chapter headings, and index if they have one, and make a list of interesting areas. Then we can divide them up between us to get through the content quicker. Anything that contradicts Hettie will have to be considered carefully. I say we go with her as the authority.'

'Sounds good. And that's not including the online forums. I started, but haven't got far.'

'There must be Facebook groups or something else on social media. Forums are kind of nineties.'

She smiled. 'I guess so. Maybe there will be someone ranting on YouTube. You never know, people put all sorts of things online these days.'

'Especially if they're recruiting. Didn't you say there was a few of them?'

'In the vision maybe a dozen?' She closed her eyes and tried to bring the image into her mind. The group were in a field, at night. They wore pale lightweight robes, which the wind whipped around them. Hands outstretched, they turned their faces up to the sky, mouths moving in a chant she couldn't hear. As she concentrated, the vision expanded; at first she had only had a flash, now she was able to watch it as though in real time.

'Freya, stop.' Jacob put his hand over hers and she fluttered open her eyes.

'What?'

'I can feel you drawing power. Whatever you're doing we have to wait until we're shielded.'

Freya frowned. 'Damn. I thought I was remembering, but I must have been using power to try to get more information. Why did you let me throw out the pouches? I'll have to get more tomorrow.'

'It was your idea to throw them out. But I agreed with you, I thought we were in the clear.'

She pushed her plate away and clenched her fists. 'Can't change the past now.'

'I'll clear up if you want to get started on the books.'

'I'm sorry, babe. You made me dinner and I didn't even eat it.'

'I know what it's like to be consumed by something, and if this is anything like last time, I don't want to be caught not taking it seriously. We could have died. A lot of people could have died.' He stood, resting one hand on her shoulder as he bent to kiss her forehead.

*

From the books' chapter headings and indexes, Freya and Jacob each started to compile a list of the areas that warranted further research. It wouldn't be done in a single evening, but it was reassuring to hold the books in her hands; it felt like progress was being made.

For reasons she couldn't quite pinpoint, she found herself drawn to the sections on blood magic. One of the books, written by a woman named Star Eagle, had an entire section focussed on menstrual cycles and how powerful this fluid was for rituals. Part of Freya was grossed out by the idea, but part of her resonated with it too.

A witch may collect the blood during her moon cycle, this can be used to create a powerful magical totem object. A cast iron receptacle should be procured, a small cauldron will do, an iron bowl or pot can be substituted. Into the cauldron, the witch should place at least a tablespoon of her moon fluid, along with the charred wood of a cedar tree, and an opaque quartz crystal, cleansed in moonlight.

A small amount of each of the following dried herbs are to be added: arnica flower, barberry, bay, caraway, lady's mantle, marshmallow, rowan, and star anise. Add two tablespoons of cleansed rock salt. Allow the cauldron to sit open until the mixture is fully dried.

This is now a powerful vessel to channel and increase your power. Store the vessel inside a ring of salt. Ensure this vessel is protected from enemies, if it were to fall into the wrong hands, damage could be done to you.

'I'm going to make this,' she said, showing the page to Jacob.

'The blood cauldron? Why?'

'It seems like a good idea.'

Jacob frowned. 'It's the stuff that could make a new person, so it makes sense it would be imbued with power, but it's a bit disgusting.'

'According to Star Eagle, men have been trying to shame us about our natural creative abilities in order to remain in control.' Freya closed the book. 'I think it's kind of weird too, but I feel I should do it.'

'You're the boss.'

'Do you think Dinah would do it?'

'I . . . don't know. You would have to ask her; I'm not comfortable doing it.' He laughed, a tight nervous sound.

'You're her brother, it would be weird.' Putting the book back on the pile with the others, she levered herself off the couch, stiff from sitting so long.

'Did you see anything I could do, y'know, similar?' Jacob asked, his voice weak and uncertain.

'She's pretty woman-focussed, so I don't think I came across anything.' She smiled, turning to see his face sheepish and eyes downcast. 'You would probably replace the blood with cum. Isn't that what men have for creative juices?'

Jacob's mouth formed an O of mock shock. 'I figured that, but I wasn't expecting you to be so blasé about it.'

'These feminist practitioners challenge squeamishness about bodily functions and fluids. Maybe I'll stop shaving.' She raised an eyebrow.

'As long as you love me, you can do just about anything you like.'

She chuckled. 'Good.' Freya leaned down to kiss him, her mouth hungry for his, his scent filling her nostrils and her body hummed with arousal.

'What did we say about sex magic?' he said, pulling away.

'Dammit.'

'Yeah, I could just . . . but I won't. Time for bed I think.' He squeezed her hand. 'Time for sleep I mean.'

Chapter 4

The next day Freya went to the the magic shop in the arcade around the corner from her office for supplies. The shop was more open and welcoming than Theo's bookshop, perhaps they were more interested in attracting tourists.

The last time she'd visited, the shop assistant had felt her power, but a different assistant was there this time. Freya grabbed a small basket and walked purposefully to the section she needed at the back, where herbs, crystals and small velvet pouches could be found. She added a couple of other items which seemed like a good idea to her basket.

At the counter, the shop assistant had raised an eyebrow.

'Looks like you know what you're doing.' She was a woman in her late forties, short and plump with a long plait of salt and pepper hair slung over one shoulder.

'I have a little experience.'

Freya touched the shop assistant's hand when she handed her credit card over to pay for the purchase and they both pulled back in shock as though a jolt of electricity had passed between them. Freya's mind was filled with a jumble of images from the woman's life, until she pushed them away.

'You're a real witch,' the woman said, her voice hushed.

'I hope you can keep that under your hat, I don't want people to know.'

'Of course. I won't tell a soul.' She put a watery smile on her face, but the fear and awe remained in her eyes.

There's no way that woman will keep that to herself, Freya thought as she walked back to her office.

The protection pouch was straightforward; put the ingredients in a small bag and say a few words, so she made up hers at her desk, whispering the words so as not to freak out her colleagues. Once it was done, she slipped it around her neck, tucking the small bulge into her shirt. Now if she wandered off into thoughts about the vision and started to seep power into the surrounds, it would be less noticeable.

At home that night Jacob was sitting in her armchair, deep in one of the books when she arrived home.

'Hey, babe,' she said, ducking her head down to give him a kiss hello.

'I've been reading this.' He waved the book in her direction, '*The Book of the Law*, by Aleister Crowley. Most of it's wild, but some of it is interesting.'

'Theo said he was as mad as a cut snake, but powerful. Coming from him that says something, don't you think?'

Jacob laughed. 'Yeah, well. Your book yesterday was all about blood, and Crowley is obsessed with cum.'

'Does that mean you've found a recipe for your cauldron?'

'Not yet, it will require some more thinking but there is some stuff in here about the power of words and the voice. I wonder if my skills work when I'm not singing, can I entrance people just with my voice if I tap into the right . . . timbre or something.'

'If you can do the Jedi mind trick, that would be very useful.' Freya's belly growled and she remembered that all the way home she had been starving, having had only a sandwich from the convenience store since breakfast.

'There's leftovers from last night in the fridge,' Jacob said. 'I can warm some up for you?'

'It's okay, babe, I'll do it for both of us. You look comfy there.'

Freya pulled two neatly packed containers from the fridge and placed them in the microwave. As she watched the spinning food, her hand drifted up to the purple velvet pouch on a string between her breasts.

'I got you a pouch from the magic place.' Grabbing Jacob's from her bag, she handed it to him. 'The woman in the shop had a strong reaction when I brushed her hand.'

'Oh?'

'Like she got an electric shock or something off me. I got a jumble of images from her life, I assume she hadn't intended to show me. She seemed a bit shaken, and I get the feeling she's going to blab to everyone she met a real witch.'

'You're not a witch.'

The microwave pinged and Freya went back to the kitchen to tend to the dinner. 'That's what she said to me, "you're a real witch".' She pulled the tubs of food out of the microwave, gave them a stir and transferred the contents into bowls before returning them for a little longer.

'I don't think of myself as a witch, but these,' she waved her hand over the collection of books spread over the coffee table, 'are magic books. I'm a practitioner of magic, by that definition I'm a witch.'

Jacob was holding the Crowley book in one hand, his finger wedged between the pages as a bookmark. 'I don't know about you, but I don't care for the power we have. I don't want to keep it after we finish. To be a witch, in my book, it's a more or less permanent transformation, a lifestyle choice, if you will.'

'Because we're magic tourists we don't count?' Freya's mouth tugged up in a half smile. 'I'm not sure it would stand up in court, but I like it.'

'You have to self identify, I reckon. Only you can decide what you are. If you don't feel like a witch, then you're not one.'

Freya leaned her right shoulder against the doorframe of the kitchen, arms folded loosely, watching her boyfriend. 'It seems like semantics but you may be right. I'm not a real witch, I'm pretending until we finish the job, and everything goes back to the way it was before. Did you put your pouch on?'

'Of course,' he said, reaching into his shirt and pulling up the small velvet sack, identical to hers.

'Good, because I've been dying to do this.' She closed the gap between them in two swift strides and straddled her knees over his lap. Jacob grinned up at her, his eyes sparkling. Their lips came together and the frisson of electricity between them jolted her, running straight down her body to her groin. She leaned into him, deepening the kiss, her breath becoming shallower, quicker, as she drank him in.

The microwave pinged again, but she ignored it, her hunger was no longer for food.

'Are you going to get that?' Jacob pulled away long enough to ask.

'I was going to stay here with you, maybe move to the bedroom.'

A gurgling sound came up from between them, both of their stomachs protested.

'Alright, we'll eat first.' She sighed, pushing herself away. He tasted so good, but he would still be just as hot in an hour or two.

After dinner, she texted Dinah.

I got stuff for protection pouches, and some other ingredients for a couple of new spells I want to try. You wanna come visit me and Jacob on the weekend?

Not long afterwards she got a reply.

Yeah. I've got some stuff to show you off the forums. It's way more interesting than Chem

revision, but tell Jakey I've been doing my homework too. :P

She showed the text to Jacob, he laughed. 'We couldn't expect her to leave it alone. I know I'd be much more interested in looking for a rogue coven than learning the periodic table.'

'Me too.'

*

Freya and Jacob met Dinah at the train station a couple of minutes' walk from their apartment after her soccer game on Saturday morning. Dinah was still in her uniform, black knee-high socks, black shorts, with an enormous blue sweater on the top, carrying a large bag with her overnight things inside Freya hoped.

'You didn't even take your shin pads off,' Jacob said when he saw his sister.

'It's nice to see you too,' Dinah replied. 'They're attached under my foot and I'd have to take my shoes off. It's a whole thing, and I was too excited to get over here and see you two.'

The siblings hugged. 'You better have a shower too,' Jacob added.

'This outfit gets a bit wiffy.'

'It's lovely to see you again,' Freya said once they had greeted one another. 'You've really gotten tall.'

Despite only having been a few weeks since they'd seen each other, Dinah seemed taller and thinner. She was now as tall as Freya and almost as tall as Jacob, although of a much slimmer build.

The walk took them past leafy gardens in front of the rows of terrace houses the inner northern suburb was famous for. Workers cottages for the local factories in times gone by, but were now trendy residences for wealthy up and comers. It was outside of Freya's budget to buy one of these small brick houses, which regularly sold for upwards of a million, but she enjoyed the atmosphere they created in the streets.

Freya couldn't concentrate on the play by play description of Dinah's game as they walked back to the apartment, she hoped Jacob was doing a better job of listening.

'I have some great juicy stuff to tell you that I found online,' Dinah said.

'We shouldn't talk about here,' Freya said, pulling her mind back to the conversation. 'I know it's overly cautious, but I would rather do some shielding stuff and be inside.'

'But I need to tell you,' Dinah said, her voice taking on a mock whining tone.

'I know you do; I'm dying to hear all about it, but we don't want to be overheard.' Jacob looked up and, following his gaze, she saw the ravens circling above them. 'These two are watching to make sure we don't get into trouble,' he added.

When they got home Dinah showered and changed while Freya set up the kitchen table for lunch; fresh sourdough bread, cheese and chicken and salads to make sandwiches.

'Dinah, this is your new protection pouch. You need to wear this everywhere, same as last time.' Freya said when they were all seated, then handed over a small purple velvet pouch. 'I've been doing some reading and I think I can do a little shielding spell for a "cone of silence" around us. I've also been practicing with some small works to get my stamina up, but I don't know how much energy spells are going to need ahead of time, which seems like an issue.'

The other two nodded. Freya closed her eyes and muttered a chant under her breath from one of the books Theo had given her. There was a faint pop, as you might get when clearing your ears in an airplane. When she opened her eyes, the room looked the same, but something had changed.

'The air feels . . . gloopy,' Dinah said, putting out her hand into the space above the table.

'Did you hear the pop?' Jacob asked.

'Yeah, it's strange, isn't it? The book said this would hold for about an hour before it needs to be refreshed.' Freya's stomach growled and a wave of tiredness passed over her. She loaded up a slab of bread.

'Am I allowed to tell you all my goss now?' Dinah asked. Both adults nodded.

'I found a YouTube channel that looks like a full-on cult. Someone was posting about it in the forums, saying how the leader was amazing and would change the world and everyone should go listen to what he had to say—'

'The leader is a man? I'm surprised I hadn't figured that out from the vision,' Freya said.

'Yeah, the main dude calls himself Vali, apparently because the world is going to end and he's going to survive it with all his followers.'

'Good, a doomsday cult,' Jacob said with a roll of his eyes.

'Yeah, it's intense. Anyway, he's been recruiting people to become the Children of Vali who will survive the apocalypse with him,' Dinah continued.

'Does he say what the apocalypse is going to be?'

Dinah chewed her mouthful before speaking again. 'Unclear, but I get the vibe he's planning to make it happen. He wants to open a door to Jotunheim I think he said, where the giants come from, and where the wisdom of the worlds is kept. Or something.'

'And his stuff is on YouTube? That's new. Did you find out where he was or how to contact him?' Freya asked.

'He had a website and an email on his contact page. He's looking for people to join up so I'm sure he wants people to reach out. As for his location, he seems Australian, the website says they're in regional Victoria.'

Freya thought for a moment, her mouth full of crusty, chewy bread. 'Do we make contact?'

'You mean join up? Like undercover?' Dinah said, her voice raising in pitch and excitement.

'Let's not get ahead of ourselves, Deens.' Jacob cupped his mug with both hands, eyebrows drawn together. 'Though it wouldn't be a terrible idea to get in with the group.'

'I wanna join the cult.' Dinah beamed.

'We need to consider the implications first. It's no good joining a cult only to let the leader know we're trying to stop him. If he knows we're shielded, he'll be suspicious and if we're not shielded, he'll know exactly what we're up to.'

'We don't know he has any power; he needs people around him to provide that,' Dinah said.

'I say we wait and observe for a while. Knowing their channels will be enough to start. Perhaps we can join the online forums as well, it's harder to get a psychic reading over the internet, especially if you haven't met in person,' Jacob said.

They were quiet for a while, each eating and thinking. Freya would have to spend some time going through Vali's videos to get a feel for his mission and his timeline. If they were trying to open a portal and bring about an end of the world scenario, knowing whether it would be tomorrow or next year would help for planning. She sighed.

'You okay?' Jacob asked, putting a hand on her forearm.

'I think so. That spell took more out of me than I thought. It's dissipated now anyway.'

'It might be easier and last longer next time,' Jacob said.

'Yeah, first times are never as good as when you've had practice,' Dinah said. Both Freya and Jacob whipped their heads around to look at her.

'What?' she asked.

'Is there something you need to tell us?' Freya asked, carefully keeping her voice neutral. Dinah's cheeks flushed bright red and she looked at her now empty plate.

'No.'

The silence stretched out, Dinah's ears turned deep red.

'There is a boy I like. We kissed a bit. It's not a big deal.'

Jacob coughed and took a sip from his mug before he replied. 'It is a big deal. I don't need to tell you about where babies come from, right?'

'Oh my God, gross. I know all about that.' Dinah briefly looked up at her brother, her eyes wide.

'Thank God.'

'If you do want to, y'know, talk about it, that would be okay,' Freya said. 'I know we're saving the world and everything, but I'm here if you have boy questions as well.'

Given your mum lives in Perth and your dad seems distant at best, she thought but didn't say aloud.

Chapter 5

The afternoon passed with each of them researching; Dinah, seated next to Jacob on the couch, had the books from Theo, Jacob had Crowley's Book of Law, a fat text which dealt with male magic, while Freya was watching Vali's videos from the armchair.

'Why has this page got a sticky note on it?' Dinah asked, breaking the silence.

'Show me,' Freya said, pulling off her headphones.

'This one on making a cauldron.'

'I was going to talk to you about that.' Freya took the book and let her eyes drift over the ritual. 'I was going to make one, it's a way to focus some power into an object.'

Dinah leaned over to read the page over her shoulder. 'But it's full of period blood!'

'I know. Our bodies are powerful, filled with natural magic we can tap into. Especially now our talents have been magnified by Odin, or whoever.'

'You sound like my mum. She's always going on about how it's natural and beautiful, but it's messy and painful and gross.'

Freya chuckled. 'We don't have to get into it right now, but there is a lot of misinformation around about menstruation. It's not as gross as we've been told, and it's what would feed a baby if there were one growing inside us.'

'But dried blood? In a cauldron?'

'I'm willing to give it a try next time my cycle comes up. I encourage you to consider it. I don't know if Jacob's found anything in Crowley's book that would be similar, but we know all the magics are worthy of study, so we should give things a go. Especially when they call to us, like this one did to me.'

Dinah's nostrils flared and her mouth turned down in disgust.

'Crowley is really obsessed with . . . cum and shit. I don't know why, or if that's better.' Jacob's cheeks became pink, talking like that in front of his sister. 'He's got a ritual for increasing a man's potency, magical and otherwise, which has some similar elements to your blood ritual. I'll give it a go if you do.'

'Do you have to jizz in a cauldron?' Dinah asked, giggling.

'Not exactly . . . you put in a few things, crystals and herbs and stuff, and it's a sort of talisman.'

'I thought a talisman was a necklace.'

'It can be, but doesn't have to be,' Freya added. 'Anyway, you'll have a little while to think about it before your next cycle.'

The videos she had been watching held very few clues as to when this apocalypse event was to occur. Like any good end of the world prophet, Vali rhetoric was vague, but urgent. She thought back to 2012 with all the talk about the Mayan calendar predicting the end of the world. A few self-proclaimed prophets had clung to the idea that this was a literal doomsday event and had had to swallow their words when the date passed by without an asteroid, rapture, or cataclysm of any kind.

'You've been listening to too many conspiracy theories. Try going back to the forums or something,' Dinah said, interrupting her stream of thought. 'I get stuff from you even when you're wearing the pouch, especially if we're in the same room.'

'Maybe I should try harder to shield myself,' Freya said, mostly to herself.

'If Vali has mind-reading talents, or someone in his entourage, they'll know you're shielding if you have absolutely nothing coming from you. It's as obvious to me as someone with a blank oval instead of having a face.'

'We said we weren't going to try to get into the group ourselves.'

'We can't send anyone else. If they're not skilled they'll be an open book.' Jacob didn't look up from his book. 'We'd have to be so careful about who we sent any way. Someone like Theo, would end up telling Vali all our secrets instead of helping stop him.'

'Vali's only interested in recruiting women,' Dinah said. 'I've had enough of research; can we try some magic?'

Freya looked to Jacob, who finally looked up from his book. 'Do you have anything in mind?' he asked.

'Victor tried to hit us with like, smoke. I don't even know what that was. Can we try some fighting moves or something?' Dinah said.

'Not in the house,' Jacob said quickly. Dinah's mouth moved up and down as she tried to come up with a reply.

'We need a place away from people where we can do some practising. An abandoned warehouse maybe,' Freya said.

'Because there are so many of those floating around.' Jacob sighed.

'No need to get snippy. We're still trying to figure out what's what.' Freya's mind went back to the moment she found her best friend lying motionless, eyes empty of life, on her bed the last time they had to save the world.

'Can you ask the ravens?' Dinah asked.

'I could try it. I've never called them down to ask something before.'

The three of them walked out onto the balcony of Jacob's apartment. The sky had become leaden, grey, burdened with low hanging clouds, although Freya doubted any rain would come. The spring afternoon still held the warmth of the day, and the wind had an edge of chill.

'Take my hands,' she said, holding them out and looking towards the clouds.

She took a deep breath and visualised a silver thread from Jacob and Dinah's hearts, running through their arms and up to her heart.

Fleur Blüm

I invoke you, Huginn, Muninn, answer my call. Come to my aid. She sent the thoughts out into the universe, hoping they were strong enough to get one of the birds' attention, and directed enough to keep her safe from anyone who might be eavesdropping.

That was cool, d'you think it'll work? Dinah's voice echoed in Freya's mind.

'I dunno,' Freya said aloud.

'I know they're magic ravens, but do they have to fly like regular ravens?' Jacob asked.

'I have no idea.' Freya said. 'Let's have a cuppa while they make their way over, just in case.'

They went back inside, Jacob put the kettle on as Freya kept her eye on the railing from behind the lace curtain across the front window. Despite knowing more than she had the last time their directions were still vague.

'Tea, babe.' Jacob appeared next to her with a hot mug in his hand.

'Sorry, miles away.'

'I used to think it was unrealistic that the gods in Greek myths were so obscure in giving instructions, especially if the Oracle of Delphi was involved, she did things to suit herself more often than not.'

Before she could murmur her agreement, Freya spotted a flutter of black wings outside, and went to greet them.

'Hey there, buddy,' she greeted the bird, who regarded her with his head cocked to the side. A moment

later another identical black raven settled next to the first.
'You know I can't tell you two apart, right?'

Both birds clacked their beaks in a conversational
way.

'I haven't called you straight like that before, I wasn't
sure you'd come. Is there anything you can show me?
How to get to Vali? How to practise our powers?
Anything really.' Freya tried to keep her hopes in check,
there was every chance they would show her the same
vision in the field. She slowly approached both birds,
hands outstretched, and ran the back of her fingers down
the silky black breast-feathers.

Her vision clouded, grey mist appeared in front of her
and when it cleared she was standing in a dark, open,
empty space; a warehouse. The ceiling was at least
twenty metres above her, the only windows were a single
line around the tops of the walls, many were broken. The
interior was stained with rust and decay, and the air
around her felt cold.

Where's this? she asked in her mind. The vision
moved outside the warehouse, her view glided upwards
as though she were flying, seeing through the raven's
eyes. Two identical dark green buildings, both in
moderate disrepair, surrounded by a large, gravelled area,
grass and weeds sprouting all over. A gravel track led
about two hundred metres back to a main road. On the
other side unkempt fields spread, dotted with scrawny
trees. Towards the horizon she saw a row of buildings,
perhaps a farm, and an overwhelming feeling of

loneliness and desolation. Her view soared along the track towards the road, bringing into view a large sign which had seen better days. Through the cracked and peeling paint, Freya could read the name: *Mindina Fruit Packing.*

'Mindina Fruit Packing,' Freya muttered to herself, trying to stick the name in her brain to find later. As she spoke, the grey mist came across her again and when it dissipated this time, she saw a small iron cauldron, the contents on fire, with blue green flames dancing around the lip, before the vision faded and she was back standing on her balcony.

'What was that last part about?' she asked, but the birds merely cocked their heads. 'Thank you.'

The bird on the right fluffed his feathers up, clacking his beak a couple of times before launching into flight. The other raven bobbed his head and a sensation flowed up her arm that she could only describe as though her insides had been filled with warm honey; a nurturing, euphoric experience she sometimes had after an interaction with the ravens. She grinned, and he took off to follow his brother.

Back inside Dinah and Jacob were both perched on the edge of the couch looking at her expectantly.

'That fire thing makes no sense,' Dinah said.

'We should probably let Jacob in before trying to decipher the message.' Freya smiled; Dinah was always trying to run before she could walk. 'The ravens showed me a big warehouse, and a sign for Mindina Fruit

Packing, which looks like a good place to do our practice. Isolated and far enough away from Vali that he won't sense us even without shielding.'

'Never heard of it, but seems promising,' Jacob said.

'The second image was a cauldron on fire. I get the feeling it's a spell we should look into. Perhaps it will solve the problem of having no thoughts when we're shielded. At least, I hope that's what it's for.'

'I'm not getting anything else from you, maybe if I held your hand for a bit I could,' Dinah said.

'Can't hurt.' Freya sat in the armchair and offered both hands to Dinah palms up.

'Your tea's there, when you're ready,' Jacob said. His eyebrows were drawn together in thought.

The sensation of Dinah poking about in her head disconcerted Freya each time. She doubted that would ever change, and she tried to ignore the feeling of being tickled inside her brainpan. After several minutes of silence Dinah sighed and leaned back.

'Anything to add?' Freya asked.

'I'll have to have a think about it. There's something in the back of my mind that I feel like I should be able to remember about the fire, but I've filed it somewhere very safely,' Dinah said.

'Burning effigies is a standard sort of thing, magically speaking. Maybe using your power bowl, that's what I've decided to call the bloody cauldrons because it seems like a better name, as a surrogate for your thoughts?' Jacob said.

'How would that work?' Freya asked.

'I read something about making a stand-in for yourself if you wanted to distract an enemy, like a voodoo doll but in reverse, where the doll takes the damage instead of you.'

'Sounds more like the portrait of Dorian Gray,' Freya said.

'That too.'

'Who's Dorian Gray?' Dinah asked.

Jacob smiled, turning to his sister. 'He's from a novel by Oscar Wilde. He sells his soul to remain young and beautiful forever and makes a deal for a portrait of him to age and decay in his place.'

'Your face says that doesn't go well.'

'No, the painting gets old, and disfigured, while Dorian remains young but becomes more and more conceited and twisted. In the end he destroys the picture in order to hide any evidence of his deal, but of course the picture is him, so when Dorian destroys the painting, he dies,' Jacob said.

'It's not a perfect analogy. We don't want the doll to be destroyed and kill us, just to be a false beacon to prevent being sniffed out by people with your sort of power Dinah.' Freya bit her lip. 'I don't understand yet, but if you go back to the spell, Jacob, it will become clear.'

*

'I found the fruit packing site. There are a couple of satellite photos but it's not clear how long ago they were taken,' Freya said a few hours later, turning her laptop towards the others.

'Where is it?' Jacob asked.

The afternoon had slipped by and it was dark outside. 'Up near Blackwood. It's a small town northwest of Melbourne. Trentham way. Doesn't look like the area is known for fruit orchards, maybe that's why it's empty.'

'Can we go now?' Dinah asked.

'It's over an hour's drive away.' Freya looked to Jacob since he was the designated driver.

'On one hand, we're less likely to be seen if we go at night, on the other hand, anyone who does see us will know we're suss straight away,' Jacob said. 'But all this reading about spells has made me antsy to try some.'

Freya's eyebrow rose. 'We don't have to get Dinah back to your dad's till the morning. If we grab something to eat on the way there we could go now.'

Dinah squealed in excitement and clapped her hands together. 'Can we get McDonald's?' she asked.

'No,' Jacob and Freya said together.

'We can do better than that,' Jacob added, smiling at his kid sister.

They scrambled to get shoes and jackets and torches and books together to find the warehouse that would be the centre for all their magical experimentation. Freya ordered burgers from a local place using an app on her phone and collected them on the way.

'I'm not driving an hour smelling your food without being able to eat mine,' Jacob said, the two women had agreed. They sat in the car to eat them before continuing.

As they drove, Freya watched the trees caught in the headlights along the narrow, dark country road. She never got used to the depth of the dark outside the city lights. The radio played softly under the hum of the engine and the tyres on the road. They hadn't said much, and an energy buzzed between the three of them, but Freya wasn't sure how it would manifest when they found their lair.

She wanted to try out her powers but was scared to draw attention to herself. Until they figured out a way to be near Vali or his followers without them knowing what they were up to, she worried about being discovered. Lying had never been her strong suit, even in her day job glossing over the negative aspects of a portfolio or selling someone a product she didn't believe in made her uncomfortable.

'How's it going back there?' Jacob said, addressing his sister via the rear-view mirror. Dinah looked up from her phone, her face lit with the light from its screen.

'I'm just chatting to some friends.'

'Friends? Interesting. It wouldn't be this boy that you're so keen on, would it?'

'Don't tease her,' Freya said. 'Young love should be left to bloom unimpeded by adults meddling, even if she is going a hilarious shade of bright red.'

'I thought we were saving the world,' Dinah said, crossing her arms, her lips pushed together in a pout. Freya and Jacob both giggled and said nothing further.

Another half hour of country roads took them to the gate of what used to be Mindina Fruit Packing. They missed the turn the first time and Jacob slowed, turned the car around and pulled into the driveway. The headlights shone on the splintered wood and faded paint of the sign. A metal and wire farm gate blocked their passage onto the property, the gravelled path beyond was patchy with weeds and the occasional pothole.

'I'll get the gate.' Freya jumped out of the passenger side door. The gate was chained closed, the padlock looked sturdy, if tarnished from the weather. She gave the lock a tug, but it was firm.

She wondered if now would be a good time to try channelling her power into an object. In their hurry none of them had thought about how they were going to break into the property.

Holding the padlock between her palms, Freya imagined blue fiery lightning flowing from her centre down her arms and concentrating on the lock mechanism. For a long moment she thought nothing was happening, but the lock became warm, then hot, in her hands. Just as the metal became too hot to hold, she heard a sharp clunk, and the lock body slid off the shackle.

'That was so cool.' Dinah had her head out the window of the car.

'I wasn't sure it would work.' Freya couldn't help grinning. She pulled the shackle away from the chain and unwound the length to swing open the gate. Jacob drove through, waiting a little way beyond so she could close the gate and join them.

'Did you see what I did? Or do you know because I knew?' Freya asked.

'You were a little bit glowy, in an energy sense. I don't think muggles would be able to see it. But mostly I knew because we're connected.'

'It was convenient, otherwise we would have had to jump the fence and walk all the way up here,' Jacob said. The headlights fell onto the first of the two large warehouse buildings; the wooden walls were painted a dull forest green. At the top of the walls, a row of windows, many of which were broken, sat under the eaves of the shallow pointed, corrugated iron roof. Despite being obviously uncared for, the property didn't feel creepy.

'This could be really cute.' Dinah said, launching out of the car as soon as they had stopped. She raced up to the structure and laid her hands on the wood.

'Getting any vibes?' Jacob asked. He turned off the engine and grabbed the torches from the back. Freya's torch was heavy, in a bright yellow plastic casing, and had a surprisingly strong blueish LED light, Jacob had taken the older torch, a long black baton-type with a warm yellow beam. They swept the light over the building, looking for the main door. Around the corner a corrugated iron roller door, painted the same dull green, with a smaller door, or wicket gate, cut into it to allow pedestrians easier access.

'Do you reckon that's the only way in?' Freya wondered aloud.

'Looks like.' Jacob was jogging back from the opposite end of the building having made a circuit.

'I'm pretty sure it's empty,' Dinah said, her footsteps crunching on the gravel behind them. 'I don't get much off objects, but it was worth a try, right?'

'Definitely.' Freya ran her hand over the roller door and the wicket gate set into it, sensing no vibes coming off either. She pushed the gate and was not surprised to find it locked.

Freya held her hand over the keyhole and brought the blue light into her mind again. With each breath she concentrated on sending the energy into the lock. It didn't take as long this time before she heard the snack of the lock giving way beneath her hand. She pushed open the door cautiously.

'I'll have a look first,' Jacob said, striding into the dark. It was almost black inside the building, what little light they had outside did not reach the interior.

'Is it okay?' Dinah asked.

'Other than being an empty warehouse, yeah.' He swung the beam of his torch back towards the door. 'Just watch where you step—there's junk on the floor.'

Inside the air felt colder than outside, Freya supressed a shudder. She swung her torch around; steel I-beams held the ceiling up in a row down the centre, beneath the roof peak, otherwise the space was vacant except for debris; bits of wooden pallets, crumpled water bottles, and assorted other rubbish.

'There isn't much we can break in here,' Dinah muttered.

'Perfect for practising magic things then,' Jacob replied. The mood among them was subdued.

'Now what?' Dinah asked, flipping her phone over and over in her hand nervously.

'I don't know,' Freya said. She flicked her torch over the wall near the wicket gate looking for the lights. She tried each of the switches, to no effect.

'We'll have to set up some rings of salt or something, make some protection circles. I haven't got any with us.' Jacob said. 'But if you want to try something we're here now.'

'I want to try moving something with my mind,' Dinah said.

'Let's start with something small.' Freya picked up an empty plastic water bottle and placed it in the middle of the empty warehouse. She walked back to stand beside Dinah and shone her torch back onto the bottle. 'Imagine the energy coming from your chest, and out your fingertips.'

Dinah slipped her phone into her back pocket, rubbed her palms up and down her thighs, as though wiping off sweat, and held her hands out towards the bottle, wrists together, fingers splayed as though holding a ball. She breathed in and out steadily, eyes narrowed in concentration. After a few moments, a sort of shimmering began to appear in the air around Dinah, although it wasn't something Freya was seeing with her eyes. The air smelled like a warm photocopier. There was a pulse, a jolt in her belly, and the bottle flipped into the air, then dropped to the floor and skittered away.

'Holy shit, did you see that?' Dinah squealed, clapping her hands together.

'That was cool,' Jacob said. Freya couldn't see his face, but his voice was hollow as though he was shocked it had worked.

'How do you feel?' Freya asked.

'My fingers are tingly. I feel buzzed and light-headed. I wanna do it again.'

'We don't want to overdo it, but one more will probably be okay.' Freya picked up a mangled cardboard box and set it up in the middle of the warehouse. When she'd joined the other two near the door, she said, 'go ahead.'

Again, Dinah rubbed her hands over her pants before holding her palms out towards the carboard box, wrists held together. She inhaled deeply, the shimmering around her body was more pronounced this time, before pushing her hands away from her. Something made a buzzing sound and the force Dinah had been directing at the box was scattered around the warehouse, Freya felt it hit her chest like a deep vibration. Dust and particles flicked into her eyes and face. It took a moment to regain her breath and blink away the flecks, then she realised Dinah had collapsed on the floor.

'Dinah,' Freya cried. Jacob was already rushing to his sister's side.

'What happened?' he asked.

'I don't know, she was doing okay, drawing more power but it seemed okay, she lost control somehow.'

'Deens, honey, wake up.' Jacob was cradling her head and patting her cheeks gently. The space between his taps and her taking a breath seemed to take an age, but she fluttered open her eyes.

'Ow,' she said, bringing the heels of her hands up to press on her temples.

'You okay?' Jacob still held her head on his knees.

'I—' she looked around. 'Did I get you?'

'I don't know what happened, the force went all around the room,' Freya said.

'I was visualising a ball in my hands, it was a sort of smoky green blob, and then . . . my phone vibrated and I lost concentration.'

'What would make you lose focus like that?' Jacob said, turning to Freya.

'It was a message from the boy, wasn't it?' she asked.

Dinah scrunched her eyes closed, her cheeks reddening. 'Yeah.'

'If you're having conniptions every time he texts you, I think it might be a bit more than a crush,' Jacob said.

'Be nice, she's just had a little magic backfire.'

'I can't hear you,' Dinah said.

'What do you mean? You're talking to me,' Freya replied.

'Your mind, I can't hear it, or feel you. Oh god, I've lost my magic.' She started to take short, quick breaths, edging towards hyperventilation.

'It's okay. Stay calm. Can you sit up?' Jacob said, helping her into a seated position. 'There we go. Deep breaths, in through the nose, out through the mouth, that's it.' He stroked her hair and murmured to her as she calmed down.

'Can you hear Jacob?' Freya asked a little while later.

'Yeah, but he's touching me, and he's my brother.'

'You've probably just overdone it. Rest and recuperation should fix it. Here, let me try something.' Freya pulled the pouch of protective herbs and spells up from inside her shirt and slipped it over her head. Once the connection was broken, she was sure her thoughts would be clear to Dinah.

'I hear you now,' she said with a sigh. 'You'd better put that back on though, you're really bright and loud.'

She smiled, and the tension she hadn't realised she was holding in her shoulders slipped away. 'That might be enough excitement for tonight, don't you think?' Freya said. Jacob made a tutting sound; she turned her torch onto him.

'I wanted to give something a go. You and Deens both got to try out your mojo, and I did all the driving.' Jacob squinted into the torch light.

She couldn't begrudge him trying it. 'Were you gonna try moving things or something else?'

'I hadn't thought it through. My talents are linked to my voice, so I thought I might try an incantation.'

Freya's eyebrows raised. 'I'll have to read this Crowley book.'

'Yeah, he's off his tree, but I think I could maybe get something to happen if I used the right words and intention.'

'I'll sit with Dinah while you try,' Freya said.

Jacob stood up and brushed the dirt from his pants. He walked over to where the cardboard box sat, it hadn't moved far even with all the wind Dinah had scattered through the room. For a while he just looked at the box, then set his torch down on the ground and shook out his hands and let them drop to his sides. He took some deep breaths, and Freya started to see a shimmering around him she knew was his power building.

'Up,' he said to the box. The shimmer of power held, but the cardboard didn't move.

'You need to push the power onto the box. You're still holding it,' Freya said. Jacob nodded, inhaled and tried again.

'Up.' This time she saw the shimmer move from him towards the box. It shivered, one corner lifted as though touched by a strong wind, before dropping back to the floor.

One more, you almost had it, she thought.

Jacob stood up straight, shook himself, and took a breath in, and pointed to the box. 'Up,' he said. His voice boomed through the space and the cardboard box floated into the air about a foot, wobbled there for a moment, before dropping onto the ground.

'That was cool,' Dinah said softly. Jacob seemed to crumple; his shoulders slumped in fatigue. He walked back to the two women, offering a hand to help them up.

'Impressive. I didn't know you could do magic with your voice.'

'I didn't either, but since my singing worked to put people into a trance, I figured I could use it for other stuff too. Crowley talks a lot about stating intentions, I'm not sure he meant it to be literal, but after seeing you and Dinah, I wanted to try it.' He was beaming, but his skin had turned pale and waxy.

'Let's go back to the car. It's too bad we didn't pack any snacks, we could all do with some quick calories.'

Jacob helped Dinah to the car, she had improved but was unstable on her feet. In the car they turned on the radio and sat without speaking for ten minutes before Jacob sighed and started the engine.

They drove back the way they had come, quiet except for the burbling of the classic rock station.

'Can you find a service station or something? I need a snack and maybe some caffeine to get all the way back,' Jacob said, his voice heavy with fatigue.

'Sure.' Freya used her phone to find nearby roadside conveniences where they could recover a little before the hour-long journey back to their apartment. She looked at the clock, it was after midnight, no wonder they were all tired and that wasn't taking into account the toll on their energy stores of performing unfamiliar magic.

In the backseat Dinah stared out the window, she seemed vague but otherwise unscathed from the blowback of her spell. Time would tell if there were any lasting effects.

The fluorescent lights of the service station and rest stop appeared up ahead on the left, as they did Freya's belly growled and she realised how hungry she had become.

'Do you want to come in, Deens?' Jacob asked.

'Hmm?' She looked up, as though just coming to awareness that they were stopped.

'Food. Do you want any?'

'I don't know, chips and a coke I guess.'

Jacob nodded and shut the door, coming around the front of the car to take Freya's hand as they walked in. 'I feel like I've been hit by a truck.'

'I know what you mean. I've tried a few more spells, perhaps I'm a little more resilient, but I want to sleep for about three days.'

He squeezed her hand.

Freya had a hot chocolate from an automatic machine which mostly tasted like sweet hot water, and banana bread of indeterminate age, Jacob bought a meat pie, and a coffee from the same automatic machine, no doubt it also tasted mainly of sweet hot water. They ate before driving home mostly without talking. Dinah fell asleep after a while, Freya stayed awake to make sure Jacob had company.

Chapter 6

The trip to the packing shed had demonstrated their need to practise using their powers, and their under-preparedness for the journey there and back. The shed wasn't connected to electricity; they would have to resolve that before going back. And there was the decoy thought cauldron spell to do.

At work on Monday morning, Freya found it hard to focus, a mental fatigue lingered. A long run after work had not helped her mind but it had tired her body so she slept.

By Wednesday her focus had returned, it had been over a week since her last visit to the occult bookshop, and she wondered if Theo had had any luck with his network.

When she entered the shop, he startled. 'I didn't know you were coming.'

'Hello to you too,' she replied, smiling at his confusion. 'My shielding is better this time if you didn't anticipate me coming at all.' *You must have expected me to come back at some point though,* she thought.

'Yes,' he said, pausing to look at the other customers in the shop and lower his voice. 'You don't give off anything at all, it's very unnerving.'

'That's what Dinah said. Like I don't have a face or something.'

'More of a psychic black hole, there is nothing to detect. It's a sucking nothing, rather than a bland nothing.'

Freya wrinkled her nose. 'Sounds unpleasant. And noticeable if I encounter someone with psychic talent.'

'It is a strange feeling, certainly noticeable—memorable, which I'm sure you don't want.'

'No. I came to see if you'd heard anything about someone calling himself Vali. He's gathering women around him and plans to use their power to bring on Ragnarök, which he insists only he and his children—his followers—will survive.'

Theo put his hand against his collarbone in a theatrical manner. 'My goodness. Ending the world again, how original.'

'So have you heard anything?' Freya prompted after a drawn-out pause.

'You'll have to do something about this vacuum. I don't know if you've found the part in Star Eagle's book about creating an item which will act as your power centre. If I recall correctly, you can make a talisman which will read as a mind to a psychic. You can put thoughts and emotions into it so that people are not looking at the . . . blankness.'

'I found it, although I'm not clear on the talisman part, she describes making a beacon to amplify one's abilities. But you didn't answer my question about Vali.'

'Mmm. I need a cup of tea and to sit down to gather my thoughts.'

Freya was tempted to force her way into his mind to see what he was plotting but decided demonstrating her power was not in her interest before she knew a little more about Vali and his reach on the magic world. Theo muttered to himself while he boiled the kettle and then brought out two mugs of tea with far too much sugar for Freya's liking.

'The ritual involves writing the thoughts you want to imbue onto a piece of paper, one for each idea. You must concentrate; any time your mind wanders to the shopping list, what's on T.V. later, or the mission, it will leak into the talisman. When you've got about five, put them all into the cauldron you've already imbued as your beacon, and burn them with cedar and salt. Then any psychics in your vicinity will have something to see or hear when you're around and they won't be immediately suspicious of your very powerful shield. No novice could be such a void.'

Freya nodded and sipped her tea, determined not to ask a third time what he knew about Vali. The silence stretched until the couple of people browsing had exited the shop.

'I've seen them in here a few times recently, it's not yet clear whether they are interested and not yet confident enough to buy something, or whether they are trying to get information from me. My very moderate psychic ability had proven useless in this case, so either they're blocking me, or perhaps they have no power.'

Freya made a noncommittal noise of encouragement.

'I made some enquiries of my circle of influence, it will be easier now I have his name I'm sure, there isn't a lot on the grapevine.'

She concentrated on not rolling her eyes at his "circle of influence".

'All I've heard is there is a group out in the country. The leader, one assumes it's this Vali fellow, has been courting women from the community who perhaps are recently single, or who have been through something difficult, and befriending them. He's very charming, handsome and magnetic in person, perhaps he's using influence magic, but more likely he's a natural manipulator. There have been a few people who have moved out to live with him, up near Castlemaine I believe.'

'That matches what I've found,' Freya said. No new information, other than a geographic area. 'If that's everything, I should get back to work. You'll keep an eye out, won't you? And let me know anything of interest.' She put her intention into the statement, attempting to imitate what Jacob did with his voice.

'Now, now, no need to use your mojo on me. I'm a friend, you can trust me.'

Freya's eyebrows rose. 'I wasn't sure that would work.'

'You are much more powerful than you give yourself credit for. A few years ago, it was different, you were a reluctant practitioner, an uncut gem. Now I sense something different, you're embracing this world, curious about what it can do for you, and I dare say, your talent has increased.'

'Perhaps.' She put her empty mug of tea on the counter and stood to leave the little alcove behind the register.

'I'll be in touch if I find anything. Be careful of who you use your talents on, shield or no, anyone with talent will know your power if you shine it on them.'

She walked back to work without seeing the people passing her, her mind filled with this new complication. If she exposed herself by using her power to influence people, perhaps it was as good as not having the power at all. The afternoon at her desk passed by without her notice as well, she went through the motions of her job, an email from Eva popped up, but she set it aside to attend to later, her mind was preoccupied with other things.

As usual, Jacob was home before her.

'Hi gorgeous,' he said, rising from his spot on the couch to give her a kiss. 'Are you alright?' His hand lingered on her forearm, comforting her.

'Just thinking.'

'While you're thinking, Vali put out a new video today. I got a notification from his channel. You wanna watch it together?'

'Sure.' Freya dumped her handbag in the bedroom and changed into some tracksuit pants and a hoodie. After the day she'd had, she wanted to be comfortable.

Jacob had brought up the video on the smart TV for them to watch together.

'It's nearly an hour long.' Freya flopped down next to him.

'Maybe we'll be able to skip some bits, I can put some leftover lasagne in the oven and we can take a break in the middle if you want.'

'You read my mind.' She leaned over to kiss him before he extricated himself to attend to the dinner. It was times like this, the quiet domestic moments, that she loved him.

When he returned, she laid her legs over his lap, and they sat to watch this new video from Vali.

Jacob had paused the video on an image of Vali sitting in front of a brightly-coloured piece of fabric. Around the edges of the fabric shabby blue-grey wallpaper was visible. He sat at a table, with a woman on either side, his usual set-up, although these two women had not appeared on his videos before. Vali himself was very handsome, with a long narrow nose, pointed chin, high forehead and an abundance of light brown hair falling around his face arranged seemingly carelessly, but it looked contrived. He looked elven, youthful, but perhaps older than he appeared. It was hard not to stare into his gorgeous honey-brown eyes whenever he caught the lens directly.

'The set hasn't changed, so that doesn't give us anything,' Jacob said.

'I didn't tell you yet, Theo's heard whispers he's in Castlemaine.'

Jacob nodded and pressed play.

'Greetings to you, my beautifuls. We, who are the followers, the Children of Vali, the chosen ones, celebrate today because we are joined by two new members.' Vali gestured to the women sitting beside him. 'I would like to introduce Tove and Sigrid, they have joined our family since the last update. We've been working on the most magnificent ceremonies, preparing for the big day.

'Both of my beautiful ladies have left their homes, and all their worldly possessions and troubles to join me here at our home base. It's such a joy to see how much they have both grown in themselves since becoming one of my children.'

'He sounds like a cult leader,' Jacob said.

'He is a cult leader. They're giving up everything to join him as he predicts the end of days. It's cheating though, since he's going to bring it on.'

'The end is coming,' Vali said, as if on cue. 'We're busy preparing the rituals and our home for the next phase. My visions of the coming event are unclear, as with all predictions our actions create uncertainty, but I feel the energy building, my children.

'Tove, why don't you tell us about the destructive life you had been leading up until you joined us here?'

'Oh, well, thank you Vali. It's so lovely to be here really. I am so lucky to have found my path. In my other life I was a hairdresser. I didn't do well at school so I left at seventeen to start my apprenticeship. Of course about a year in I met a guy and ended up pregnant and married by nineteen. I went back to hairdressing but then I had a second child, their father was a salesman but he never did sell much so I was the main breadwinner. In the end, he ended up falling for a younger woman, and—not to get into to many details, but I didn't handle the divorce very gracefully and he has custody of the two kids with his new wife.'

'Sounds very tough Tove, what brought you to us?'

'Well I always knew I had a talent, I could tell what people were thinking sometimes, and after the kids were gone, and I had much more time on my hands, I started drinking too much and dabbling in the online forums, and then I met Vali. You've really turned me around. Stopped the drinking, given my life meaning, and boosted my confidence. I feel alive in a way I haven't had for a long time.'

'They didn't really understand you, did they, my beautiful Tove?' Vali put his hand on the woman's arm, she was transfixed, a slight flush spreading across her cheeks.

'They must be sleeping with each other,' Jacob said.

'Definite chemistry. She's loving it, he's very handsome.'

Freya tried not to get hung up on appearances, Tove was a plump woman in her early forties, neither ugly, nor beautiful, a person who would easily blend into the background. Being the centre of Vali's world, even temporarily and shared with the others, she was in heaven.

Jacob paused the video and turned to Freya. 'What drives a person to attach themselves to someone like Vali?'

'Other than being desired by a handsome, charming man? You heard her, she wants to feel special, to feel seen. Perhaps after all the troubles in her life she wants to feel like it meant something. You know: 'everything happens for a reason'. People like Vali can make any bad thing seem like it was building to whatever they want you to do.'

'How does someone not see how manipulative he is?'

Freya sighed. 'This kind of cult situation is just like any another abusive relationship, being intelligent doesn't protect you. Anyone can be seduced by someone telling them exactly what they want to hear.'

Jacob looked at his hands. 'Thanks for not mentioning Rhonda.'

'You've lost me.'

'I've thought about it a lot since I broke up with her. She was so negative, undermined and undervalued me, controlled me, in a few ways I've wondered if it was abusive, but I guess I didn't want to admit I'd ended up in that situation.'

Freya sat upright and turned Jacob's head towards her. 'There is nothing you did to deserve to be treated like that. Perhaps you didn't recognise certain red flags but it's not your fault. It's never the victim's fault.' She sighed. 'If the victim hurts someone while under the spell of another more dominant person, they're still responsible for that harm, but they weren't the only person at fault. I'm sure Vali doesn't do any of the dirty work himself, he gets women like Tove to do it. Like Manson.'

'Let's hope we're able to stop them in time.'

They were quiet for a moment, then Jacob resumed the video. After Tove finished, Sigrid spoke.

'My life has been pretty rough. Mum died when I was ten, and that left me with my dad and his friends. They were. . . well Dad did nasty stuff to me and shared me with his friends. I ran away at fourteen, I couldn't stay there anymore. Then I was with one bad boyfriend after another until I found Vali earlier this year. He showed me what true love could really be like and gave direction to the magic I always knew I had.' Sigrid was younger, but her face was puffy and wrinkled as though her life had left more damage than Tove's. She stared into Vali's eyes with quiet desperation.

'Do you reckon she was doing sex work?' Jacob asked.

'I was just thinking she hadn't said anything about her job. It makes sense, sometimes people with an abusive background end up in that profession. It can be unhealthy and unstable but joining a cult is definitely a step backwards.'

'Does she look high to you?' he asked.

'Her eyes are a bit glazed and red.'

'I'd probably be high, and in a cult, if I'd had her life.'
He squeezed her hand. For a man who worked with
people at their most vulnerable, she was surprised to see
him so affected by these women's stories.

Vali turned his gaze on Sigrid as she spoke, he
watched her with the sort of rapt attention Freya would
find hard to resist even knowing that he was evil. *What
does it say about our culture if people like Vali can get
followers just by showing vulnerable people attention?*

When the two women had finished their stories, Vali
turned back to the camera.

'You've heard the stories of Tove and Sigrid, now it's
up to you. Will you listen to the magic in your heart and
find your place among those who will survive the
coming storm? We welcome newcomers with open arms.
We ask only that you shed your worldly worries,
embrace our lifestyle and hone your spiritual power.
With these small changes, you will be able to pass
through the end of days unharmed.

'I cannot save everyone, the prophecies are clear that
there will be very little left after the cataclysm. Human
beings have been too selfish for too long, the world must
wash most of us away and start again. This is the word of
Vali, and my followers will be protected by my power.'

'As if you have any power,' Freya said.

'He clearly has something going for him to get these
women to join him.'

'True, but how much is magic and how much is being a sociopath remains to be seen.'

'If you want to reach out to our family, our email is in the description box below. If you have always felt like you were meant for more, ever wondered if you're psychic, or made things happen with the power of positive thinking, you might have real talent. I can give you a place in the new world. Until next time.' Vali pressed his palms together in prayer, kissed his fingers and spread his hands in front of him, his usual sign-off.

'We're going to have to get in with him to know what he's up to. Despite the video running for an hour, he said very little. What he did say repeated stuff he's said before.' Jacob's hands were clasped tightly in his lap.

'I know. We need the cauldrons, so he doesn't sense we're shielded. Theo said it would be a dead give-away if we were able to hide ourselves. Like creating a believable back story and cover identity for a spy. The ravens will let us know if things become urgent. At least, I hope they will. It's all so confusing.'

Her period was due at the end of the week, and although the thought of collecting her menstrual fluid was disconcerting she understood the power in it—both symbolically and literally. The Star Eagle book had a whole section on the power of the womb to create life, and how the shed lining had come to be seen as unclean, mostly through a narrative led by men who were afraid. According to the author these men, weaker and greedier than the women around them, had spread misinformation about the power of the womb, its ability to generate life, and the magic that could be harnessed if used in the right way.

'I'll get started on my uh . . . contributions when you've done yours.' Jacob's cheeks turned a shade pinker. 'What about Dinah? You asked her right?'

'She's less squeamish about it than you are—though I don't know if I want Dinah meeting Vali. Even watching him on a screen, I can feel the magnetism in him. Is Dinah going to be able to keep her mind on task? After the debacle the other night, setting her magic rebounding off the walls because she got a text from a boy she likes, maybe we keep her in the background.'

Jacob rubbed his chin, his salt and pepper stubble rasping. 'It's true she's a bit wild sometimes, and immature, but she's part of our circle, she's almost an adult, and we need her power.'

'You're right. I'll remind her to collect her next cycle and grab some cauldrons from the magic shop.'

*

At work on Wednesday morning Freya answered her desk phone. 'Hello, Freya Gordan speaking, how can I help you?'

'Why are you ignoring me?' Eva's bright, loud voice came down the line.

'What do you mean?' Freya spoke quietly in an effort to avoid attention from her colleagues.

'I asked if you wanted have lunch on Monday and you haven't replied. I haven't seen you in ages. And you didn't reply to my email.' Eva made a tsking sound.

'I've been really snowed under with work—'

'Everything you do is urgent. Have you had a fight with Jacob? Are you mad at me?'

At first Freya thought her best friend's outrage was feigned but the longer the conversation went she started to think it was genuine. 'I'm sorry, Eva, I didn't mean to worry you. Things have been hectic.'

'What aren't you telling me?' her friend's voice changed, dropped to a more conspiratorial whisper.

'I can't talk right now. I was going to go do a few errands today, but I'll meet you tomorrow for lunch if you want?'

'It will do. But I demand to hear all about it tomorrow.' Her friend abruptly hung up the phone. It wasn't like Eva to be moody, and she'd never hung up on her before. Freya went through her emails and found the one from Eva a couple of days previously and sent a reply.

I didn't mean to ignore you, meet you out the front of my building tomorrow at twelve and I'll fill you in. It's top secret—nothing in writing.

She hoped it was enough to pique her friend's interest and appease any anger until the next day.

The magic supply shop was in one of the small arcades near Bourke Street, a short walk from her office. It was busy, filled with various hippy types, and people in office wear looking for a novelty gift or spiritual self-help book. Despite the kitschy purple and black shop dressings and the assortment of nonsense they sold, they had the staples for doing real rituals. The woman working there today was one she'd come across back in the days when the coma plague was running rampant over Melbourne. Their eyes met briefly as Freya approached the display with their mini-cauldrons, incense holders and small pots. The assistant looked away first and Freya turned to examine whether the little vessels were what she needed. Grabbing the first cauldron with a lid, she held it in her hand, it was surprisingly heavy for its size, typical of cast-iron. It had no vibe, which made sense for something that had never been used. Even so, she would have to give it a good cleansing when she brought it home. They'd need three identical vessels; the books didn't say this but something in her mind told her they should be uniform.

'I haven't seen you for a while, I wasn't sure it was you, your aura is so different now, but how many women with your looks are going to walk into my shop?' The shop assistant's hands unconsciously fondled her long black plait.

'It's nice to see you.'

'I wish I could say the same. I waited for you to come back after all the power changed, I knew you'd done what you were supposed to do, but I still dreaded the day you were back. Are we in trouble again?' Her face paled.

Freya bit her lip.

Best not to say anything.

'You've evolved your shielding so much it's hard to look at you directly. Like my eyes want to slide away, you're uncomfortable.'

'I've been told. I didn't realise it was so obvious.'

'Most people wouldn't notice, but you just need one person who knows what it means and isn't on your team and you're in a tough spot.'

Freya mumbled agreement. There was no way she would take the protection pouch off, it would make her an even more obvious target to her enemies, but the sooner she could finish the cauldron ritual, the sooner any focus on her wouldn't see the obvious markers of power and skill. Of course, someone may see through the smoke screen of the avatar but she hoped it would give her time to get close to Vali.

'Did you need something from this section?' the assistant asked. Freya realised she had drifted off into thought.

'Sorry. I need three iron vessels, preferably identical and relatively small—'

'Don't tell me any more. These will do the job.' She grabbed one of the plain cauldrons. 'I use these myself. The more elaborate the design the more you have competing with what you want to do. Plus, they're for the tourists and not as good quality.'

'Great, have you got three?' Freya felt an urge to get the transaction done as quickly as she could, she felt uneasy in this woman's presence. 'And I need a couple of other things.'

The assistant seemed much less chatty as Freya reeled off the list of items she needed for the rituals. She hoped the woman wouldn't be able to deduce the spell she needed from the list and added a few unnecessary items to throw her off.

'You should hold that from the bottom. I hope the spell work is successful,' the woman said as she handed over the thick black paper bag bulging with her purchases.

'Thanks for your help, again.' Freya nodded to her and turned to leave. As she walked swiftly back to the office with her purchases, expensive and heavy as they were, her annoyance and discomfort faded. The feeling of being watched lingered as she approached her building and she looked up into the branches of one of the plane trees which lined many of Melbourne city streets to see the raven perched there. She slowed to pause under the tree.

Checking in or do you have something to share?

In a public place she didn't talk to them aloud.

The bird bobbed its head and croaked softly. In her mind, Freya saw the women in the circle. It was the same scene as she had seen in the past, but now as she moved her head around, she saw Dinah standing in a long flowing robe, her mouth moving in the chant.

What does that mean? Has she gone to the Dark Side? Freya's mind reverberated with questions, she knew the ravens wouldn't, or couldn't answer, but it was disconcerting to see the young woman she thought of as a sister taking part in a ritual which would bring on the end of the world.

As soon as it began the vision faded, the raven called loudly and launched itself into the sky.

'Thanks,' she said aloud.

The vision along with the dread she felt in the magic shop left her rattled. After half an hour struggling to write a report, she gave up and went to the kitchen for a cup of tea. As she dangled the teabag in the cup, staring at the wall, her belly rumbled.

I didn't have lunch. Her focus on the magic shop had completely obscured her need to eat. She hadn't brought anything with her, and she opened the fridge in the vain hope there would be something to tide her over until five, when she could head home. The only stuff in the fridge was clearly other people's food. Ready to give up and try to get by on a few of the sweet biscuits, she saw fruit on the communal table. An apple and a banana would see her through, and perhaps with some food in her belly she would be able to concentrate on her work.

The afternoon crawled by, but Freya managed to get the report done and submitted. On the way to the station, she grabbed a couple of sushi rolls and ate them on the train. The image of Dinah in that ritual circle was stuck in her mind. Although she had pushed it aside at work, it was ready to come back as soon as she let her focus slacken. What did it mean that the vision had changed?

Should she tell Jacob or keep it to herself and try to find out more?

There were no lights on in the apartment as she approached, then she saw the silhouette of Muninn sitting on the railing. Her heart pounded in her throat as she climbed the stairs and approached the slick black bird.

'Hello again,' she said, swallowing although her mouth was dry.

Muninn clicked his beak. She put the heavy black paper bag down in front of the apartment door and went to approach the raven. His breast feathers were soft, warm, and soothing as she stroked him.

'Is something wrong? Where's Jacob?'

A sensation of calm flowed through her, a vision of Jacob driving with his sister beside him swam before her.

'He's taking Dinah somewhere? Why didn't he text me?' She pulled out her phone only to realise it had switched itself off. 'Damn it.' She tried turning it back on, but it refused.

The raven cawed softly, clacked its beak once more and flew off.

'Bye.'

Fancy coming down here just to tell me Jacob was fine.

After the disturbing image of Dinah with the Children of Vali she wasn't sure what to believe. Freya let herself into the cool, dark apartment. She put the shopping down and changed into more comfortable clothes, before making something for dinner. She plugged her phone into the charger in the kitchen and tried turning it back on.

A text from Jacob came through, the time stamp said it was sent just before five o'clock.

Dinah's having a meltdown. Big fight with Dad, details unclear. I'm bringing her to our place but will be late home.

Why didn't he call me? Freya thought to herself as she dialled his number.

'Hey,' Jacob's voice seemed far away, obscured by a lot of background noise.

'Are you driving?'

'Yeah, I've got Deens in the car with me, we're about twenty minutes away.'

'Is everything okay?' she asked, his voice held an unusual strain.

'I'll tell you about it when we get home.'

'Okay, see you soon.' Freya held the phone in her hand, her mind racing. She put some extra pasta into the pot to boil, the sauce would have to stretch to three instead of two.

By the time Jacob and Dinah came through the door the meal was ready waiting for them.

'Do you want food?' Freya called from the kitchen, before turning to greet them. Dinah was ashen-faced, her shoulders hunched double.

Freya's eyes widened in surprise.

'I'd love some, I dunno if Deens is up to it just now,' Jacob said throwing a worried glance his sister's way.

'Of course.' Freya wanted to know what had happened but maybe it was too raw. 'Come sit down love.' She held the teenager's shoulders to guide her to the couch. She felt frozen to the touch, and Freya shivered.

She turned to Jacob with a frown. He shrugged, perhaps Dinah hadn't told him either.

'A nice hot cup of tea I think,' she said.

Jacob followed her into the kitchen, his face held still as though to keep it from betraying his thoughts. 'I'm really worried about her,' he said, his voice a low whisper.

'You can say that again. What the hell?'

'I don't have details yet, but Dad found all the books she had on magic and witchcraft, they had a big blow up. It seems she's done something to him—I don't know if she knows what—but he's forgotten about the whole thing and thinks she's hanging out with us for a fun midweek break.'

'You mean she cast something on him by accident?' Freya understood why the girl was so pale and cold, if she'd used uncontrolled magic—she would be exhausted and confused.

'It seems like it. I didn't push, she seems quite guilty about blasting him.'

'It's a worry.' Freya finished making the cup of hot sweet tea and took it out to Dinah. She'd hunched herself into a ball. Freya wrapped a blanket around her shoulders and returned to Jacob.

They sat at the kitchen table to eat, although she didn't taste the food. 'I got all the stuff for avatars.'

'Dinah's much stronger than she knows. She needs to control herself. That backfire in the warehouse, and now with Dad. What if she blasts someone and really hurts them? We don't know how to heal a magic-induced wound.'

'I didn't mean to,' Dinah said, she had appeared in the kitchen doorway and Freya and Jacob both jumped in surprise.

'Are you feeling a better, love?' Freya asked, some of the colour had returned to her cheeks and she was standing straight again.

'A bit.'

'We were worried about you,' Jacob said as Dinah took a seat at the table. 'Do you want to talk about it?'

Freya grabbed a bowl of pasta and slid it towards her without a word, hoping that she would tell them what had happened, in her own time.

'I was sitting at my desk, supposed to be doing homework, but I was procrastinating by looking at stuff about Vali online, and Dad walks in to check on me and sees the video on the screen and he asks what's that? And I say nothing and close it down, but he was suss by then, so he looked at the stuff I had open on the desk, you know the Star Eagle book, and he saw the rituals and he started asking all these questions and—'

Words were tumbling from her until she suddenly stopped.

'And?' Jacob prompted gently.

'I just wanted him to put the book down and go away, so I told him it was nothing, but he was getting angrier and angrier. I tried to use your voice trick Jacob and he went all slack like he was in a trance. Then I told him he didn't remember coming in and didn't want to ask me anything, and he went back out into the lounge and sat on the couch. But he was like a zombie, and I felt like I'd been hit by a truck, so I texted Jake I thought I was going to pass out, so he came round.'

'Okay.' Freya looked to Jacob; his brow was furrowed in concern.

'He was still sitting there looking vague when I got there,' Jacob said. 'He came good when I said hi. He was surprised to see me, but I went with the first lie that came into my head, that I was there to take Dinah for the night, like we'd planned. He didn't question it.'

'You're sure Dad was okay?' Dinah asked, her fork full of food halted on the way to her mouth.

'Maybe a bit vague. Whenever I used the voice on people in the past, they were fine, but foggy. I don't think he'll suffer any long-term effects.'

'Thank fuck.'

'Dinah, language,' he said.

Freya put her hand on Jacob's hand. 'We've all had a big day, I'm sure it will be alright. You did the spell on purpose then? It wasn't an accident?'

'I didn't know what I was doing, coz I was panicking, but it was on purpose.'

'That's something then. We were worried you'd done it without meaning to. We'll need that practice after all. I got the cauldrons, and the ingredients today.'

'Oh, cool,' Dinah said. 'But the assistant was weird?'

'How—yeah, she was weird. I tried to put her off the scent but I'm not sure it worked. The sooner we have something for people to read instead of a void the better.'

'Yeah.' Dinah shovelled the last mouthful into her mouth and sat back. She was almost back to her usual self. 'I need to sleep for a week.'

'Good idea,' Jacob said. 'You can take the bedroom if you want, Freya will sleep with you, and I'll take the foldout in the spare room.'

Dinah nodded before she pushed herself up and wandered off towards the bathroom.

Freya and Jacob waited for Dinah to go to bed before reopening the conversation. They did the dishes and pottered around while Dinah cleaned her teeth and said goodnight.

'Your dad is okay?' Freya asked, as they sat side by side on the couch.

'He'll be fine.'

'Are you okay?'

'I don't know. It's a worry to have my little sister going around blasting people with magic, even if it was on purpose. We don't know how much attention that blast might have drawn.' He held up his hand to stop

Freya as she opened her mouth to reply. 'I know we're shielded but the last thing we need to do is to have Vali turn up on our doorstep.'

Freya's mind returned to the new vision that Muninn had sent her earlier. 'One of the ravens came to see me today.'

'You didn't say anything about that.'

'We were busy. I saw Dinah in the circle with Vali and the others. What do you think it means?'

Jacob pressed his mouth into a line. 'We said we were going to infiltrate the group, maybe it's good.'

'It didn't feel like good news.'

'Oh.'

'I'm worried Dinah's going to be sucked into the cult. Or do something that reveals us before we're ready and Vali defeats us, and she joins the Children instead of being part of the solution.'

'That's not very nice, thinking she would betray us like that.'

'She would never hurt us on purpose, but she doesn't know her own strength—she's impulsive and we've seen that today.'

Jacob put his hand around Freya's where they lay in her lap. 'I know my sister; she's a bit of a ninny but she's not going to join Vali. I get that you're worried, I'm worried too, but suspicion of each other is the worst thing we could do. We're the three musketeers, nothing can stop us if we're together.'

'I hope you're right.' Freya sighed.

Chapter 7

Freya found it hard to fall asleep with a different person in bed with her, and she woke several times to Dinah whimpering in her sleep. Jacob had offered his spot in the bed to Dinah rather than give her the lumpy fold-out couch.

Jacob was still sleeping in the spare room, when Freya went out into the kitchen to make breakfast. She watched him sleeping for a moment, his face calm, almost happy, free from the burden of their mission, and wished she could leave him like that.

'Time to wake up, hun,' Freya said, shaking his shoulder.

'Oh God.' Jacob groaned before he opened his eyes. 'Next time you get the fold-out couch.'

'That's fair. I'll start on coffee.' She hadn't dreamed much the night before, as was the usual way when her sleep was disturbed. Surprising given the momentous vision Muninn had shown her, although perhaps having had the vision while awake, it didn't come to her dreams.

Going through the motions of making coffee Freya focused on what to do with Dinah. She heard Jacob stretching and getting up, but nothing from the bedroom.

'Has Dinah fallen asleep again? She takes her hearing aids off to sleep.'

'I can take her to school if she's ready when I'm leaving,' Jacob said.

'Come on Deens, you need to get ready for school.' Freya brought the girl coffee into the bedroom in the hopes of coaxing her out. Dinah was playing on her phone.

'I mean it, let's get going.' Freya leaned over to take the phone away, but Dinah pulled it out of reach.

'I'm coming.'

'Can you do it quicker then?' Freya said. 'Please?'

With a dramatic groan, Dinah got out of bed and shuffled into the bathroom.

*

Work was busy, Freya was called into a meeting as soon as she arrived which lasted over two hours. She started on her usual work and was lost in thought when her phone rang at half past twelve.

'Are you coming down? Or do I need to come up and get you?' Eva's voice held a laughing quality, at least her friend wasn't genuinely annoyed.

'Oh my God. I'm sorry, I'll be there in two ticks.'

She locked her computer and raced down to meet her friend. They hadn't seen each other for several weeks, Eva had been caught up with this new man she'd started dating for a few weeks before the ravens showed up, and Freya was keen to hear the details, if there was time. They would talk over the new situation with Vali and the cult first, but she wasn't sure how Eva would feel knowing her magic was back and someone else was threatening to create an apocalyptic portal.

'My darling! Look at you, you're positively drawn,' Eva flung her arms around Freya in a hug as flamboyant as her usual dress sense. Today she was wearing a fuchsia and carrot orange patterned all in one jumpsuit with a sapphire blazer.

'That is an amazing ensemble,' Freya said. Her own typical black and white palette always seemed plain in comparison to her best friend, then again, she couldn't pull it off even if she wanted to.

'I have the best fashion sense of anyone you know. The fact you're constantly surprised is mind boggling.'

They turned to walk down the hill towards Spencer Street to the hole-in-the-wall sandwich place they both liked.

'Honestly darling, are you feeling okay? You seem a bit off, and I don't just mean the bags under your eyes.'

Freya hesitated. 'I wasn't going to say anything yet.'

'What do you mean?' Eva stopped in her tracks so suddenly that Freya had to turn and walk a few steps back to her friend. 'What aren't you telling me?'

'Uh.'

'Freya. You're scaring me.' Eva grabbed her arm.

'I'll tell you, but you need to take a deep breath.' Freya inhaled, and they both exhaled together. 'I have magic again.'

'Oh my God, oh God.'

Fearing Eva would hyperventilate and faint, Freya wrapped her arm around her friend's shoulders and steered her to a bench seat a few metres down the street. The stream of people flowed around them; Freya's attention was on keeping Eva upright.

'It's not like the other time.' Freya knew it might even be worse but saying so to Eva would not help. 'Jacob and I have a plan. We know what we're doing.'

'How do you have magic again? Am I going to get withered again? I couldn't stand it, you'd have to kill me.' Eva's usually deep toffee coloured skin, due to her Indian heritage, had paled to a worrying shade of grey.

'Like I said, it's not like last time. There's no portal open. As far as I know there is no plague. I know it's scary for you but there is nothing to worry about.'

Yet.

'Okay. Alright.' Eva took some deep, shaky breaths and some of the colour returned to her face. 'I must have PTSD or something.'

Freya stroked her friend's upper arm waiting for the panic to subside. 'Do you want to know the details? Or shall we get a sandwich, and I can tell you when we're in the sun, out of the shadow of these buildings.'

'Sandwich and sun. Yes.'

Freya bought the sandwiches and led Eva to their usual spot. A sloping grassy hill looked over Southern Cross train station. Not quite big enough to be a park and still surrounded by the bustle and grind of the city, it was an oasis of green. They sat on the edge of a block, with the sun on their left.

'I got you chicken and avocado,' she said, handing her friend a baguette wrapped in brown paper.

Eva's eyes were glazed, she took the baguette, opened it without looking, and took a bite.

'I was afraid to tell you. I know it's been tough and with the magic back would be harder. I was going to wait till later, when you'd had something to eat and I'd gotten the goss on your new beau.'

'You seem different.' Eva frowned at her.

'Yeah, people keep saying that. I've shielded myself so people can't sense my thoughts, but it's off-putting. I'm working on it.'

'It's better if I don't look directly at you.'

Freya nodded and took a bite of her egg and salad baguette. They ate in silence for a while.

'How do you know something is happening, you know, with magic?' Eva asked.

'The ravens visited.'

'And?'

'I wasn't sure how much you wanted to know.'

'I want to know everything you know. I deserve that.'

Freya sighed. 'You're right. Tell me if it's too much, okay? There is this guy calling himself Vali.' Freya laid out what they knew in an uninterrupted monologue, her partially-eaten baguette in her hands. Eva nibbled at her lunch, nodding occasionally, but seemed mostly to be focussed on the patch of grass directly in front of her black suede shoes.

'You said he has videos online?'

'Yes. But I don't think you should look into them. He's quite charismatic, and I don't know if you're maybe in danger of being swayed because of your... history.'

'I'm sure I can manage not to join a cult.'

She looked at her friend, unsure whether she had taken offence. The small upward turn of her lips reassured Freya she was kidding.

'In that case.'

'It might be interesting to watch them. I could help you out with research or something.'

'You want to get involved? I would have thought you'd want to be as far away from the whole thing as you could get.'

'That's very tempting, but another part of me needs to know my enemy.'

'Okay, I'll send you some stuff to look at. I don't totally know what he's planning, but he says Ragnarök is coming and in order to survive it we need to be in his group. It's standard cult leader stuff, but it seems to be true. The last portal between one of the nine realms and ours nearly caused an apocalypse, if a very slow one.'

Eva poked at a tuft of grass with the toe of her shoe, the soft green blades crushed under it started to unfurl slowly as she moved her foot back. 'I want to help. I can't do anything, you know, magical, and meeting anyone in person would be too much but watching and talking to you and Jacob would be okay. Do you think you could get me some of the protection stuff you have? So people don't see me?'

Freya squeezed her friend's hand. 'You're so amazing. I'll get you a pouch to wear like mine, I'll try not to make it so strong so you don't end up with the weird emptiness I have, that's almost as bad as not wearing the pouch at all.' She touched the place on her breastbone where the pouch hung on its string around her neck.

'And you're sure they're not draining people? I'm not in any danger of that again?'

'No, there's nothing to point to that. I think that was a special side effect of the deal Victor made. Vali seems to be working in a different area of magic.'

'And Dinah did the Jedi mind trick on her dad? I can't believe that worked.'

'I was surprised, more that she had done it almost without intending to. She needs to get better at controlling her emotions—'

'Do you remember what we were like at that age? Enormous blobs of emotional chaos bumbling around, wrapped in the most precarious layer of decorum and sanity.'

Freya laughed. 'I do have a vague memory of being angry with the world at her age.'

'I'm sure she'll put in the work; the vision could mean anything. Maybe you all join the cult to take it down from the inside.'

'That's what Jacob said.' She looked at her watch, it was time to head back to work. 'Are you going to be okay?'

'It was a shock, at first. I had thought I'd never have to deal with magic again.'

'Same.'

'But you're more confident this time. And I'm going to help, behind the scenes. I'll be okay. You have to keep me in the loop, okay? No more surprises.'

'I promise. I'll add you to the group chat now so you can keep up with everything. Want me to walk you to your office?'

'I'm going to sit in the sun a bit longer, thanks for lunch.' Eva turned to hug her.

Freya walked back up the hill to her office, her prosthetic eye itched, and the scars on her eyelid prickled. Maybe it meant something, maybe it didn't. At least she didn't have mind-numbing visions without warning anymore, all the shielding and work on control were having a few positive effects.

At her desk that afternoon, she patted the pouch of herbs she wore around her neck where it sat under her blouse. It was soothing to remind herself it was there, although she would have to curb the habit before she met the Children of Vali, they would understand the significance of such a pouch.

*

By the weekend Freya was impatient to try out some more spells, she'd been reading over the books and re-

reading the hand-written books left by Hettie. Power sung through the pages calling to her; enticing her to flex her new muscles.

Dinah texted the group on Friday night.

Dad won't let me hang out with you on the weekend. I have an English assignment due on Monday, and ever since, y'know, he's been all clingy. I've created a monster, LOL.

'I guess that means we're free to do whatever this weekend then,' Freya said to Jacob as they lay in bed.

'Let's go up to the packing shed and practise first thing tomorrow. Maybe we can have the day off all this on Sunday and go see a band or something on Sunday afternoon.'

Freya turned to him. 'That sounds great, you haven't wanted to see a gig for ages.'

'I lost my mojo. Singing didn't have the same appeal when I lost all that power, and playing guitar without singing wasn't as much fun.'

'And now?'

'I have it all back. Maybe I can tamp it down. I'm better at controlling it now, but I want to feel the music again.'

'That sounds nice.' With all their shielding and with Vali and his minions all up in the country it seemed low risk, but still, a cold trickle of dread seeped into Freya's belly.

*

Fleur Blüm

The drive up to the packing shed was much more pleasant in the daylight. They listened to the youth music station on the radio; even though both of them had aged out of the demographic.

Freya's breakfast of toast and coffee sat in a lump in her belly, her anxiety was not helped by the fact she had started her menstrual cycle during the night.

'What's up? You're in a mood this morning,' Jacob said, flicking his eyes to her as he drove.

'Nothing.'

'Is that true or do you not want to talk about it?'

She turned to watch the trees sliding past. 'I have a bad feeling.'

'Can you be any more specific?'

She hesitated, and turned back to Jacob. 'I know you want to sing but I'm worried.'

Jacob said nothing, his hands on the steering wheel. The song played on, their indifference to it highlighting the tension between them. Freya knew she shouldn't have brought it up in the car.

'How about this, I'll give singing a try today while trying not to use my talent, and if it works then we'll do the open mic tomorrow?'

'Thank you.' The tension she had been holding drained away; her shoulders dropped and her gut unclenched.

The packing shed seemed smaller in daylight, the ominous shadows and dark spots were pushed away by the sunlight. The sky overhead was bright blue, so sharp it hurt Freya's eyes as she looked up at it. Circling over them were the ravens, and the chill of concern in her belly returned.

'Look,' she said, pointing up at them.

'We have company,' Jacob replied.

The ravens continued to swoop around above them, making no move to join them on the ground. 'Maybe they're not saying hi today.'

They had brought a set of bright battery-operated LED standing lamps, the sort sometimes used for car maintenance, with a bright yellow handle and blinding if you looked into them directly. The door was still unlocked, from when Freya had broken the padlock on their last visit. Jacob had purchased another padlock to keep the lights and other stuff in the shed secure after they left today.

Even with bright light, the interior of the shed was dim. Rubbish and debris were strewn all over the empty floor. 'Do you wanna play with our powers first? Or should we tidy up?' Freya wanted to play but the rubble-covered ground seemed unsanitary.

'Better start with a nice space. No good throwing power around if we're gonna get dust in our eyes.'

'You can be very domestic when you want to be, Mister Olsen.'

'That's why you love me.' He winked at her and handed her a large stiff broom, brought for the purpose. By the time they'd collected up all the detritus and swept the floor, Freya was hot and sweaty and not at all satisfied with her work. Usually when she'd finished a big cleaning job there was a sense of achievement, but it was only the first in a series of hurdles for the day.

'Coffee break?' she said, leaning the broom against the wall near the wicket gate.

'We've earned it.'

Before they left home, Jacob had filled a large thermos with coffee and they stopped at a bakery on the way up to get some sweet treats and sandwiches to keep them going. They sat on the back ledge of his silver four-wheel drive and had a picnic of sorts.

'Our friends are still here,' Freya said, pointing to where two ravens were sitting on a fence.

'Maybe they're reporting back to the big cheese, whoever that is.'

'They're Odin's familiars so I guess to him. It's weird to know that Odin is a real—not a person, but a real entity.' She giggled, it was one thing to know she had magical abilities, powers that came from outside of the natural order of things, but it was quite another to believe that the gods of mythology were out there.

'Do you think they're waiting for us to try some stuff out? To see whether we blow our heads off?'

'They're on our side.'

'We hope they're on our side.'

'I can't imagine Odin, or whoever, wants some dipshit cult leader bringing on Ragnarök. I guess the end of the world will come at some point, but Vali is not the guy I'd choose to do it.'

'I'm sure the Aesir want to destroy the world themselves.' Jacob shoved the last piece of vanilla slice into his mouth with more force than necessary and then had to chew hard to get it down.

She brushed off the crumbs on her pants and stood. 'Wanna do some magic?' It was hard not the be excited about the idea of flinging her power around. Sure, it would be tiring, but the only way to improve her stamina was practice. She would need all the strength they could muster when it came to trying to fight a whole coven with only three.

The first thing she wanted to work on was telekinesis; moving things at a distance would be very handy when it came to a fight. They headed into the now sparce but mostly tidy warehouse.

'The books suggest I should be able to channel energy from the universe through myself to move things.'

'Right. What are you going to move?'

'I thought I'd start with the thermos—see if I can get it to rise off the ground.' She had brought it with her, and now placed it on the ground.

'What should I do?'

'Can you observe and make note of what sensations you have? I want to know if you can feel or see me working.'

He nodded and stood behind her, his face set in concentration.

Freya took a deep breath, closed her eyes and imagined the silver-white threads of magical power in

110

the universe. It flowed like water past her mind's eye. All she had to do was redirect some of it to her, and then out to the thermos. In the blackness behind her eyes, she reached out with her imaginary hand, dipping her finger into the stream and dragging it back towards her. Her fingers felt both hot and cold at once and she almost pulled away from the sensation. When the stream of power connected to her chest she felt a jolt and then a hot and cold shivery sensation.

Freya fluttered her eyes open, brought her hands together in front of her and raised them while imagining the thread of power flowing from her chest out her fingers and into the thermos. She poured her concentration into the action, clenching her teeth, and just as she was about to give up and try again, the thermos wobbled and fell over.

'Was that you?' Jacob asked, breathless.

'I think so.' She released her concentration and the hot and cold flow of power left her. 'Did you feel it?'

Jacob shivered. 'It's hard to describe. It was prickly, like I needed to sneeze but not that, and then I felt a bit sort of hot.'

Freya nodded. 'And when the thermos fell, any different? And now?'

'No, it felt the same when it fell, but the prickling was gone as soon as you spoke.'

'I let go. It feels super strange to channel like that. Did you see or hear anything?'

'No, just the sneezy feeling. Can I have a go?'

'Sure.' She explained what she had done, Jacob nodded, he had read the same books. They swapped positions, Freya stood behind him, to the side so she could see his profile. He closed his eyes and took a breath. She felt the prickling in the air, her skin tingled and her throat itched as though she needed to sneeze or cough. Jacob opened his eyes, held out his hands and exhaled. The tingling in the air wobbled, briefly intensifying then dying away. He let out his breath in a grunt.

'It didn't work.'

'I felt it. You might not have moved the thermos this time, but it was working.'

'Really?' he turned to face her, his face alight with joy.

'Yes.' She smiled back, it was so long since she'd seen him so excited. 'Let me try again.' She stepped forward, reached towards the stream of silver-white light, pulled some to her chest, opened her eyes and instead of forcing the light towards it, she imagined the thermos rising. The hot-cold prickling in her fingers increased as the power flowed out of her. The thermos wobbled, tipped to the left, straightened and hovered a centimetre above the ground before dropping down again.

'You did it.' Jacob was leaning forward on his toes, almost bouncing with excitement.

'I got it up—' she giggled at the word choice, but also in relief that it had worked. 'Did it feel the same for you?'

'Yeah, pretty much.'

Jacob stepped forward, and Freya moved back to give him some space. He held his eyes closed longer, and moved his hands forward and out slower, his brow furrowed in concentration. Around her the air prickled even more than last time, she could almost hear it buzzing.

Just let it move through you, you don't have to force it. As before, the prickling energy disappeared as quickly as it had come on and Jacob stood, shoulders hunched in defeat. Freya put her hand on his upper back.

'It's no good,' he said.

'The thermos didn't move but it felt more powerful from where I stood. You'll get there.' She dropped her hand to her side and a wave of fatigue washed over her. 'I think I need a little sit-down.'

'Me too.' Jacob ran his hand through his hair and scrubbed it down across his face. 'The back of the car is empty now, we could chill on the blankets.'

Freya nodded and they went back into the sunlight. After spending so long in the shed she squinted and threw an arm up to shield her eyes. They lay down on blankets and pillows in the back of the four-wheel drive. Jacob had folded down the back seats, their feet sticking out a little. It wasn't the most comfortable place to rest but her eyes drifted closed.

*

Freya woke a while later; the sun sat low in the sky. When she looked at her watch she was surprised to see several hours had passed Jacob was spooning her, breathing softly on her neck, his body pressed against hers.

'Are you awake?' she asked.

'No.'

'You want to try one more time before we head back to the city? Or maybe singing?'

He raised his head, peering over her shoulder to look at the sky. 'It's getting late, we must have slept soundly.'

'I definitely did, even without any padding on this.' She rolled onto her back and stretched, feeling the stiffness that had crept into her body from sleeping on the hard surface. 'Next time we'll bring foam for the back.'

'Agreed.' Jacob groaned and pushed himself out of the car. The temperature had dropped with the late afternoon, and they both shivered in the chill breeze. 'I want to try to lift the thermos one more time, then I'll give singing without using my talent a go. What about you?'

'I have a few other things I want to try, but maybe I'll just give the telekinesis another try with more control or for a longer time. It's one thing to levitate the thing, but another to be able to do something useful.'

Back inside, Jacob tried, but failed to make the thermos move. When Freya tried a third time, she focused on being casual, coaxing the power from the source rather than dragging it to her with her own energy. She allowed the power to flow through her, directing the thermos to rise, hold in the air and placed it back down a foot or so to the left. She released the silvery energy and grinned.

'That was impressive, but what did you do? It hardly even felt prickly that time.'

'It's hard to explain but I tried less.'

'Right, I'll give that a go.'

Jacob stood, his feet placed wide, shoulders pulled in and tensed.

This isn't going to work, he's forcing it.

As before the prickling crept through the air, making the hair on the back of her neck stand up, but the thermos didn't move.

'I can't do it. This sucks.'

'You'll get there. I think it's about practice and getting the right . . . touch.'

'Easy for you to say, you got it first time.' Jacob's lips pressed together as though he was trying to suppress a pout.

'Do you want to try singing? Or have a little break?'

'I'll have a breather.'

Freya removed the thermos from the centre of the shed and put in its place a plastic water bottle from the junk they'd tidied earlier. She walked a few paces back and set up her focus. Each time she did it, there was less resistance, and she didn't have to think as hard about it. In her mind's eye she visualised the bottle crumpling and flying back towards the wall of the shed. With an exhale she pushed her hands out from her chest, letting the silvery power flow from her. The bang when the bottle hit the wall startled her and she lost her grip on the thread of power.

'Was that you?' Jacob had covered the space between them in a couple of steps, looking around the space for the source of the noise.

'I thought it would be a fizzer like the first time.' The water bottle was in a ball at the bottom of the wall about forty metres away. A few feet up the wall was a mark where it had hit. Freya ran her fingers over the spot.

'Wow.' Jacob picked up the ball of squashed plastic.

'Imagine if it had been something more solid. I'll have to be careful, don't wanna punch holes in our practice room.' She laughed, a breathy sound she hoped wouldn't betray the concern she felt. If not used carefully the power could harm someone she loved, or herself.

'All that and hardly even a prickle in the air. I only noticed because I knew you were doing it. Alright, my turn and we'll call it a day?'

Freya nodded. Jacob hadn't brought his guitar with him, he took a breath and started to sing one of his favourite warm-up songs. With eyes closed, she focused on the air around her; when he used his power to sing a sense of euphoria and trance-like calm fell over people. She was less susceptible but still felt the effect. He moved on to an original song he'd written a few months before they'd met, a melancholy ballad of love unrequited. She started to sway, and the melody trickled into her, a smile spreading across her lips.

'I used it, didn't I?' he said.

She opened her eyes. 'I don't know. I really liked it, but it might have been in a regular way, not in a magic way. I've missed your singing.'

'Thanks.' Jacob's cheeks turned pink. 'Maybe I'll try some practice at home tomorrow and we can see if it's still non-magical.'

'Deal.' She leaned forward to kiss him, feeling more hopeful than she had for weeks knowing he might be able to control his power, at least to turn it off.

Freya drove home, Jacob had used an enormous amount of energy through the afternoon to force the power to do what he wanted, while she felt relatively fresh. The technique of inviting rather than dragging the silvery thread through herself was much less taxing on her body, although she caught herself yawning more and more as they neared the apartment.

Once she pulled up, she shook Jacob's shoulder gently, his head lolled back. 'We're home.'

'Hmm?'

'You fell asleep, get out of the car and come into bed.'

Jacob looked around, the warm, amber glow of the streetlights fell over the apartment parking area, it wasn't late, but no one else could be seen.

*

In the morning Freya woke to find Jacob already making breakfast. He looked much refreshed after falling asleep almost immediately after arriving home.

'Morning, gorgeous.' He held a cup of coffee in her direction. 'I was going to come in and wake you when the food was ready.'

'Maybe I smelled it in my sleep.' She smiled, something about the set of his shoulders, his easy grin, made her think some of the tension he'd been carrying had drained away. 'Did you sleep well?'

'I must have, I feel great this morning. I don't think I even dreamed, which is a relief, I've been having all these dreams about Vali and his minions finding us and doing awful things to you and Dinah.'

'You never said.' She reached out to touch his shoulder.

'I didn't want to worry you. They're not visions, like you have, just dreams, but it's been a recurring nightmare. I'm in a field watching you fight Vali and you lose.'

'Sounds awful, I'm glad you were able to have a break from it.'

He must have been really worried; I can't believe I didn't see it.

With everything she'd been considering it hadn't occurred to her that Jacob would be overwhelmed and anxious. He was such a strong, competent person, never let his worries show on his face, but in the couple of years she'd known him, she should have learned that just because he didn't say anything didn't mean he wasn't thinking about it.

'Music used to be my way of getting out of my head, but since the last time, I haven't trusted myself to play. I didn't want to accidentally put someone into a trance—I thought the magic was gone but didn't trust it.'

'Are you going to give it a try today? With a little practice, I'm sure you'll be able to sing without entrancing people.'

'Ask me again after we've eaten. Here.' He handed her a plate of steaming French toast with strawberries on the side. The syrup and cutlery were already on the kitchen table behind her.

They were quiet over breakfast, Freya gave Jacob space to talk if he needed to, but he seemed content to sit in silence. After breakfast there were chores to do, her usual Saturday tasks had been put off so they could get out to the packing shed early. They needed groceries too, but it could wait for a couple of days.

When Jacob was ready to practise singing, she would need to be there to give him feedback on whether he had been using his talent, in the meantime, she did the dishes, put on a load of laundry and pottered around the house.

The twanging sound of a guitar string filtered through to her from the spare bedroom. It was sorely out of tune, and she hoped that none of the strings snapped after so long not being used. He didn't do any vocal warm-ups, but went into one of his favourite covers, *Wonderwall*. The air around her shimmered a little, the thoughts running through her mind drifted away and she was mesmerised by the music, despite a couple of fumbles.

The next song was one he'd sung yesterday in the shed, and this time she felt less of a drag on her attention. Bringing up the washing she was holding in her hands, she put it onto the clothes airer for drying and realised her hands were cold and damp from having held it through the first song.

'How was that?' Jacob called from the other room.

'Good babe, seems like you still remember the songs.'

'I meant, y'know, did you feel any powers?' Jacob put his head out of the door into the lounge this time, his voice softer as though nervous.

'The first one definitely, I forgot what I was doing and was all slack-jawed and glassy-eyed. Second song seemed better, I could concentrate, did you do something different?'

'Sort of the opposite of drawing power—I visualised a barrier of cotton wool between me and the silver stream of power.'

'Good plan. I wonder if there's some in you too, maybe you need to wrap cotton wool around that, in your mind, as well?'

'Good idea.' Jacob smiled and retreated again into the spare bedroom. He played another four songs, which had almost no effect on Freya's mood, at least in a magic sense. She bobbed her head along with the rhythm and noticed herself smiling. It was good to hear his singing again, the rich, gravelly, bass voice always sent thrills of attraction through her body. Despite usually being uninterested in sex when she was on her period, she wanted to run to Jacob and pull him to her.

A little while later Jacob emerged from the spare bedroom grinning. 'How was that?'

'Mmm, lovely,' Freya replied, her mind was full of pleasant fantasies of when they first met, how they had such intense chemistry, even of the time they'd nearly given themselves away to Victor by taking off their protection pouches while making love. Victor had found her apartment from the signal, and it had never felt safe to be there afterwards. Even now, with all her new knowledge and skill with her talents, she was anxious about creating something big enough to get noticed without meaning to.

'I meant did you feel any magic?'

'Oh.' She sat up a little straighter in the armchair and tried to banish her lustful thoughts. 'No, I think we're safe.'

'I'd forgotten how good it felt to noodle around. I used to do it all the time, you know, before I met you.' He stood behind the armchair, resting his hands on her shoulders and gently rubbing them. He had such strong, sensual hands.

'I think I better go for a little walk. I need to clear my head.' Freya stood up sharply.

'Do you want company?'

'No, I'll be back in a bit.'

Jacob's face fell, but he said nothing. She slipped on her running shoes and went out the door with her keys, phone and headphones.

A walk will do me good, I can't jump his bones today, it's not safe until we have the cauldrons set up, we're too close to muck it up by sending up a flare of sex magic.

An hour or so later she returned to the apartment, the late afternoon sun sank low and the air had started to get cold, although she barely felt it. She'd walked hard and fast keeping her mind on putting one foot in front of the other.

She opened the door quietly, unsure how Jacob would react to her leaving.

'You're back,' he said, the furrow between his brows lessening in relief.

'Sorry.'

'What are you sorry for?'

'I thought you might have been mad . . .'.

'I didn't understand it, but we've had some heavy stuff happening lately. I was getting a horny vibe off you, but then you left.'

'About that . . . you were right. But I don't want to set off any light shows.'

'Is that why you haven't been interested lately? I thought it was stress, or something. I never thought about the fact we have powers.' He patted the couch next to him. 'Maybe we'll take a rug up to the shed next time and give it a try. At least that way we're not at home, and we should be far enough away, with the dampening pouches and stuff.'

'That sounds like a great idea. I'm sorry I didn't say anything earlier. I wasn't sure how to bring it up.'

'It can be tricky, but I'm not going to be angry with you, if you need something, or you want me to change, you just have to tell me.'

'I know.' She turned to him, 'I worry you'll think I've turned into your ex, wanting everything just so, and being demanding.'

'You could never be Rhonda. She didn't want a boyfriend so much as a man-shaped accessory. You see me as a human being, you're safe from comparison to her.'

*

The bar where the open mic was to be held was in Northcote, north of their apartment. The suburb had been the hub for live music for years but was starting to become too expensive for the musicians and student types that made a music scene thrive to live in. The stage where the open mic would be held was at the front, the windows open, and concertinaed flat so smokers outside could hear the performers, further inside the venue was a pool table, then the bar along the left wall, and tables opposite. A couple of people played pool, two were hanging around at the bar, and the rest of the crowd, all four of them, were sat around one table at the back.

'It's really jumping tonight.' Jacob's breath was warm on her ear.

'At least it's not too big a crowd for your first time back. I'm sure they're all performers too, so they'll be forgiving if anything goes awry.'

'Thanks for the vote of confidence.'

'You know what I mean—prepare for the worst, and when it goes well, you'll be pleasantly surprised.'

'I'm going to find the organiser, and put my guitar out the back, you wanna grab us a couple of beers?'

'Sure.' Freya leaned forward to give Jacob a peck on the lips. 'For luck.'

A small square table near the stage offered a good view of the room, and meant she didn't encroach on the group, or the pool table.

'Should we have invited friends?' Jacob said, sitting next to her on an identical hard wooden chair.

'To stack the audience?'

'They could use the patronage.'

'Next time. Eva would come, maybe we could rope my brother in.'

'Is he a musician?'

'No, he wishes he were. He's got an arty look, but no talent.'

'Is that fair?' Jacob sipped his beer, a local IPA the barman had recommended.

'His words, not mine.'

'That's different.' He smiled, dropping his free hand onto her thigh. The warmth permeated her black jeans, the weight of it familiar, comforting. Her beer was a golden ale; she didn't like strong beer, preferring wine instead, but she suspected the beer would be better than the wine in this place.

The man organising the open mic was named Jonathan, a tall, thin, fey-looking man with long, dead-straight, strawberry-blonde hair. He stepped up to the microphone on the stage.

'Greetings, my beauties, welcome to another night of merriment and song here at the Grumpy Giant. We have a fantastic line up for you tonight, many of our regulars are here again,' he swept his hand out, indicating the scattered crowd, 'and a new face or two, for a little extra spice.' Jonathan went on for a while longer, telling an uninspired story about changing a lightbulb in his share house, before introducing the first act; a sullen-looking youth with an angular electric guitar and a pedal board with eight effects pedals. Despite looking like a metal head, he played a meandering prog rock song which involved a lot of looping and went for the entire fifteen-minute allotted time. He had not put any distortion over his vocals, but Freya had no idea what he said nonetheless; he seemed to mumble into the mic rather than sing, thought the impression was pleasant.

After this first act, the host came back to relate another rambling anecdote, allowing time to change equipment. The second performer was a tall, round-faced and round-bodied man wearing a trucker cap. He played all covers of popular country songs on a battered acoustic guitar. His voice sounded more like gravel falling down a metal pipe than singing, but it suited the style. He played five songs before the host hustled up on stage.

'Thank you, Brett, plenty of material as always.'

Freya turned to Jacob and raised her eyebrows. 'Overstayed his welcome.'

'Fifteen minutes isn't long, perhaps Brett has done that before.'

Next was a duo, a petite slim woman of indeterminate age, and a man of similar proportions. The woman sang, the man played an electric piano.

'Do you think they're a couple or siblings?' Jacob whispered in her ear as they applauded the end of the duo's first song.

'Hard to tell, but I'm going with siblings.'

'A big round of applause for Ross and Gemma, great to see you both back here after a hiatus of a couple of weeks. Up next, we have Jacob, new to our little community. You wanna get yourself ready up here, Jake?'

Beside her, Jacob stood abruptly and jogged to the back of the room where his guitar waited. The host covered with banter about the woman working behind the bar and their ongoing disagreement over the proper topping for nachos. As Jacob was setting up, Freya's belly tightened and she clasped her hands together. If anyone with talent was in the room tonight, they would know if he let any magic out. The protection pouch would hide him a little, but in the same room it would be impossible not to feel the trance. The normal people, without any magic in them, would feel stoned and perhaps have a notion of him being good but no proper memory, but practitioners would know.

Jacob strummed out the intro to his first song, one of his original compositions, Freya sat forward on her seat, preparing for the lyrics to start, but the guitar kept going.

She smiled broadly.

It'll be okay, you can do this, she thought, hoping he would pick up her vibe if not her message. The first words he sang were wobbly, his throat tight with nerves, but after the initial phrase, he fell into his normal deeply resonate tone. Her shoulders dropped, there was no tell-tale prickle of electricity in the air and she was happy and calm, but not in a magical way. Some of the lyrics came back to her and she mouthed the words along with him, becoming caught up in the moment, loving watching her partner on the stage for the first time in over two years. He looked at home up there even though his stance was tight.

As he strummed the last chord of the song and took a half step back from the microphone the small audience applauded wildly. Even without using his magic Jacob's voice was enchanting. Freya cheered and clapped and Jacob beamed back. It was such a joy to see him able to do something he loved after being afraid of it for so long.

The second and third song were equally successful, both originals, and his final song was Wonderwall, the one he liked to end with. Halfway through the second verse, Freya felt, rather than saw, a shimmering in the energy in the room. His concentration was slipping, perhaps he was so wrapped up in the performance he hadn't maintained the dampening around him. She waved her hand in front of her chest, indicating for him to tone it down. He glanced at her, registering the gesture, and there was a surge in the energy, like she had been dumped in it before it disappeared as quickly as it had come. A blip as he tried to hold concentration on the song and the spell simultaneously.

'Thank you very much,' Jacob said, giving a small, tight bow. The room was silent for a long moment until Freya started to clap, which brought the audience out of their reverie, and they all followed her.

'Wow, Jacob! Where have you been all my life? I've never heard anyone do such a phenomenal job on their first try,' the host said taking the microphone from the stand in front of Jacob. 'Another round of applause for the dark horse. Come back and see us again soon, Jake.' He winked at Jacob when he said this, Freya thought he was flirting.

Jacob packed up his guitar and came back to take the seat next to her. 'I'm sorry, babe, this was a mistake. I shouldn't have come.'

'What do you mean? You were amazing, you were inspiring. I haven't seen you that happy for a long time.'

'But the . . . I felt it blast out of me.'

'You were leaking a little, and there was a moment where it was full power before you got it under control, but I don't think it will attract attention, and I doubt the patrons will have any memory of it.'

'What if one of them is a child of Vali? They're all over the internet, any one of them could be in with him.'

'So far, I haven't clocked anyone giving the "why don't you seem to feel right" look I get from people who can sense the shielding, and I haven't felt any power in the room, so I think, I hope, we'll be okay. Sometimes we have to live and not spend our whole lives waiting for an apocalypse.' She put her hand on his thigh, and he rested his hand on top of hers. Jacob's other leg was bouncing up and down, perhaps burning off some of the nervous energy. Despite her words, Freya worried the slip was obvious enough to tip off someone in the room. Just one person who knew what it was could get on some forums and the word could get back to Vali. It was a risk they'd both agreed to, but she wondered also if it had been worth it.

'You were so great, Jake, just fantastic.' The host sidled up to them an hour or so later after the last act. He had been staring at Jacob ever since he stepped off the stage, and Freya had a solid ball of dread forming in her stomach. 'I wondered if you have enough material for a full set, forty-five minutes, I run band nights and I'd love to have you on my list.'

A frown flitted across Jacob's brows, before he plastered his friendliest smile on. 'I'm just getting back into performing, ask me again next time?'

'Playing hard to get, I see. Here's my number, call me if you change your mind, otherwise, I'll see you here next week, maybe.' He winked again, his hand lingering on Jacob's longer than seemed necessary.

Jacob was silent as they walked out until they were both in the car, seatbelt on and key in the ignition. 'I think he was flirting with me.'

Freya laughed. 'You might be right.'

'I never know when someone is interested, especially not men.'

'I don't think he gave you his number only for professional reasons, let's say that.'

'As long as he doesn't know I'm a witch.' He smiled, and put the car into gear. There had been a wobble or two, but overall, a successful evening. Control was important in defeating their enemy, not only having the power, but wielding it well was their best hope for winning.

Chapter 8

The days after Jacob performed at the open mic, Freya checked the forums and videos of Vali and his disciples, in case they had caught wind of something.

She had collected as much of her menstrual fluid as she could and added it to the cauldron. The ritual to create an avatar would require her energy and focus, and she wanted to wait until they were all three together to create a more powerful circle. Dinah had started her period a few days after Freya and would be finished by the weekend.

'Can we get Dinah to come up to the shed on the weekend? We should have all the stuff for the cauldrons,' she said to Jacob as they sipped tea in front of the TV on Wednesday evening.

'She can come hang out after soccer practice on Saturday. If we pick her up, we'll probably get another hour with her, especially if the game is late in the afternoon.' He looked into middle distance for a moment. 'I'll have to get my deposit ready, won't I? I mean, how much do you think I need?'

'You're the one who read Crowley's spell. I have like fifty mills, so about that much?'

'I never thought I would need to know how much I produced in millilitres.' He laughed but his fingers gripped the cup so tightly his fingertips were white.

'It's awkward, but the sensible next step. Unless you're angling for me to give you a hand.'

'I can manage it myself. If you insisted, I'd have to allow you to assist.'

It had been a while since they had fooled around, on top of her cycle she hadn't wanted to test whether they would make another beacon. 'Better not.'

'You're right.' He leaned over to kiss her, lingering on her lips, his scent was enthralling, Freya's throat tightening, breath hitching, thighs pressing together suddenly aware of what lay at the apex. And then he pulled away. 'What a great way to get started.'

She watched his round, tight bottom as he walked into the bedroom and longed to follow him. *Next time at the shed*, she thought.

While Jacob was taking care of things, Freya texted Dinah.

We need to do the cauldron ritual. I've got mine, you're nearly there, Jacob will have his soon. This weekend come round to stay with us and we'll go up to the shed.

Once they were shielded and had avatars to prevent others from realising how they were blocking their power, it would be time to approach Vali. She didn't know how long it might take to get into his inner circle, to uncover his real goals. The content online, in the forums, hinted at his plan, but he didn't go so far as to state he wanted to cause Ragnarök and punch a hole to Jotunheim.

Freya had subscribed to Vali's YouTube channel, and signed up for the email newsletter, which was a rambling, stream of consciousness rant every other day, often rehashing what they'd said in the live streams.

All the other ingredients she needed for the avatars were sorted out, having purchased them from the magic shop a few weeks ago. Which reminded her, she hadn't heard anything from Theo. Not that he contacted her unless she went into the shop. Then she realised she'd never given him her phone number or email address, and he hadn't asked. Perhaps he didn't want to contact her, in case he had to do more work.

That's an errand for tomorrow, she decided. Fifteen minutes passed before Jacob re-emerged.

'That was weird,' he said, placing the small black cauldron back on the shelf behind the TV.

'What do you mean?'

'It was fine, but I kept thinking about what I was collecting for, and then I got distracted by how Vali is evil and I hate that we're doing this again, saving the world, and it made it very difficult to finish.'

'Oh.' She wasn't sure she would have been able to concentrate with all of that going through her mind, but he'd done the job. Her phone buzzed on the coffee table and she grabbed it.

'Dinah says she's in for the weekend. She'll meet us here about one.'

'Cool.' Jacob sat next to her, resting his head on her shoulder as the show she was watching automatically rolled over to the next episode. She knew it was possible to turn the feature off, but sometimes, having the streaming service make decisions for her helped.

*

Work on Thursday was steady, not too hectic, and Freya took her lunchbreak a little before one to stroll down to the occult bookshop.

Up the secluded set of stairs, the little shop looked much as it always did; as though it should be dusty despite being clean. Perhaps it was the light filtering in through the opaque windows at the top of the room, or the thick smell of incense and old books. Theo was in a far corner discussing something in hushed tones with a young woman. Her hair was an unnatural blue-black that matched her dark clothing and chipped black nail polish—perhaps a witch in the making, or a rebellious youth trying to gain the attention of her parents. Freya had looked much the same in her teens and early twenties. At least she didn't have any regrettable tattoos to permanently mark her dalliances, some of the young people she saw nowadays had covered themselves in ink they might regret later.

After another minute of urgent whispered conversation, the young woman followed Theo to the counter to make her purchase. Freya tried to look innocuous and buried her attention in a pulpy-looking pocket guide to reading tarot cards.

'You're back,' Theo said, interrupting her studious pretending.

'Good to see you too.'

'You haven't fixed that black hole yet.'

'There is an element of timing in that.' She assumed he knew what the ritual involved, he'd given her the books after all, but perhaps he didn't understand menstruation in the way some men had of remaining obstinately oblivious.

He made a surprised grunting noise, before scribbling something down on a notepad beside the till. When he looked at her again, he seemed to have pulled himself together. 'I don't have anything to report. There's nothing much going around the circles I travel in.'

Freya raised an eyebrow. 'Nothing to report?'

'I'll put the kettle on.' He slipped behind the little curtain, and she heard the tap running and the electric kettle switch on.

'Rumours, people talk. These children of Vali are getting their fingers into things they shouldn't be. Stepping on a lot of toes, and some people are miffed about it.'

'That tracks, they're zealots.'

'A few women have left groups they were part of for years to be part of Vali's harem. People with real skills and who should know better, but somehow don't when it comes to him.'

'Skills?' Freya prompted after he'd been silent for a time. There were no other people in the shop, she sometimes wondered how he stayed open.

'A friend of a friend, Bianca, very talented at predicting events, usually romances or break-ups, and finding things, especially if they were high in sentimental value. She lost her son in a car accident about a year ago. It was a traumatic time for her, and all on top of the whole—well we don't need to talk about that.' Theo prepared the tea and handed her a mug.

'After two very challenging years one on top of another, she was lost, looking for someone to tell her how to be happy again, and along comes Vali. He has the message down to a fine art, exactly what you need to do to hone your skills, to get what you want in life. He provides meaning to people who have tragedy in their lives. She started watching the stuff online, you know, then going on retreats, very expensive of course, and fasting, going on restrictive diets, and before anyone knows what's happening, she's cut herself off from her circle, a group she joined some thirty years ago, and only listens to what Vali says.'

Freya nodded. She'd heard it before, the allure of certainty. Gurus all through time had used the same techniques to attract people who had been betrayed, by another person, or by their belief in a benevolent power, and were looking for someone to guide them.

Theo sipped his tea. 'Her coven is furious. She was one of the founding members, a pillar of the community, and to see her fall prey to this charlatan with no gifts to speak of, it's put a lot of people out. And, of course, it's the same all across Melbourne. Possibly further abroad, although my sources are not good outside Victoria.'

'A list of members would be handy.' Freya spoke, almost to herself.

'I'm keeping track of people who seem to have been seduced, yes. I won't be able to tell you all of them, especially if they weren't in the scene before joining, young people or people new to the community, but I have four on my list already.'

'I saw twelve or thirteen in my vision.'

'Those are powerful numbers, and if they're all as strong as Bianca, then no wonder the powers that be want you to deal with them.'

It had been a surprise to realise only her, Jacob and Dinah had their powers back. Unlike last time, when the magic from Vanaheim had been spilling into their world, there was no portal open, yet, and their power must have been coming directly from Odin or some other higher power. 'The list?'

'Yes, yes, I'll make you a copy. I'll keep mine and add to it when I hear of anything else.'

'Is that all you have for me?'

'Well, I heard a whisper about Vali's real name. Joseph Barrow. It's unconfirmed so I wasn't going to tell you.'

Freya raised an eyebrow. 'You need to contact me when something important happens. I can't keep dropping in in the hope something has come to light. Here's my phone number and email.' She handed him a small square of card onto which she'd put her details. 'If you have anything sensitive, you know, a real bombshell, don't tell me over the phone, let me know you have news and I'll come and see you. Better safe than sorry.'

Theo's mouth pinched together, and he nodded curtly. 'Alright.'

'No more holding out on me either. If Vali continues with his plan, he'll cause the end of the world, and I doubt either of us will make it through that.'

His eyes widened, as though he hadn't thought of what it would mean if Vali succeeded. Theo opened his mouth as if to say something but closed it again, glancing to the shop door.

'I'll leave you to it,' Freya said as a customer came into the shop. A prickle of energy followed the woman in, she was average height, shoulder length wavy mid-brown hair, wearing a dark grey pants suit that was too big for her, as though she'd lost weight. Something about the woman seemed familiar, Freya turned to Theo intending to silently ask who she was, but his face had blanched. He shook his head, a tiny no movement.

'I'll call you when that order comes in,' he said, eyes darting to the door.

'Thank you.' Freya frowned but from the look on Theo's face he wanted her to get out.

I'll give him a ring when I get back to the office, she thought.

As she passed the other woman on the way to the door, the woman looked up at Freya, confusion spread across her face. She recognised Freya was shielded, even if she didn't know how it was done, the fewer people who knew the better. Whether Theo recognised the woman, or only that she had the talent to spot the emptiness, Freya needed to leave.

The rest of her day at work she couldn't get the other woman out of her mind, that niggling thread of recognition. They'd met somewhere before but she couldn't bring to mind where.

*

Back at the apartment Freya walked in to find Eva sitting with Jacob in the living room.

'Hey, I didn't know you were coming around.'

'I dropped in because, well, I know you said you were handling it, but I wanted you to see what the children of Vali posted today. I'm freaking out.'

'Have you seen it?' Freya asked Jacob.

'We were waiting for you,' he replied. The atmosphere in the apartment was tense, Eva's usually bubbly laugh and sing song tones were replaced with a hushed voice and a slumped posture.

'I've got it up on the TV.' Jacob pressed a button and the YouTube video of the Children of Vali's latest upload, a short one dated the same day, started to play.

'We're updating live today, one of our siblings encountered a truly evil person.' The woman speaking had appeared on the channel before, but whose name escaped her, addressed the camera. Her cheeks and neck were flushed as though she'd been exercising.

'I received a panicked phone call from one of our children, a woman who has not yet joined us here in the community, but who is none the less dedicated to our shared vision. She was in the city, in Melbourne, when she came across a woman who was empty.'

Freya sat forward on the couch.

'Some of the Children have skills, talents, this woman's talents are in feeling things which she should not be able to feel—psychic knowledge. She came across a woman who was not just impossible to read but sucked energy into her, drowning it with a dark swirling void where her soul should be.

'The woman she encountered was tall, slender, with very short jet black hair. She wore a long black coat and grey dress, and her right eye is surrounded by pale scar tissue.'

Freya couldn't breathe, the air around her felt as though it was full of honey, not air, a ringing sound blocked her hearing.

'She's talking about you, isn't she?' Eva's voice cut through the ringing. 'Freya, say something.'

'It was only a matter of time before someone recognised the spells we have protecting us.' Jacob's voice sounded far away.

'The moment Theo's face lost all its colour, what little there is of it, I knew—maybe she didn't know at that moment what was wrong, but it was enough to ask her group, and they recognised it.'

'What are we going to do? They know you now,' Eva said, she sounded strangled.

'Let's keep watching and see what else they say.'

Jacob resumed the video, and the woman on the screen continued to talk about the spectre of their enemy.

'We expected someone would try to stop what we're doing. People like this Empty Woman who don't want us to reach enlightenment, who want to keep us here on this plane where we are powerless, where we suffer. But Vali, our great leader, will deliver us. He has seen this woman; he knows her ways now. We must follow his teaching and he will protect us. Anyone who sees a tall thin woman with scars around her right eye, especially one who seems to suck the air out of the room, should contact us as soon as possible. She drains your energy without your consent, like a vampire, and she wants to stop Vali. Together we much keep her out of our community and out of paradise.'

'Shit.' Freya sighed. 'If I hadn't been so impatient to get information out of Theo this wouldn't have happened.'

'You couldn't have known you would run into one of Vali's people there.' Jacob laid his hand on her thigh.

'I'm so stupid. I was walking around looking like a black hole to anyone with even a hint of magical ability but I couldn't wait one more week to ask, until after we'd done the ritual. She wouldn't have noticed then.' She stood up and started to pace the length of the lounge.

'Why didn't I get a vision? Something to warn me not to go.'

'If Odin, or Muninn or Huginn, didn't know she was one of their followers, maybe they couldn't warn you?' Jacob said.

'It could be part of the plan?' Eva added.

Freya laughed, a bitter bark. 'I don't think there is a plan. This isn't a Christian "God works in mysterious ways" kind of thing, this is the god of wisdom, war, victory. He's not going to give us powers to stop Ragnarök and then hamstring us by letting me walk into something so catastrophic, is he?'

'The same god that had a raven peck out your eye and get you to save the world with no instructions and very little resources last time. We're working with a lot more this time, maybe this is a test?' Jacob said.

'Great.' Freya curled her hands into fists by her sides, she wanted to scream. Why was everything so complicated? Just when it felt like things were under control, they slipped from her grasp again.

'You're not the only one here you know. Dinah and I are both still unknown. They think you're one person, well, one embodiment of evil. Maybe we can turn it to our advantage?'

'How are we going to do that?'

'It could be a good opening to join the forums. Dinah and Jacob could be witnesses to your evil emptiness, they could feed panicky fake sightings to the group. It's not the end of the world.' As Eva spoke, Freya remembered

seeing Dinah standing in the field with the other
disciples. This is why she was there alone—Freya
became the enemy, the big bad, that will help solidify
people under Vali's control, and it would be their way
into the group.

'I hate gods,' Freya said. After the wave of anger
passed, she felt limp, all the energy in her limbs drained
away and she came back to flop on the couch next to
Jacob. 'I wish I could be there with you and Dinah.'

'You'll be our backup. We're not defeated yet.'
Jacob's furrowed brow and wide eyes betrayed the fear
he felt, but she focussed on his words instead.

'I almost forgot, I went to see Theo today to check in
on his progress. He gave me a list of people, women,
who've left covens and other groups to join Vali. We can
do some asking around or poking through forum posts
and looking for these people. The more we can tell you
about them when you try to join the group, the more
likely they are to accept you.' She pulled the list out of
the pocket in her dress.

'Maybe if you wear a wig and go back to the eyepatch
people won't notice?' Eva said.

'I'm not a pirate.' Freya laughed. 'I'll keep it in
mind.'

'I didn't mean to be the bearer of bad news.'

'You're not, well, you are, but I don't blame you. I'm
glad you're here with me.' Freya remembered how alone
and frightened she'd been knowing her best friend was
lying in a hospital bed trapped in her own mind. They

had it a lot better this time around, but maybe their enemy did too. For a moment she thought over the possibilities, searching for an idea that would allow them to get someone else in with the group, to support Dinah, Jacob might be able to get in but given the circle was full of women, it seemed Vali had a problem with men.

'What if you were our inside man?' Freya said.

Eva looked blank for a moment. 'Me? I don't have any powers. I said I'd do whatever to help but . . . what about Jacob and Dinah?'

'Vali's sexist—all his inner circle are women, I suspect he's sleeping with most of them. It's a classic cult setup. There will be a few men on the periphery, but Jacob won't be able to get close enough to keep an eye on Dinah. Not to mention she's still at school, if we need to do stuff without getting her father's permission having an adult in the group will be really useful.'

'I want to help...' Eva bit her lip.

'But?' Jacob prompted.

'What if he finds out I'm a fraud? I don't want to end up in coma. I was so close to being lost in there. I know you have my back, but you won't be there. Freya you can't get near them now they know what you look like.'

'You're right. There is a risk. But there is a risk if you do nothing; they're trying to bring on the end of the world. I'm not going to pressure you, it's your decision. Have a think about it, you know a lot already. You could start on the forums, see if you can meet up with some people. I'm sure they have events, worship sessions or rituals or something. Just see how it goes, and you can pull back if things get hectic.' Freya gripped her hands together, she wanted Eva to be free to make her own choice while at the same time, she was desperate for another set of eyes and ears in the organisation.

'Having someone there to keep an eye out for Deens would be a real help for me, I'm sure she would never say so, but my sister doesn't want to go in alone,' Jacob added.

Eva looked from Freya to Jacob, her face shifting as several emotions passed through her. 'I'll put out some feelers. No promises.'

Freya beamed; she couldn't help herself. 'Thank you, you don't know how much it means to me to have you on the team.'

'I was always on the team. I won't leave you to deal with this alone if I can help it.'

The barb went straight to Freya's gut, she hadn't meant to insult her friend, it wasn't her fault that she had been out of action the last time, in fact Freya had spent a long time berating herself for not protecting her best friend. Finding Eva prone and immobile in her apartment had been the point at which things started to feel real.

'So that list of names from Theo?' Jacob asked after a lengthy pause, his warm mellow voice taking the edge off the coldness between the two women. Perhaps he had put a little of his talent into it, although she felt no electrical buzzing.

'I've got it here.' She held up the folded piece of paper with the four names on it. 'Theo also said he thinks his real name is Joseph Barrow. I was going to see if I could find any of them on the forums, either now, or in the past, to get an idea of who they are, or what they're up to now.'

'Let me see,' Eva said, holding out her hand for the paper. Freya handed it over, she had looked at the names, stared at them, all the way home on the train.

'Heather Whitecroft, I've seen her name somewhere before,' Eva said.

'I didn't recognise any of them,' Freya replied.

'Whitecroft? That rings a bell.' Jacob pulled the laptop off the coffee table and into his lap. He tapped and clicked without speaking for a few minutes before the video on the TV switched. 'Here. This is a few months old, they were introducing some new members to the live stream.'

'Hello, and welcome. As you know we stream regular updates for our followers, all the dedicated Children out there in cyber space, and on Sundays we get together with a few of our newer residents and talk about life in the community, here in our location in country Victoria. Joining me today is Heather Whitecroft, she's recently made the move to be with us full-time, and we're so grateful that she's here. Why don't you say hello to the people at home, Heather.'

'Goodness, what an introduction,' Heather said, the colour of her neck deepening to a pink shade as she started to speak. 'I—' she stumbled, made a small cough, then resumed. 'My name is Heather. I've been a Wicca practitioner since I was a child, both my parents were into it, and I knew from a very young age that I had clairvoyant skills—I knew what people were thinking, what they wanted, and I could always find something that was lost. Small things at first, but when I reached my mid-teens, my ability grew. I joined a group of women practitioners in my last year of high school, they were mostly older, but I needed to establish myself away from my parents. I was happy there for a long time, you may be able to tell I left high school some time ago, but a couple of years ago there was a change. We all remember the strange affliction and many in the magical communities had increased abilities.'

'It was a fantastic time to be a practitioner, all those rituals you'd never been able to make work, or had been too difficult, were suddenly achievable,' the host broke in.

'I don't know what happened, but we had been given divinity and must have proven ourselves unworthy, the powers we were bestowed were taken away months later. It was after that change, the shift back to where I used to be, I started questioning my faith. Everything I knew up until then had been guided by Wiccan principles, but I wondered if there were other disciplines that would allow me access to that power once more. I wanted to help people with it, I wanted to be able to make a difference,' Heather said.

'Is that what drew you to Vali? And his followers?' the host asked.

'Yes, I came across the Children several months later, and I was sceptical at first, what could this guy know that I hadn't been able to find out with all my education, but when I started to watch to his videos, and try some of the stuff out at home, I knew this was the person I wanted to follow. I met some of the Children at an open house Vali was hosting and when I met him, I just…'

'It's very hard to describe the first time you meet him, isn't it?'

'If you had said to me, I would meet someone and want to dedicate your life to them on the spot, I would have said you were crazy, but that's what I did.'

'And now, four months later, you're an integrated full member of the Children, and you've moved to live with us here. What is it you hope to achieve by being a part of Vali's plan?'

'We're going to create a place where we're all loved and are all powerful in our own way. I want to help Vali make that a reality, whether my part is peeling potatoes for the meals, or doing rituals to draw down and direct power from the universe, it's all to serve Vali.'

Jacob paused the video. 'There's another hour of this, but I think we've seen what we needed to see. She has definitely drunk the Kool-Aid.'

'She's not there by accident, nor is she there against her will, it would seem,' Freya said.

The three of them were quiet for a moment. Freya didn't know what to do next.

'I should get back to my apartment and start building up my profile in the forums. I'll start asking what Vali is all about and try to get someone interested. I'm sure they would much rather think they've recruited me than if I try to force myself in.' Eva rubbed her hand on her knee, her orange silk trousers whispering under her strokes.

'You'll do great. I'm believe in you.' Freya took Eva's hand, silencing the silk. 'Get in touch with Dinah too, you can both be in the forums, maybe get to know one another there so when one of you is invited in the other can tag along.'

Eva glanced at Jacob, who seemed lost in thought. 'Are you going to try to get in, Jacob?'

'Hmm? Yeah, I've already started poking around. No doubt you and Dinah will find it easier, but we all have to get in, since Freya can't go near them.'

'Gee thanks. As if I don't feel bad enough already.'

'Don't be like that,' Jacob said. 'There's nothing else we could do. It's bad timing but maybe it's part of the great plan.'

We're talking in circles. Freya's belly grumbled and she realised she had had nothing to eat. There were no leftovers tonight, they'd finished the last of the curry last night, so it would have to be toast, and maybe a can of baked beans if she was lucky. She was hurt Jacob was being so defeatist and pessimistic. She hadn't intended to reveal herself to Vali's followers, and while she hadn't mentioned she would be seeing Theo that day, she couldn't imagine Jacob would have stopped her. After the weekend they would solve the protection black-hole problem, allowing them to get physically closer to Vali's people, but they needed information on what he had planned to figure out a way to stop him.

Freya stood without another word and went to the kitchen, her mind swirling with thoughts and half-formed plans. Finding bread and dropping it into the toaster was mechanical. She tried to calm her mind, imagining white cotton wool surrounded her, the icy lightning trickle of universal power flowing nearby. It wasn't a spell, it was something natural, intuitive. The flow of power hummed in her mind, sound, but not sound—beyond sound.

In her inner eye she saw the circle of witches, standing in the field, their long robes flapping, hands clasped as they muttered incantations she couldn't hear. She looked around her, like before Dinah was there, part of the circle, and she followed the chain a few people down to see Eva. She could feel the ripples of magic coursing through her hands, or the hands she was inhabiting in the vision, there was no way Freya was in her own body for this ritual. The toast popped up, her vision faded and she had learned nothing new. If there was a way to butter toast angrily, she managed it.

In one moment, everything changed. Being online meant Vali had much greater reach than Victor had, he was charismatic and attractive, even on screen. His people were everywhere, Freya didn't dare to think about how many people might know she was the enemy now, how many people would be looking for her and reporting back.

'I'm going to work from home until we get the avatar up. I can't risk people being on the lookout for me in the city.' She walked back into the room carrying her toast and Jacob and Eva sprang apart from their huddled conversation. 'What's going on?'

'Nothing,' Eva said.

'We—I wondered if you were okay. You don't usually go so quiet. I'm sorry, it sounded like I was blaming you,' Jacob added.

Freya's eyebrows rose, but she remained silent.

'I hate this. knowing you won't be there is freaking me out, I've always known you're the powerhouse of our team. We have to get in with the Children, full of experienced magic practitioners and one crazy dude at the top, it seems impossible now.' Jacob's face was pale.

'Which of the two of us has the gift of the golden voice? Who can calm people without them knowing? Influence them to your way of thinking?'

'I do.'

'Exactly. You don't need me to be there. You'll be great. Eva and Dinah will be there, with your powers combined who can stop us?' She took a bite of her toast to give her a reason not to speak.

'I didn't think of it like that.' Jacob's mouth pulled up in a half-smile. 'Is there any bread left? I'm starving.'

'There's a few slices.'

Jacob had cheered up, she was always envious of his ability to live moment to moment and not get stuck in his own head, like she did.

Chapter 9

By the time Saturday came around Freya was itching to get out of the apartment. She was able to access her work from home with a little bit of technological negotiation, although her manager wasn't too pleased.

She woke early, restless. 'I'm going to the coffee shop. I need to get out of the house. You want me to bring you one back?' she asked, although Jacob's eyes were still closed in an imitation of sleep.

'I'm not awake, but if I was, I would say yes to coffee.'

'Okay.' She leaned down to kiss his forehead. Getting back to normal domesticity was what kept her going when she thought about how difficult their task was. The constant fight to feel safe and the fate of the world hanging over her head made Freya edgy, and being stuck inside for days didn't help.

She shoved her feet into her runners after slipping on some gym pants and a hoodie. A surprising number of other people were out, nine o'clock on Saturday was a popular time, perhaps for parents whose kids woke them at six each day this was late.

It was cool, despite the bright sun, and she was glad of the excuse to wear large sunglasses and keep her hood up—no good being recognised by her scars if she could help it. Each time she passed someone she second guessed them; one person looked too long, and she was sure they knew, another's eyes slid off her as though she weren't there and Freya worried they were trying to avoid notice because they recognised her. The walk wasn't as stress-relieving as she had expected.

'What can I get you?' the woman behind the counter seemed frazzled.

'Two café lattes to take away please,' Freya said, keeping her voice as neutral as possible. She and Jacob were regulars and she hoped to avoid being drawn into a conversation.

'Big night?' the woman asked as Freya waved her bank card over the machine to pay.

'Something like that.'

'Won't be long. Can I help you?' The question was addressed to the person behind Freya, another regular she knew by sight, but not by name. She stood in front of the shop, her back to the large plate-glass window, the sun warm on her face.

'Freya!' the waitress called her name and Freya jumped. 'Coffee's ready.'

'Thanks.' She took the two cups, sneaking a grateful sip from hers, hoping the caffeinated drink would calm her nerves. The walk back to the apartment was a little over five minutes, she tried to focus on remaining calm, not looking at passers-by, but when she let herself back into the apartment she sighed with relief.

'You okay?' Jacob said, emerging from the bedroom at the sound of the front door. He slept in boxer-briefs, without a shirt, his chest hair formed a layer of salt and pepper to match his head and stubble. It had been a while since she'd really looked at him; the cool air had made his nipples erect. He took the coffee from her hand and crossed his arms over his naked torso. 'You looked spooked for a moment, but now I feel like you want to eat me.'

'Would you blame me?'

'Never.' Jacob sipped his coffee and sighed. 'See anyone on your walk?'

'No, but I got myself in a lather trying to figure out if people were looking at me funny. Probably why I looked odd when I came in. It never occurred to me how many people stare. Everything seemed suspicious. I can't wait till we have the avatar ritual finished; I can't live with the stress of that as well as trying to save the world.'

'Come here.' Jacob sat on the couch and beckoned her toward him. 'Sit here and I'll give your shoulders a rub.'

The feel of his hands over her shoulders and neck was like magic; the stress she had been carrying was forgotten and the spark of arousal that had started earlier was fanned into a burning desire. It wasn't long before their coffee was forgotten, and they had gone back to the bedroom, but keeping their protection pouches on.

*

'Oh shit.' Jacob sat bolt upright, the sheet slipping down his chest. 'Dinah'll be here in a minute.'

'I'll shower while you straighten this and get started on the sandwiches. Then we'll swap.' She glanced at the clock on the bedside table. 'We've got twenty minutes.'

When she came out of the bathroom a few minutes later Jacob had started on the snacks and preparations for the trip up to the shed.

'Bathroom's free.' Although she enjoyed showering with a partner, in times of stress or where efficiency was key, they made better time splitting the tasks. Freya threw on some old, comfortable clothes and went to take over the packing in the kitchen.

Jacob padded from the bathroom to the bedroom a little while later, humming under his breath. She had to smile to herself, it was nice to be touched, to luxuriate in exploring each other's bodies the way they used to when they were first together. A knock at the door startled her.

'Hi Dinah,' she said through the closed door as she swung it open. It took a moment to register that the woman standing in front of her was not the teen she'd expected. 'Eva?'

'I wanna come to the shed.'

'Uh, come in.' Freya stepped back to welcome her friend into the apartment. 'Did I tell you when we were meeting today?'

'No, Dinah did. I want to be part of it.'

'Right,' Freya said, more to buy herself some time to think than because she agreed.

'Dinah and I have been texting, first to coordinate our approach to the forums, then we developed an online friendship so when we both join the cult we can seek each other out legitimately.'

'Right,' she said again. 'So why do you want to come to the shed?'

'Dinah thinks I might have powers, she wants me to give it a try.'

'Is that Eva?' Jacob looked out of the bedroom, his hair damp from the shower.

'I'm coming with you.'

Jacob glanced from Eva to Freya and back.

'I don't see the harm,' Freya said. There was another knock on the door, this time Freya felt the teen's presence on the other side.

'Hey—oh cool, Eva's here.' Dinah entered the apartment with an enormous sports bag, which she dumped on the floor by the door.

'Were you going to tell us you had invited Eva?' Jacob asked.

'What's the problem? She's on the team, and she can help.' The girl shrugged. It was hard to fault her logic, but something in Freya still resisted. Back in the kitchen she threw some more snacks into the picnic bag. The other items they would need for the avatar ritual were gathered in a plastic craft crate near the T.V.

'Did you bring your blood, Dinah? If the avatars are the only thing we do this weekend, then all the better.'

'It's in my bag.' A sly smile crept up Dinah's face. 'You know I can tell what you've been up to.'

'I don't know what you mean,' Jacob said.

'They make . . . ripples in the magic when they boff,' Dinah said to Eva, who giggled. 'But the shielding is still good. I only felt remnants of it when I came in the house, not from outside, and definitely not from halfway across the city like that other time.'

The tension in Freya's shoulders released, at least they hadn't created any big, obvious magic.

'Shall we get on the road?' Jacob asked, keys and duffle bag in hand. Freya slid her backpack on and grabbed the plastic crate, careful to keep it level so as not to spill anything.

Chapter 10

They listened to music and chatted about nothing in particular on the way to the shed. Eva looked at scenery slipping past the windows. Jacob drove up, they would have to assess who had the energy to drive back later.

'One time, can I drive up? I need to get my hours for my licence.' Dinah said.

'You've got two years to get your hours, but I'll think about letting you drive up there one day. I should ask Dad, I don't want him to be suss if you have a bunch of extra hours in your log book.'

Dinah sighed in the loud way only a teenager can. 'Fine, I'll get Dad to call you about it.' She folded her arms; Freya suspected their father would be less than enthused to have his daughter driving without him. He could be overbearing.

'You feel anything, Deens?' Jacob said as they approached the turn off. Dinah closed her eyes for a moment, concentrating on something the others couldn't experience.

'No, I don't feel anyone around.'

They turned into the driveway, Freya jumped out to open the padlocked front gate, then closed and locked it after the big silver car was through the gate. The sheds looked the same; big, empty, and unloved.

'I hadn't expected them to be so big,' Eva said, as she stepped out of the back seat to look at the large green wooden structures.

'They're fruit packing sheds, or they were. Much bigger than your average garden shed.' Freya smiled at her friend, then looked to the sky. 'Good to see we have supervision.'

'Are they the ravens?' Eva asked.

'Yeah, they follow us around when important stuff is happening. Also, sometimes when not important stuff is happening,' Dinah said.

'How can you tell which is which?'

Freya laughed. 'I can't. I don't think they mind.'

'They're quite nice when you get close,' Dinah added.

'So, what's the plan?' Jacob asked, starting to unpack the items from the boot.

'We'll start with the avatars. Eva, you'll have to watch those, then probably take a break, then maybe Eva can try some spells. After that I don't know.' Freya had only thought as far as getting the avatar ritual done.

Inside the shed was just as they had left it, Freya breathed a small sigh that no one had found it. They set up a circle of salt in the centre of the big open interior space. Eva sat on a folding chair off to the side.

'The ritual requires us to combine the relevant objects, charred wood, crystal, herbs and salt into the cauldron. We then use some words to imbue the totem object, that is the cauldron, with the essence of ourselves. Or in this case a particular version of the essence of ourselves.

Then when we're shielded other practitioners will be able to feel the totem object's presence and not our blocked nothingness. We'll start with mine.'

She had placed all three cauldrons next to the circle of salt but brought only hers inside the circle. Inside was her monthly fluid, five small pieces of paper, and the other ingredients. It looked like a mud pie but was still too wet for what the spell book had called for.

'I cast this circle in the name of Odin, All-Father, and Freya, the giver. I call on the spirits of the North, South, East and West to watch over us as we do our work,' she said, drawing the circle of salt closed behind her. 'May the circle protect us under his watchful eye.'

In her mind, she reached out to the silvery stream of magical power, encouraging a small stream of it towards her. 'This vessel, I imbue with my essence. May it protect me and hide my true self from my enemies. May I be safe while it remains safe.' She repeated the words three times, while imagining the silvery light flowing from her hands over the cauldron, drying the contents and allowing some of herself to be imprinted on the contents. It was easier said than done, she wasn't sure exactly what her essence was, and how it would be put into the tiny cast-iron cauldron, but in magic it was the intention, and not knowledge of specific mechanisms that was the important part—if you had the right ingredients, and the right belief, anything could be achieved.

The contents of the cauldron burned briefly with blue-green fire, before flickering out.

After she finished repeating the words, she looked to Dinah and Jacob. They were both sitting cross-legged, eyes closed, holding hands. There seemed nothing else to do, so she ended the spell.

'I thank the spirits of the North, South, East and West for watching over us as we did our work. I thank Odin, All-Father, and Freyja, the giver, for watching over us as we did our work. The circle is now open, but never broken.' She pushed her finger through the line of salt to open the circle and a rush of wind seemed to pass over them.

'Is that it?' Eva said.

'I think so,' Freya replied. 'Dinah, you need to test whether you can feel me now.' She stood and stepped over the circle on the floor, in case being inside it made it more difficult for Dinah to know whether the spell had worked. 'Anything?'

'Give me a second. There's lots of, you know, energy and stuff floating around.' Dinah closed her eyes and flicked her hearing aids off so she could concentrate on her inner experience. She stood still and quiet for a minute or two, the prickle of magic working floating in the air, Freya felt as though she barely breathed.

'I think it's worked. When I feel for you with my mind, I see a bunch of stuff, you at work, going for a run, having a coffee, very boring, and no matter how hard I probe, that's all I get.'

'It worked, then?' Eva said. Freya had almost forgotten her friend was there, she had been waiting silently in the shadows for so long.

'I guess so,' Freya replied.

'There is a possibility that someone will know that what they can read from you is y'know, a mask, if they're as strong as I am and they can't get anything more that those little scenes, they might be suss, but for the average punter, someone who isn't going poking around and doesn't know they should, there's nothing to notice about you. When I look at Jacob, he's still a black hole.' Dinah sighed.

'Let's have a snack break, you might have used a bit more juice than you intended with that probing,' Jacob said, wrapping his arm around his sister who had gone very pale.

They sat in the sunshine outside, sitting with their backs against the shed wall on a picnic blanket. Eva was quiet, unusually so for her, as was Dinah, whose colour returned slowly as her energy was replenished.

'I felt a sort of prickling in the air when you were doing the ritual, and then again when Dinah was testing out the avatar, is that what the magic feels like?' Eva asked.

'It's hard to describe. Kind of like a sneeze coming on, or the tail end of pins and needles,' Jacob said.

'Now you know what you're looking for, you can concentrate on tapping into that feeling. We have two more cauldrons to imbue, then we'll give you a go.'

Freya stood, dusting off the crumbs and dust. The others followed her lead, packing the rug back into the car before they set up the second ritual.

Since it was Dinah's cauldron this time, she would have to say the words of power, to close the circle and pour her intended images into it. Then Jacob would do his, they didn't need to open the circle between the spells. Freya would need to feed the power to Jacob, his control and talents were not so easily directed as hers, although Dinah would probably be able to complete her ritual unassisted.

Eva went to her spot in the background, and the other three stepped inside the salt circle sitting on the floor. Dinah took the salt and closed the circle, reciting the words. She closed her eyes again, took Freya's hand and there was a faint tickle as she connected to the stream of power and drew it into her.

'This vessel, I imbue with my essence. May it protect me and hide my true self from my enemies. May I be safe while it remains safe.' Dinah said this three times, all the while power pulsed through Freya's hand. It felt rawer somehow than when she had done it, as though the stream was an ocean compared to her small stream. In her mind Freya visualised a calm mountain creek, perhaps only a few feet wide, this was the power they tapped into, it was mild and malleable and would respond to their influence.

Blue green fire danced over the contents of the vessel, and Dinah let go of her hand. She looked to Jacob and took his hand. Their eyes met and he nodded. Freya reached inside herself, to the place where she accessed power and drew a small amount towards her, she allowed the silvery light-energy to flow through her hand and into Jacob. He gave a small jolt as he felt the magic pass into him. They had discussed how they would do it earlier and again in the car on the way up, but perhaps it was still a surprise to be tapped into the source in that way.

'This vessel, I imbue with my essence. May it protect me and hide my true self from my enemies. May I be safe while it remains safe.' Jacob repeated the phrases this time, his low, gravelly voice giving it a different feel to Dinah's. Freya could feel the pull of him through her hand, and concentrated hard on maintaining a steady flow. The ritual created an object of great power, and usefulness, but only needed a small amount of energy to complete. Jacob's understanding and control of the flow needed a little more work.

When he had finished speaking, the blue green fire flared briefly, and when she looked into the cauldron, it had turned to an ashy colour, dry and gritty with herbs and salt. Both Dinah and Jacob gave a nod when she turned to them, and she said the words to open the circle and end the ritual. After breaking the line of salt and stepping outside of the line, she felt a rush of fatigue and hunger pass through her. She closed her eyes for a moment to regain her balance and when she opened them again everything was as it should be. Jacob felt different, the urge to touch him was so strong she almost kissed him right then.

I guess there has been a barrier between us, the emptiness that I couldn't see but still felt in a way, it's all gone.

'How did it get so late?' Freya asked, the day seemed to have slipped away from her, it was after four in the afternoon.

'I don't know.' Jacob looked tired, no doubt she looked the same.

'Let's have a break.'

The sun was lowering in the sky, its rays bright but not very warm. They went out to the rug again; Freya lay on her back on the ground and remembered thinking it was rather uncomfortable before she slipped into a light sleep.

The ravens circled over the shed, she called to them, but they didn't respond. Next to her, as she lay on the blanket in the silvery half-light of the dream world were Jacob, Dinah, and Eva, their chests rising and falling in the deep rhythms of sleep. The ravens called out, and started to move away, Freya followed them down the side of the shed towards the abandoned orchards behind them. The scene stretched and distorted as she walked through it, and she was suddenly in a wide, open field at night. The grass felt dry and brittle under her feet, although she heard no sound. The air around her was hot, sticky, and thick with the smell of rain close to falling.

She was alone on the field, it felt heavy as though something bad had happened.

As she walked, a black mark appeared on the ground—a charred circular depression. The centre glistened as though wet, but as she approached, she realised it wasn't water that gave it that look. A shudder ran through her as she realised where she had seen that shimmering black-beyond-blackness before; the portal to Vanaheim. Her feet kept moving, as though being pulled onwards by a will other than her own, the closer she came to the black mark, the colder she became. Her skin rose in goose bumps and she wrapped her arms around herself.

Looking up, Freya saw the ravens. They hovered above the mark, waiting for her to do something important, if only she could remember what.

'Freya? Are you awake?' Jacob's voice broke through the fog of her dream, and she opened her eyes to the fading afternoon.

'Hmm?'

'Eva wants to try a couple of tricks but maybe you should be there to help, you know guide her, like you did with me.'

Freya blinked. Her mind felt slow. 'I dreamed I found a portal. I guess this one must be to Jotunheim. It was summer, there was a thunderstorm in the air, but it was cold. I think we failed.'

'We'll be fine. It was just a dream. Even people with psychic powers can have a dream that doesn't mean anything.' Jacob wrapped his arms around her briefly, the familiar smell of his body, the clean woody smell of his cologne, helped to ground her in the present.

'You're right, it was probably just a bad dream.' She didn't believe it, but maybe saying it aloud would help to make it true.

Eva and Dinah had already gone back into the shed. Dinah was kneeling on the ground in front of the three cauldrons, her face set into deep concentration.

'What you up to there, Deens?' Freya asked.

'I'm just checking them out. It's really weird to probe them with my mind and they feel like you, or more accurately, you feel like these and not like real people but it's almost impossible to tell the difference. We did a good job on them.' She smiled up at them, her eyes clear, but purple circles had started to form below them.

'You've done a lot of working today, you don't want to overdo it,' Jacob said.

'Thanks, Dad.' Dinah stuck her tongue out but stood up and moved away from the totems none the less.

'Do we leave them here?' Freya asked.

'I feel unsafe having them so far away from the apartment, if something goes wrong, but at the same time, no one knows we're using these sheds, so they're probably safer here than if we bring them home.' Jacob rubbed his chin, his stubble rasping against his fingers.

Freya made a non-committal noise. 'I don't really want to be hanging around here after dark, so let's get you started, Eva.'

Jacob and Dinah sat towards the back of the shed, both seemed like they could use the rest. Eva was wide-eyed and leaned forward on her toes as they stood by the salt circle.

'We're not using the circle for this, it's not a ritual like what we did earlier. It's more like channelling the power directly, telekinesis if you like. Jacob and Dinah are both able to do it, I seem to be the strongest. I don't expect you'll be able to do anything the first time, or the first couple of times, and maybe not at all, but you wanted to try.'

Eva nodded.

'When I do it, I close my eyes and imagine a big black empty space,' Freya paused. 'You could close your eyes and do it with me if you want.'

'Right,' Eva said with a small nervous laugh.

'In the big empty space there is a tiny silver stream. It's a little way off. Do you see it?'

Eva was silent for a moment. 'I think I have it.'

'Now, move closer to the stream. Just gently float over to it . . . once you're there, picture yourself reaching out to touch the stream. This stream is the universal power source, it's what we tap into to do magic.'

Eva stood still, eyes closed, a slight frown drew her eyebrows down.

'What does it feel like?'

'It's a bit like the feeling I had when you were doing the ritual earlier, like I need to sneeze, but also tingling in my fingers,' Eva said.

'That sounds right. The first thing we want to do is to try to redirect some of the stream to you. I won't force it; more invite it to flow up your arm into your chest.'

Eva's eyebrows rose up her forehead half a second before she opened her eyes. 'Oh my god.'

'What happened?'

'Power started to come up my arm, it felt like ants all over my skin and I freaked out and let go.'

Freya smiled. 'That's alright. Let's try it again now that you know what to expect.'

Eva took a deep breath, shook her hands and arms out then closed her eyes. Freya didn't speak again until she felt the prickle of power flowing into Eva.

'Do you have it? Is it in your chest?' she asked.

Eva nodded. 'Now, try to hold onto it but open your eyes.'

Eva flickered her eyes open, the prickling wavered, steadied and then disappeared. 'I lost it.'

'That's okay.' Freya took her water bottle from the back of the shed where Jacob and Dinah were watching and placed it a few feet in front of Eva. 'This time, when you feel the power sitting in your chest, I want you to push it out and topple the bottle.' She was sure Eva wouldn't be able to move the bottle, but having an object to focus on might help. Jacob had taken several tries, and he had access to a lot more magic than Eva, whose abilities were small in comparison.

For almost an hour, Eva tried to move the water bottle, each time she got a little closer, but the bottle remained.

'It's not possible. I can't do it,' she said, throwing her hands in the air.

'You'll get there.'

'Show me.'

'Alright,' Freya said. She hadn't been practising much, they didn't dare use their power at home, and she'd used a lot of juice earlier in the day, but this should be a simple task. Freya calmed her mind, reached out to the source, drew a tiny trickle into her and pushed it out to the water bottle. She was able to do all of that in the space of one breath in and out. The bottle flew back as though punched, then scuttled spinning end to end across the floor clanging as it hit the back wall of the shed.

'Holy shit,' Eva said, her mouth forming an O of surprise. 'I thought you were taking the piss and couldn't really do it.'

'That was cool, I barely even felt that,' Dinah said. Freya turned to her; she'd almost forgotten they were there.

'I didn't use much, just enough to move the bottle.' She shrugged.

'You had plenty of punch—it's all the way at the wall.' Eva's face had schooled itself back into a normal shape, although a tinge of jealousy remained in the tightening of the eyes.

'Don't feel bad Eva, she's got more juice than me or Jacob. That's what you get being the chosen one. On the other hand, she doesn't have her right eye so . . .' Dinah dropped her voice for the second part, although Freya still heard her.

'Let's go home,' Freya said.

Before they could leave, they had to find a place to store the totems. 'In the circuit box, I reckon.' Jacob waved his hand in the direction of the electrical boxes on one wall.

'It's probably safer to keep them away from the apartment, you're right.' Freya stepped out into the clear early night air as Jacob secured the electrical boxes closed again. The sky overhead was free of clouds and the stars pricked the deep blue canopy. The moon, over by the horizon, was a thin crescent, and the blue tinge over everything made Freya want to weep with exhaustion.

They all piled into the car, Jacob drove back, although Freya was concerned he would be too tired she reconciled herself with knowing he had been able to rest while she and Eva had been trying to move things. She sighed, as disappointed as she was Eva hadn't shown great potential straightaway, maybe it was for the best. Having a lot of power would make her a target for Vali and going in undercover it would be better to be one of the pack, than to stand out. It was another reason she wasn't keen on Dinah going in alone—she had plenty of power that, while protected with the shielding and the avatars, would make her a threat to Vali and his followers if it were discovered.

On the drive back, Freya drifted in and out of sleep. Dinah and Eva, in the back seat, were silent, as was Jacob. Everyone felt the fatigue of the afternoon's activities and the weight of the task ahead.

'Can I crash on your couch?' Eva asked, as they approached the apartment building.

'Of course, Dinah's staying on the fold-out in the spare room. You could ask if she'd share,' Jacob said, eying his sister in the rear-view mirror.

'Sure. Dad says I snore but,' Dinah said.

'I'm so tired I'll sleep through anything.'

Freya and Jacob had already pulled out the couch in the spare room and made it up with sheets, pillows and blankets. They said goodnight and retreated to their rooms.

Walking up the stairs to the front door had been a massive effort, Freya was sure she would fall asleep as soon as her head hit her pillow, but as she lay there, eyes gritty, she couldn't find the calm she needed to drift off. She kept thinking about the dream of the orchard and the feeling it was more of a vision than a dream. Did it mean she would fail to stop Vali, and he would open the portal to Jotunheim? If he did, would it set Ragnarök into motion? Was the ritual she'd seen in her other dreams the one that opened the portal? If Dinah and Eva were there, did it mean they had helped to open the portal, which was against everything they were fighting for.

Freya couldn't shake the idea that they would be seduced by the rhetoric of Vali and change sides once they were in his presence; he was handsome, charismatic and somehow able to get people to do what he wanted. No matter how many times Jacob told her it wasn't her fault the woman in Theo's shop had clocked her, she was still angry with herself for not being able to support them in person.

When she finally did fall into an exhausted sleep, Freya dreamed of the field and the inky black stain. It was calling her. She knelt beside the charred grass, the blackened blades stiff, and pushed her hand towards the centre. The coldness she felt earlier was much stronger now, a shiver ran up her arm as her fingers approached the edge of the wet, ink-black patch.

As soon as her skin touched the shiny area in the centre she felt as though she were falling through a frigid dark tunnel. As she fell, the air around her rushed past, as though caught by a strong wind. She opened her eyes and found herself in a pine forest, the night sky was blacker than any sky she'd seen before, although the snow on the ground glowed and pulsed with a strange half-light.

This must be Jotunheim.

A frozen land covered in forests and grim mountains, where only the hardy giants survived. Freya looked around and couldn't understand why anyone would make a portal here. Her breath hung in a cloud as she exhaled, her fingers and feet ached from the cold before she remembered to pull her hand out of the portal.

She woke with a start in the blackness of their bedroom at night. Jacob slept beside her, his gentle breathing steady. Her heartbeat was loud in her ears, and she was hot and sweaty even though the room was cool. Slowly her breaths became deeper, and her panic subsided. Shuffling over a little she pressed her cheek on his shoulder, the contact soothed her, and she fell asleep again.

Over and over Freya dreamed of Jotunheim. The dream was always the same, the field, the black inky hole, the frozen forest. Each time she woke in distress and had to calm herself before falling asleep and doing it all over again.

'You look terrible,' Dinah said when she finally emerged from the bedroom a little before ten the next morning.

'Good morning to you too,' Freya said.

'For real, you don't look okay.'

'I had bad dreams, visions, of Jotunheim.'

'What do you mean?' Jacob asked from the kitchen.

'I dreamed about the portal, and it leads to Jotunheim. Like the scar on the beach connected to Vanaheim last time.'

Dinah shuddered. 'But we're gonna stop him, right? Your visions don't always come true.'

'No, not always. I can't tell which will end up being real predictions, but we need to be prepared.' She didn't add that she had concerns her friends would cross over to the other side and were the reason Vali succeeded,

175

although she planned to tell Jacob later. 'Anyway, I kept waking up in a panic. I'm surprised Jacob slept through the whole thing.'

'I was dead to the world. I didn't do as much as you, babe, but I was bushed. I always forget how draining it is to play with magic.'

'I feel like I've been hit by a truck,' Eva said, her smooth dark skin looking drawn and blotchy.

'We did what we needed to do this weekend. Now when we're out in the world we won't be easily recognised. And we proved you have the potential to work magic, Eva.'

Eva harrumphed, Jacob had made them all coffee and brought out four steaming cups.

'So, we just go back to infiltrating the Children now? I thought there'd be more action.' Dinah sounded disappointed.

'There will be plenty of action soon enough.' Freya thought again of the circle of women. Eva dragged herself out of the apartment not long after she finished her coffee. Dinah was due back at her Dad's in the afternoon, and was occupying herself studying on the couch. Freya had gathered the cups and plates from where they were scattered around the living room and started to run hot water into the sink for washing them. Firm hands slid around her waist, and she leaned back against Jacob's warm, reassuring body.

'You okay, babe?'

She hesitated. 'I'll tell you about it later, I don't want Dinah to know.' She thought of the girl's strong ability to read their thoughts.

'Good idea.' Jacob leaned down to kiss along the side of her neck, causing shivers of delight to pass over her body.

*

Dinah said very little until they got close to her father's house. 'What didn't you want to tell me before?'

'What do you mean?' Freya said, pretending not to know.

'In the kitchen. I heard you.'

'You were using your talent to spy on us, weren't you?' Freya said.

'I was getting a hostile vibe and I wanted to know why, so yes, I was eavesdropping.'

Freya took a deep breath. 'I'm worried about something and I haven't been completely transparent with you and Jacob.'

He pulled the big car into the kerb and switched it off, the silence after the hum of the engine felt like a weight on her.

'In my vision, you're participating in this ritual. You and Eva.'

'I know that.' Dinah crossed her arms.

'I get the feeling that maybe you aren't trying to stop him. And now my visions are full of portals to Jotunheim.'

177

'You think I would do that? Get sucked in by some arse-hat and try to end the world when I literally bled to stop the last apocalypse with you?'

Freya glanced at Jacob, his brows were furrowed and his mouth set in a thin, straight line. 'I don't think you would betray us on purpose,' she added.

'That's even worse. I'm too stupid to even know I'm bringing on the end of the world.' Dinah scrabbled to grab her things together. 'I don't know why you have me on the team if you think that. I'm not stupid. You can save the world on your own.' She dived out of the car pulling her bags with her before stomping into the house.

'I fucked that up, didn't I?' Freya asked.

'It could have gone better.'

'I was trying not to keep secrets from her, I know she can read me, and I know she's sensitive to being left out.'

'She's also sensitive about suggesting she'd switch teams,' Jacob said.

'Fuck.' Freya looked at her hands. 'Do we go after her?'

'No. Stay here. I'll see if I can talk to her . . . just to be clear there is no evidence she betrays us? You only saw her participating in the ritual which is totally compatible with the expectation that she infiltrates the group.'

'Yes, it's just a feeling. I'm sorry.' Freya glanced at Jacob; his face was soft but he didn't agree with what she had done. She turned back to looking at her feet as she listened to him leave the car and walk up to his father's house.

He was gone for twenty minutes before he appeared again, slipping into the car with a sigh. Freya held her breath and waited for him to say something.

'Dinah's livid. I think I've convinced her it was a mistake; exhaustion and stress affected your judgement. I explained we both love her and would never believe she would hurt us on purpose. But she kept asking what she'd done to make you think that of her, I didn't know what to say.'

Freya opened her mouth to reply, before closing it again to consider her answer. 'Nothing. She's done nothing. I know how much she's put into this, and how hard it must be for her. I don't know why I said it. I don't know why I dreamed it, over and over.'

'It'll be okay.' Jacob cupped her chin and turned her to face him. 'It will be alright.'

The tears that Freya had been trying to keep in check started to spill over her cheeks in prickly hot streams. 'I'm so sorry. I don't want to do this again. It's too hard. Vali is so much more powerful than Victor—he has a coven of potent witches who think he's the messiah. We've got no hope of stopping him.'

'Shhh.' Jacob gently brushed away the tears on her cheeks. 'We're much stronger than we were the last time. Remember how you sent that water bottle flying yesterday? It barely caused a ripple, you can do that with a tiny amount of power, imagine what you can do with a lot? Even with twelve other witches at full strength, they don't have the access you do to the source. The ravens chose you. And me and Dinah. We've been given this job because the gods, wherever they are, have faith that we stop Ragnarök. They wouldn't do that without cause, would they?'

'I have no idea what gods would do.' She tried to laugh but it came out bitter and hollow. 'We've never seen any evidence they exist except for the ravens. The parallel with my eye and Odin is clear but . . . I felt Jotunheim. I felt the cold, bleakness of it. It's—' she stopped herself.

'It's what?'

'Maybe that's why I was convinced Dinah's doing something wrong. The influence of Jotunheim in my dreams is corrupting my thinking.'

'How would that work? You haven't been there.'

'I don't know. The dream version, the future version, is icy and empty and inhospitable—it might be enough to put me off balance.'

'We'll keep an eye on it. Maybe you can have a nice bath, or do some meditation when we get home.'

'That would be nice. Thank you.'

It was early evening and the sky was darkening when they arrived home. Freya headed straight to the bathroom to run herself a bath with lavender oils and pan flute music. The weekend had taken more out of her than she had realised, on top of being named on Vali's YouTube channel as an enemy.

She sat in the hot water, a rolled-up towel behind her neck and rested her head back, closing her eyes.

When she opened her eyes again, she realised she had fallen into a black dreamless sleep, the water had become tepid and her fingers were deeply wrinkled.

'Why didn't you come get me? How long was I in there?' she asked when she returned to the lounge room wearing her charcoal-grey terry-towelling bathrobe.

'I looked and you were asleep. There's dinner in the kitchen, I didn't wait for you.'

Freya stuck her tongue out at him, but then leaned over the couch to plant a kiss on his lips. 'Thank you. I feel better, but still very tired.'

'Eat your dinner and then go to bed. You've got work in the morning.'

'Don't remind me.' She groaned and padded into the kitchen. She ate while Jacob finished watching his show on the TV and then both got ready for an early night. Freya was mortified she had accused Dinah of being a traitor but hopefully, the damage was reparable with grovelling and time.

*

On Wednesday, at work, it occurred to Freya, that Eva might need a protection or shielding charm as well, now they had established she had some talent. In the magic shop near her office Freya bought the necessary supplies without having much interaction with the woman working there. It was a new person, not the one she'd encountered previously, and Freya was relieved to find neither her presence nor her purchases were cause for interest. On her way back she dropped in to see Theo, to check in on him and to ask what he felt in her presence. She would have to do some research into the protection spells and charms to make sure Eva wasn't shielded so much that she became a black hole like the others had.

A range of emotions crossed Theo's face before he schooled his expression. He settled on a polite smile and tried to seem relaxed while the tiny muscles around his eyes contracted and twitched. 'Freya, I wasn't expecting you.'

'Nice to see you, Theo.' She looked around the rest of the shop, there were no other customers today. 'I came to check on you.'

'And to show off your new persona I suppose, it's very impressive.' Theo let his smile fall but the tension in his eyes remained. 'I wouldn't have expected you to be able to wield such complexity of magic after such a short period.'

'I'll take that as a compliment.'

'I mean no harm, I'm impressed, but also . . . intimidated. Not that I expect you not to be able to do anything you set your mind to, of course.'

Freya frowned at the grovelling manner Theo had reverted to. He was a weak character and in times of stress or uncertainty he often fell to the placating, people-pleasing behaviours she found distasteful. 'What do you sense in me? Do I seem ordinary?'

Theo's eyes narrowed and he steepled his fingers in front of his lips. 'Let me see. I sense a little bit of work, normal stuff, office banter and the like, I see some love, Jacob and your mother, is it? And that's it. How marvellous.'

'Mmm,' Freya murmured. It was the same as Dinah had seen, which reminded her that she hadn't heard anything from her since the weekend and made a mental note to follow up. 'I guess it worked then.'

'Yes, yes, very effective. On casual inspection one wouldn't know anything was out of place, you and I know the sort of power you should give off, but none of that is present—' he stopped abruptly and closed his mouth.

'But?'

'No but . . .caveat, that with extended contact, or very careful examination and probing, it would be clear it was a veneer. If someone were to realise you had put up a screen of this nature, they would know immediately you were very skilled.'

It was a risk they had to take, without it they wouldn't last five minutes before someone knew they were threats.

'Not that it makes any difference. It's the only thing you could have done to hide your ability.' Theo nodded as though satisfied he was telling her something valuable and not repeating himself.

'And no news from any of your contacts?'

'Since you last asked? No. No news.' He picked up a notepad from the counter before putting it back in almost the exact same place.

'What are you not telling me?'

'Nothing. Why would you think I was hiding something?'

'You're a terrible liar.'

'I'm not lying.' He hesitated. 'I did have someone come back a couple of times to ask if I knew you—the woman with the scars on her eyes and the empty soul...'

'What did you tell them?'

'They had seen you here, I said you'd come in once or twice, but I didn't know who you were, and that you always paid in cash in case they wanted to press for your name.'

Freya pressed her lips together as she considered this information. 'You don't think they read you?'

'Not without physical touch, I can block that sort of thing when I know they're trying to do it.'

It seemed like a stretch but there was nothing she could do about it now. Perhaps coming back had been a mistake. 'I'll get going then. Remember to call me if there are any urgent developments.'

'Of course,' he said, bobbing his head. She showed herself out and hoped he hadn't given anything away about her without realising. Her life consisted of keeping a series of plates spinning on precarious perches. It was exhausting, but she couldn't do anything but move forward.

Chapter 11

Freya sent a message to Eva as soon as she was back at her desk.

I need to drop off a protection pouch to you – are you around after work?

The pouch needed a little bit of ritual work to be effective but she could do it at Eva's place. She had managed to keep the apartment in the city even while she was trapped in the coma for months but the memory of having lain in her bed, soiled herself, and waited for Freya to find her were too much she said. Eva had moved into a set of apartments in converted warehouse on Spencer Street.

Eva replied not long afterwards.

Sure. I'll come by your office and we can walk to mine. How's 5:15?

Freya breathed a sigh of relief; after putting her foot in her mouth with Dinah she worried Eva resented her too.

I need to lighten up, this gloomy attitude is not helping anything, Freya scolded herself.

The afternoon crawled by—her normal work tasks were less engaging than usual, although she managed to get a few tasks ticked off her list. When her phone rang she was surprised.

'Hi,' she said.

'I'm downstairs, you ready to go?'

'Is it after five already? Let me just finish one email and save everything and I'll be there in two minutes.'

'I'm going to wait exactly two minutes.' Eva sounded tired. Freya hung up and quickly finished the sentence she was part way through. Eva's abruptness worried her, as she descended in the lift to the foyer, she hoped what she'd said to Dinah hadn't got back to Eva.

Standing with her back to the building, Eva's small frame was offset by her long, straight black hair, which hung down to her waist. It was a mystery how she kept it so smooth and tidy all day. Her trousers were fitted around the waist and ankles, and ballooned out over the hips, the fabric a striking mix of green hues in a paisley pattern, on the top she wore a canary yellow jacket; at least her friend's style had stayed the same.

'Hey, sorry I lost track of time,' Freya said.

'That's okay,' Eva said, turning to greet her. Even though her skin was as deep brown and luminous as ever, her expression tight and weary.

'Are you alright?'

'I haven't slept much since the weekend. Nightmares.'

'You'll have to tell me all about it.'

'Not here. I'll tell you at home when I'm out of these heels.' Eva's feet were covered by beautiful high-heeled strappy pumps the colour of her skin; stylish but not comfortable. Eva's apartment was only two blocks from Freya's office, at least the walk wouldn't take long.

When they arrived, Eva flopped onto the couch with a dramatic flourish. 'Can you help me with the shoes?'

'Sure.' Freya approached her friend's feet, trying to ascertain how they worked.

'There's a zip, in the back,' she said. For all their complicated appearance, they slipped off with minimal effort. Freya sank onto the chair opposite and let the silence between them stretch out.

'I've been dreaming about a forest. Creepy, pines and oaks, with snow and ice.' Eva addressed the ceiling from her position flat on her back. 'I'm lost and I can't find the way home. Everything feels scary.'

'Sounds awful.'

'I thought it was just a dream, but I keep having it. The more I think about it, the less it seems like a dream—what do your visions feel like?'

'It's hard to describe. The main thing with my visions is there's no sound. I can feel cold, or hot, I feel wind and things on my skin. What tells me it's a vision is it's repeated, exactly the same, over and over.'

Eva made a contemplative harrumph and was silent for a while. 'Could I be getting visions?'

'You have some talent. That's why I wanted to give you the protection pouch. It's unlikely Vali, or his disciples, will find you if you're practising your magic at home, it shouldn't cause too many ripples, but you can also be influenced by things going on around you. Maybe since we've awoken your talents, you're being affected by something, or someone.'

Eva sat up, her brows drawn together. 'Is someone putting these in my head?'

'I was thinking it could be something the ravens are showing you. It's very similar to the vision of Jotunheim that I saw when I was up at the sheds on the weekend.' Freya paused; it was this vision and the implications of it that had caused the rift with Dinah. 'Have you spoken to Dinah about it?'

'No, I didn't want to bother her . . . she's very upset with you.'

'I know.' *That answers my other question.*

'I told her you would never say anything against her, that you were just being a dickhead. She was reassured, but who knows if she's calmed down enough to speak to you yet.'

'Jacob told her the same thing. Not in so many words, I hope.'

Eva smiled. 'I heard about that too. He would defend you to the death, although you were clearly in the wrong, Dinah decided it was sweet how much he cared for you.'

'I care about him too, and his sister. I was devastated when I realised what I'd done.' She shook her head. 'Let's get this pouch done quickly so we can shield you from outside influences.'

'I've been watching a lot of Children of Vali videos. Do you think I could be getting remote whammy from them?'

Freya shrugged. 'I have no idea. But listening to the ramblings of a doomsday cult is a downer even if they're not psychically influencing you.'

'Hmm.' Eva looked out the window. 'You want to stay for dinner? Maybe open some wine?'

'Yeah, sure. I'll let Jacob know. Should I invite him round or just us?'

'Just us. I'm not up to guests, as lovely as he is.'

'Okay.' Freya was glad of the opportunity to hang out with her best friend again, since she'd got together with Jacob, they hadn't hung out just the two of them very often.

Last minute change of plans—I'm having dinner with Eva. Be home later.

Hopefully Jacob wouldn't be annoyed she was giving him no notice. Eva stood up and got out wine and a couple of glasses.

'My dad got me this bottle from the Barossa, it's very expensive. My palette is less sophisticated than I would like.' She poured a generous glass each and returned to her spot on the couch. The wine was a rich, woody red with fruity notes.

Freya took a few sips before placing the long-stemmed glass on the coffee table so she could grab the ingredients for the protection pouch from her handbag.

'I should do this before I get too squiffy.' She had hoped to sound light-hearted but there was a tension in the room that hadn't been there before. 'I'm sure you'll feel better as soon as we're done.'

'Do I need to help?'

'If you like. I can do it alone, but it might be good experience to do it together.'

Eva nodded, putting her wine down. Freya put the pouch and the ingredients together on the table in front of her and took Eva's hand. She called on the spirits to protect them and imagined a white protective light around them to shield and protect them as they completed the short ritual.

'With these items I call on Odin, All-Father, and Freyja the giver, to watch over you and hide you from your enemy,' Freya said three times after putting the items into the pouch. 'Now you say it.'

Eva hesitated, taking the pouch from Freya's outstretched hand. 'With these items I call on Odin, All-Father and Freyja the giver, to watch over me and hide me from my enemy.'

'That's it. Put it on.' Freya smiled at her friend. Eva slipped the little pouch on its cord over her head. Freya thanked the spirits and the gods for their protection and ended the ritual.

'I can't believe how much this changes the way I feel.'

'It's wild, isn't it? Carrying around a lot of bad mojo and being buffeted by things around you might not seem like it's draining you, but it does.'

I'm so relieved it helped.

'I'm starving. Let's get Mexican, my shout.' Eva was beaming, relieving the weight of whatever it was hanging over had changed her demeanour completely. They ate far too much Mexican food; Freya's burrito was almost the size of her head while Eva had a quesadilla that would have fed two people easily. She wasn't usually a big eater, but perhaps the pouch had brought back her appetite too, as Eva got through all her food without any trouble.

'They're having an event, Vali and the Children. Not this weekend, but next. I thought I'd go, meet some of the people I've been chatting to on the forums, and get an invite to more in person stuff.'

'Sounds good,' Freya said, slightly nervous about her friend being directly exposed to Vali and his followers. 'You know he's going to be charming, right? Possibly even seductive. It's his job.'

'Honey . . . it's sweet you think I'm not all over his shenanigans. I don't know if you remember a year or so ago, I went on a few dates with a guy who told me all sorts of stuff to get me to sleep with him; he was an airline pilot and a property guru and he was rich and did all this charity work—I didn't realise at first, not till after we'd slept together a couple of times, that I was an accessory to him, and not a person. I've seen Vali's type, and I'm immune. I'll put on a good show, of course, because I want him to like me, and invite me into his inner circle or whatever he calls it, but I think I can manage not to fall into bed with him.'

'Phew.'

'Plus, I'll have you and Jacob and Dinah on the outside telling me how bonkers it all is.'

'We'll keep you grounded.'

Freya took a taxi home from Eva's place a little after eleven and expected Jacob to already be in bed. She opened the front door as quietly as she could and tiptoed into the bedroom.

'You're back,' Jacob said from the darkness.

'Yeah. I thought you'd be asleep.'

'Not yet.' He flicked on the bedside light. 'You seem jolly.'

'If that's code for drunk, then yes. Eva kept giving me wine.'

'You're allowed to have wine with a friend. I don't envy being you tomorrow though.' He laughed softly.

'Damn, I forgot about that.' Her midweek drinking days were supposed to be behind her.

'Drink some water, have a shower, and clean your teeth because they're purple.'

Freya's hand flew to her mouth to cover it a little too quickly and she smacked herself. 'I'm drunker than I thought. I'm so sorry, baby.'

Jacob laughed again. 'I'll leave the light on for you, but I might be asleep.'

'Okay.' She dropped her shoes on the bedroom carpet and went about getting ready for bed.

*

As predicted, Thursday at work was rough for Freya, but she got through it. Friday went by without note, and it was Saturday morning before she thought about trying to talk to Dinah again.

'Babe, have you heard from your sister?' she asked over their morning coffee at the local café.

'She texted last night to see if we were going up to the shed this weekend.'

'What did you say?'

'I said probably not. I don't know about you, but I'd really like to have a weekend where we do normal stuff, get some exercise in, maybe see a band. All this work is important, I know, but it feels like we've completely lost who we were.'

'Mmm,' Freya said. The time pressures of stopping the end of the world felt constant, but the next steps were with Eva, and Dinah, and the meet and greet wasn't until the following weekend. 'I haven't seen my mum for a while. Maybe we could go over tomorrow for dinner?' Freya's mother, Astrid, lived in a peculiar multi-level house in Doncaster, a suburb to the east of Melbourne's city. Her brother Axel had moved in with her a couple of years ago following a break-up and had made no moves to find another place to live. They were company for each other, and Axel's heart had been badly broken.

'Do you want me to come?' Jacob asked, a crooked smile indicated he was joking, but perhaps not entirely.

'I know you don't like her . . . New Age stuff, which is ironic, if she knew the rituals we were doing worked, she wouldn't be interested at all. I don't want to go on my own.'

'Alright then.' He sipped his coffee. 'I'm only teasing but I do find your mum a bit weird.'

'Her heart is in the right place.'

'Kindness makes up for a lot when it comes to differences of opinion.'

Freya squeezed his hand across the table. 'I'll let her know now.'

'Do you need to go visit Dinah? Should I come?' Freya asked.

Jacob frowned. 'Might be better if I go on my own, maybe this afternoon. She's still mad at you.'

Freya pressed her lips together, holding in the cranky comment she wished she could make.

'I know you're annoyed with her, and yourself. She's only a kid, you'll have to be patient.'

Freya folded her arms across her chest. 'I know. You're right. But I'm not happy about it.' She felt childish holding onto her resentment, when the fault was hers, but the longer it went on, the guiltier she felt.

Jacob left their apartment a little after one o'clock, and Freya used the time to go for a run and do a quick weights circuit at the gym down the road. Her route to the gym took her about twenty minutes to run, the pounding rhythm of her feet and the heavy pulsing bass of the dance music she played through her headphones put her into an almost meditative state. The gym was packed; one man, in his late twenties, sat on one of the benches texting for the entire forty minutes she was there and he was oblivious to the side-eyes from all the other gym patrons.

I wonder if I can get him to decide it's time to go home, she thought to herself, as she breathed hard between sets of weighted squats. When she finished the last set, she stepped away from the rack, so someone else could use it while she tried her experiment. She cleared her mind, and gently reached out to touch the source of power—the silver bright ribbon that flowed through her imagination and connected her magical energy. She redirected a tiny amount, just the merest hint, lest someone around her be sensitive to her working, and she pushed her idea out towards the man on the bench.

I've left the stove on, I've left the stove on, I've left the stove on, she thought pushing a little bit of anxiety along with the idea to encourage him to leave. After about thirty seconds of this he looked up from his phone, frowning. Then he picked up the tiny towel that had been lying on the ground next to him and scurried out the front door. Freya grinned, releasing the small thread of silver power she'd used. The sense of elation, that she had influenced someone, was like electricity in her veins. She finished her last set of exercises, brutal ab crunches and planks, before heading out the door to jog home.

As she approached the apartment the ravens were circling overhead. They dove down to rest on the apartment balcony as she climbed the stairs.

'I haven't seen you two for a little while, I thought you must have left me to get on with it.'

The ravens bobbed their heads and shifted from foot to foot.

'Did I do something wrong? That guy at the gym didn't know what hit him.'

The birds didn't answer, but the one closer to her took a side-step toward her. She held out the back of her hand, stroking it along the bird's breast feathers. Her inner eye filled with an image of Dinah and Eva at a gathering of some sort, the meet and greet next week she assumed. Around them were people wearing deep purple cotton robes, and flat sandals tied around the feet and up across the calves and ankles. They were serene looking, but Eva was talking animatedly with Vali. His golden-brown hair flowed around his shoulders and his strong, elegant nose made him more attractive than he might have been otherwise. He smiled, inclined his head toward Eva, and touched her upper arm; all signs of flirtation. She shivered and the image disappeared.

'I know it's dangerous to send Eva out to meet him, but I don't have another choice. They know me, by my scars and my eye. Jacob wants to go along too but as a man he's more likely to be seen as a threat. What am I supposed to do?'

The raven fluffed it's feathers a little, as another image floated into her mind—she was sitting in front of a mirror applying make-up to her eye. Heavy beige foundation to camouflage her scars. Then she put on a long brunette wig with a heavy fringe, and she looked very different to her usual, severe, almost black pixie cut.

'A disguise? That's your plan?' It seemed too easy to be effective, put perhaps with a different look and with the totems now working, there would be no reason for anyone to examine her too closely. 'I would feel much better knowing I was nearby in case anything gets too hairy. I'll leave meeting Vali to Eva and Dinah; I don't think there's any reason for me to get close to the guru even with my identity obscured.'

The two birds clicked their beaks in what she hoped was approval before flapping away into the dull Melbourne sky. The wait for Jacob to return from visiting his sister was interminable; she cleaned the apartment, flicked through options on the T.V., but couldn't settle on any. Her mind was whirling, and she was both restless and tired. She tried to meditate but her mind wouldn't settle, at least the attempt had used up half an hour of waiting time.

She gave in and texted Jacob a little before six o'clock after having stared into the fridge hoping for inspiration for long enough it started to beep at her.

Will you be home for dinner?

Flopping onto the couch her eye caught on Hettie's spell book. It had been a while since she had consulted Hettie and the old woman's book always had a soothing quality.

Freya held it in her hands, allowing herself to be calmed. She stroked the pages, asking Hettie to guide her to the right passage or page, before flipping the book open to a spot near the start.

Singular Purpose

My rituals have been successful, almost too successful, and I find myself becoming ever more worried about my own power. What right do I have to wield magic in this way? My ancestors were wise women, they were persecuted and hunted for their beliefs. It has always been the way that some have power, they are allowed to exist in the world, even to have weird or unexplained abilities, while others are not. The Christian faith healers, men usually, are allowed to exist, to flourish and attract wealth, while my mother's mothers were cast out.

I fear being found out. I fear also that my light will not be recognised. I fear being alone, never finding my true people, but I also fear being surrounded by influences which will entice me further down this difficult path. I will use the ritual below to call on my ancestors to provide guidance and to sooth my worries.

Freya rested the book open on her lap, was she self-sabotaging by being filled with doubt? What if she had subconsciously been worried about her own betrayal of the group, and not Dinah? Had that been the reason she had been so careless about seeing Theo before the totems were finished? An urge to cry welled in her throat. Connecting to her ancestors could be a useful exercise, her mother was spiritual although it was often expressed in odd ways. On the other hand, it was hard to believe she had been chosen to save the world, twice, without a link to the witches of old.

The ritual involved a white candle, and a clear quartz crystal to focus the mind upon. Her forays into magic rituals meant she had most things handy in the overnight bag they took to the shed. She sat cross-legged at the coffee table, Hettie's spell book open, beside her and lit the candle, before reciting the words to call on the gods and the spirits to watch over her.

'I come to you this day in the hopes of receiving guidance from the women who have come before me, my mother's mothers, to help on my journey. If you're there make yourself known.' She held the crystal between her palms, imagining the light of the source pulsing inside the crystal, along with an echo or sister light inside her heart chakra. She breathed steadily, waiting and holding her mind open to welcome whatever ancestors decided to make contact. The light in the crystal and the light in her chest swelled and receded in time with her breathing.

The flame of the candle flickered, stood tall, then started to lean to the right. In her mind, Freya saw a woman sitting across the table from her on the floor. She was elderly, her hair white and wispy, moving as though blown by an unseen wind. Her eyes were milky, as though she were blind.

My darling. You are so powerful. Why do you call us to you? The woman was speaking, but her mouth did not move.

'I don't know what I'm doing. I don't know why I was chosen.'

Singular Purpose

You were chosen because you can complete the task. Your blood is strong with the northern magic.

'Is the outcome is already determined?' Freya wasn't sure whether she wanted to know the answer.

Nothing is fixed. There are many possible futures, in many of them you succeed. But you must repair this rift. Be humble. Accept and embrace your power.

'What do you think I've been doing all this time?' Freya was surprised how angry she felt.

You are resisting. You do not believe. You are fearful. These things all create obstacles in your path. Be bold. Believe you can defeat this foolish man and you will do so. You will defeat him not because of your power, although it is great, but because of the family you bring around you, the man you love, his blood kin, the friend whose life you saved. Only together can you create the force to destroy the fool who thinks he can be a god.

Freya opened and closed her mouth. She was stunned at the bald way this ancestor had spoken to her, if her brain had been working, she might have said the woman was lying, or exaggerating but the words didn't come. As she watched, the woman faded, as though she were smoke being swept away by wind.

To her left, another woman appeared, younger than the first, but still much older than Freya. Her heart warmed at this woman's presence, curly hair, crinkles around her eyes and mouth spoke of kindness.

Fleur Blüm

It is not fair that you are here again, Freya. I wish I had been able to help you more the first time, but alas, I was drawn away.

'Hettie?'

You didn't think you could use my spell without me knowing, did you? She made a clucking sound, but as with the other apparition it was all happening inside Freya's head, not in her ears.

'Can you help me?'

You do not need my help. You have everything you need except belief. In spite of everything you've seen, you don't think it's real. You'll never be able to truly wield your power if you are waiting for it to fail. Hettie's eyes were stern but kind.

It was true, it felt like she was in a movie, yet here she was again trying to stop the end of the world. One power-hungry wannabe who thinks he can ruin everything to be the king of a pile of ash.

Hettie faded away and the candle flame flickered briefly before resuming its steady vertical burn. Freya didn't feel any other spirits around her, and had learned what she needed to know, the barrier was inside herself. She thanked the spirits and ended the ritual before blowing out the candle. It had felt like only a few minutes passed but the candle was half burned down and the sky outside was dark. As she tidied up, her belly rumbled loudly, she had been planning to make herself dinner before getting involved in talking with her ancestors. She turned at the sound of the front door opening to see Jacob walk in.

'Hey babe—are you alright?' he said.

'I did a spell to contact my ancestors, it was a little intense. I have no idea what time it is, I forgot dinner. I feel a bit odd, but I'm alright. How was Dinah?'

'It's after eight, you look tired, but calm. Dinah is okay, I think she's mostly over it. I haven't eaten either, let's get something delivered and you can tell me about your afternoon.'

They ordered from a local Italian restaurant, and Freya told Jacob about her ritual.

'Do you feel like you're ready to commit now?' he asked once she had finished.

'I don't know. It seems easy to say I believe and let that be the end of it, but I don't think it's enough. I'm afraid I'll hurt someone with my power, and that I'll fail the mission, but I need to realise that not doing everything I can is just as likely to stuff up the mission.'

'That's a hard thing to hear.' He grabbed her hand and gave it a squeeze. 'Dinah has been stewing in the same juices you have. She's very fragile at the moment but said she has forgiven you.'

'We'll also have to tell her the ravens recommended I go with you all to meet the Children next weekend in disguise. I had written it off as too dangerous but when the emissary of Odin gives you a tip, you do as you're told.' She lifted the left side of her mouth in an attempt at a lopsided grin, unsure whether she was selling it to

Jacob. A knock at the door announced the arrival of their late dinner, and as soon as the smell of garlic and tomato hit her nostrils, Freya couldn't wait to eat.

'We can tell her tomorrow. When I left she looked exhausted.'

They ate in companionable silence, and then prepared for an early night. They were in bed before eleven, and it occurred to Freya that she used to be much more exciting on weekends before she had to save the world.

Chapter 12

The group message thread between Freya, Dinah, Jacob and Eva buzzed all week. Details of how they would approach the meeting with the cult; whether they knew each other or were meeting for the first time, what they would wear, and how they would signal the others if there was a need to get out. Knowing these details soothed Eva and made Freya deeply uncomfortable—there were so many ways it could blow up in their faces.

The event was to be held at the Children of Vali's compound near Castlemaine at midday. Freya and Jacob would go up together, Eva and Dinah would go as friends, but they would pretend the two groups didn't know each other. Jacob and Freya drove up in the big silver four-wheel drive, their secret stash of magical ingredients hidden in the back.

Eva and Dinah followed in a car Eva had hired, living in the city she didn't own a car but used a car share program on her mobile phone to grab one locally when she needed to.

Freya wore a long brunette wig, with a fringe that hung low over her eyebrows, partially covering her scars.

'Stop touching your hair, or else tie it back,' Jacob said, his eyes on the road.

'I'm trying. If I tie it up my scars are too visible, and it looks more like a wig, the less attention I can draw to myself the better.'

'Constantly flicking your hair draws attention too.'

She shifted in the passenger seat, about to tell Jacob he could keep his opinions to himself, but closed her mouth again as the turn-off to the compound came into view.

Two young women dressed in long mauve robes made from cheesecloth-like fabric, stood at the gate greeting people. They waved the car over.

'Hi,' Jacob said through the lowered window.

'Hey! Welcome to our home, have you come to learn some more about the Children of Vali?' the younger of the two asked.

'Yes, we're really intrigued by the work you do.'

'Excellent. Drive up to the main house and park anywhere you like. Someone will direct you to the main meeting area where you will have an opportunity to meet the elders, and maybe even our leader Vali himself, if you're lucky.'

'My goodness, that sounds super exciting doesn't it, love?' Jacob turned to her to speak.

Freya widened her eyes in warning, his tone had slipped a little too far into sarcasm and she worried the women would notice. 'Thank you so much.'

Jacob rolled up the window and drove up a narrow winding gravel track. 'Don't give me that look.'

'I didn't want you to blow our cover immediately.'

'I would have been able to smooth them over without them even noticing,' Jacob said.

'Let's not use our talent if we can avoid it. I want them to believe we're ordinary, non-magical folk.' Freya fidgeted with her dark grey trousers.

'If everything goes south though, all bets are off, right?'

'My first priority is to get out safely, second to maintain our cover stories; if we can get out without revealing ourselves, great, but if we can't, then we can't.'

They'd had the conversation numerous times already, but Jacob needed to reassure himself. It was annoying but she reminded herself it was his way of coping. They drove for a couple of minutes, the bush around them wild and full of eucalypt trees and ratty-looking ferns. Turning around one last corner the gravelled road opened out into a wide flat space, where a number of other vehicles were already parked. Freya doubted the cult members would leave their vehicles out with the punters. Jacob pulled in next to a white campervan covered with red-orange dust, the curtains drawn over the windows, very hippy-chic.

Jacob switched off the car and took a deep breath. 'Here we go.'

For convenience they would keep their first names the same as their real first names. If asked, they were married, and both used the surname Grimm. It was a nod to the fairy tales they were spinning and to the old Norse word for mask, sometimes used to refer to Odin. Freya thought it was too obvious but both Jacob and Dinah had said it was too good to pass up.

'People aren't likely to ask for our surnames, we might need to provide contact details, so let's get an email address for ourselves in those names, and avoid putting phone numbers on anything,' Jacob had said.

The building was a large colonial-style farmhouse, with a second story rising from the centre of the roof, and a wide wooden veranda on all sides. It would be worth a lot, but signs of disrepair became clear as they approached; peeling paint on weatherboards and the dark wood veranda was grey with old varnish and exposure to the elements.

Another woman in her twenties greeted them as they approached the front door. She wore the same mauve cheesecloth dress as the two at the front gate and had an off-putting smile—her eyes a little too wide, a few too many teeth showing.

'Greetings and well met. We invite you into the bosom of our leader, the wise and powerful Vali, we are all his children.'

'Thanks,' Freya said after an uncomfortable pause.

'You can meet our leaders in the main room, there are some vegan refreshments and green tea as well, we know it's long drive if you've come up from town.'

'You're very generous to invite us all up here. We've been following the group online. I'd love to hear more about what you're doing up at the centre of everything,' Jacob said. Freya tensed as the woman at the door leaned away from him, her smile faltering slightly, as though taken aback.

'That's great you've been learning about us already. Go through and have a look as some reading material, one of the leaders will come to speak with you.'

Freya squeezed his hand as they entered the main reception space. The internal floorboards were in better condition than the veranda, polished hardwood. A large Persian rug covered most of the boards, a polished mahogany table, covered in leaflets and reading materials sat on the rug. Along one wall, a smaller trestle table held various bite-sized foods, and a large urn of hot water. The plates and cups were stacked at one end, although they appeared to have been cobbled together from a number of different sets, and didn't stack well. A few knots of people were standing in around the edges of the room, none were dressed as members. Several women seemed uncomfortable or nervous; one picked at her cuticles, one whose eyes darted around the room constantly, and another holding her elbows, her shoulders hunched. No one attempted to strike up conversation with anyone else.

'Do you want to look at the food or the literature first?' Jacob said in a low voice.

'Literature. We can hold the pages up and watch people.'

Jacob nodded and they took a couple of the pamphlets each, before retreating to an unoccupied corner. Freya counted fifteen people, in groups of two or three in the room; a man and woman both with waist length dreadlocks, possibly the owners of the van out the front. Near them, a petite woman and a larger, younger woman who looked remarkably like her, mother and daughter perhaps. Three women in their early twenties giggled in one corner, each held a steaming mug. Two couples were both women in their thirties, one trio of women in their sixties, and a man and woman in their forties, all dressed in normal clothing; smart casual, the sort of thing one might wear to eat at a mid-range restaurant.

Freya held the pamphlet up and let her focus relax, concentrating on getting a vibe or feel for the people in the room without tapping into the silvery source and drawing attention to herself.

'Are you getting anything?' Jacob whispered after a few minutes.

'Nothing much. They're edgy, the three young ones are giving off a "here for a bit of fun" vibe, the older trio seem serious, but anxious, and the others are giving me nothing. You?'

'Nothing from a magic perspective.' He chuckled softly. 'But our dreadlocked friends are tucking into the food, perhaps here for the buffet?'

'You're wicked,' Freya said, smiling. She had wondered the same thing herself. Five minutes later Eva and Dinah walked in, heads together talking in hushed tones. They went to the green tea first and tried to start a conversation with the mother and daughter. Freya looked for a suitable opening to introduce herself when a gong sounded, followed by the chime of Tibetan cymbals. A hush fell over the room, and a straight-backed, stern-looking woman wearing a deep purple linen robe walked in. Probably in her fifties, although her bearing and serene face made it hard to know for sure. Bianca had appeared in several of the Children's videos, the woman Theo said had left her coven to join the children a few weeks ago.

She's risen up the ranks fast, if she had any talent at all, no doubt Vali would bring her into the inner circle.

'If I could have your attention, please,' Bianca began, her voice clear and bell-like, her tone low and authoritative.

Freya glanced at Jacob, eyebrows raised in a question whether he had felt the little tickle of power she used, he dipped his head in a tiny nod, before turning his eyes back to Bianca.

'We're so pleased to welcome you to our learning and community centre. We're here to answer your questions and tell you about why we're here.' She lowered her voice to a more conversational level and approached the trio of older women. The three women in mauve they had seen when they arrived were also now circulating the room, each with a mug of green tea. Freya moved over to the urn and poured herself and Jacob a tea, by the time she returned he had struck up a conversation with the younger woman from the front gate, and one of the duos of women.

'Freya, this is Elsa, we met her at the gate, and Gemma and Teresa, they're first timers here too.' Jacob introduced the three women.

'Lovely to meet you, Freya, I get a really great vibe from you,' Elsa said, stretching out her hand to shake. Freya concentrated on her white protection aura so that the physical touch would not reveal anything to the other woman and shook her hand. As their skin was in contact Freya tried to absorb what she could about her new companion. It was a skill she and Jacob had been working on, trying to learn things by touch without the other person feeling it. In her mind, Freya imagined the story of the other woman flowing over her like a river, this approach had proven the least intrusive, and from Elsa's face, it had not registered.

In the jumble of images that flowed from the handshake; Elsa sitting cross-legged on the floor, holding hands with several other women, chanting. Above them, on a raised chair or throne, sat Vali, looking down his pointy nose at them; patronising but approving. The purpose of the chanting circle was unclear, in the centre of the circle lay a large pale tree branch. The wave of images didn't tell her the meaning of the branch, but Freya made a mental note to look into Yggdrasil, the sacred tree which joined the realms. They might try to use it to anchor their energy to force a portal to Jotunheim.

'What about you Freya?' Elsa asked, her eyebrows up, expectant.

'Sorry, off with the fairies, did you ask a question?' Freya was annoyed with herself that in her efforts to sort through the images she'd picked up the conversation had continued without her. Hopefully, Jacob had been paying better attention.

'I said is this the first time you've been interested in new spiritual pathways?'

'I dabbled a couple of years ago, do you remember that coma thing that was going around? A friend of mine was a victim of that, and it really made me re-evaluate the way I looked at the world around me.'

'Yes, that was catalysing for a number of people. A very rich period for magical practice, although it didn't help those in the hospital.' Elsa's eyes glazed over for a moment, as though she was remembering something. 'Vali has made some concerning observations about the state of the world, climate change and pollution, and the general lack of empathy people show for their fellow human beings, it all points to a need to restore things. That's what we're doing here, preparing to heal the world.'

'Very admirable. I feel overwhelmed by big issues like poverty, hunger and overpopulation.' Teresa's fists were closed tightly by her side. 'I'd love to be part of a group that was really doing something about them.'

'We all would, not knowing how to start is a sticking point for many people,' Freya replied.

'Weak-minded people find it easier to sit and do nothing in the face of the end of civilisation as we know it. The evidence keeps building up and their inaction becomes harder and harder to overcome. Vali has seen we need to act now to save ourselves.'

Classic doomsday cult rhetoric, Freya thought to herself. Taking the issues of the time and proposing a solution. It was what people wanted to hear, to be reassured that their contribution, their sacrifice, would make a difference.

'How can we get involved?' Gemma asked.

'You've done the hard part already, finding us and visiting our centre. We want to make sure everyone who wants to be involved can be, so we'll spend some time assessing your skills and backgrounds and assigning tasks or groups to be part of. A lot of our work can be done from home, but many of us, myself included, have decided to live on the grounds so we can do what's needed. There are so many people who need to hear our message and I'm dedicating my life to the survival of the human race by being close to Vali.'

'Do you enjoy your life here? What did you do before?' Jacob asked.

'Of course, it's beautiful. I have meaning in my life, and my spiritual self has never been better.' Elsa's voice was automatic, her words rehearsed. No doubt their leader had given them specific things to say in response to these sorts of questions. They continued to talk for another ten minutes of Elsa expounded the virtues of the group. Freya tried to keep smiling, but her cheeks ached with the effort. Jacob looked bored, his eyes roaming around the room.

Bianca approached them. 'Elsa, are you taking care of our guests?' she asked in the same low, seductive voice.

'Yes, we've been having a fantastic chat. They're all great candidates to join, if they like what we have to offer of course.'

'Of course.' Bianca's eyes fixed onto Freya, and she hoped the shielding and the avatar work were enough to hide from the gaze of this powerful witch. She dragged the white protective light around her and concentrated on exuding warm curiosity, and a non-threatening aura. Bianca dragged her eyes away to look at Jacob, who she stared at with the same intensity, holding his hand in hers. The social awkwardness of such a long handshake was nothing compared to the certainty she was trying to read them, the air around them prickled with magic; it took all her concentration to maintain the white light and not scratch her nose.

'We were so keen to see everything up close. We've been watching the videos and what Vali said really resonated with me.' Jacob withdrew his hand, his lips pressed tight and brows drawn together as though in concentration.

'He's very attuned, I believe he has a channel directly to the makers of the universe.'

'Is he a Christian? Pagan? Or something else?' Gemma asked.

'I'm sure he would prefer to be given the chance to answer for himself, but as I'm his representative in this meeting I will try to provide answers.' Bianca clasped her hands in front of her and straightened her shoulders. 'He believes in himself, as he believes in others. The theology Vali follows takes elements of many of the world's religions and combines them in a powerful, liberating way. There are parts of what we do that are influenced by Christian lore, parts that are influenced by Western paganism, including some of the Wicca traditions, but his name Vali has been given to him from the Norse pantheon. He is one of the few who sees the coming of the end of the world and manages to survive, along with a select group of followers.'

The air around her fizzed as she imbued magical influence in her words. Despite the protection spells and her white light, Freya wanted to agree.

'There are warning signs around the world; rising sea levels, pollution, billionaires exploiting workers to create ridiculous electronic devices that strip the earth and leech poison into the soil, it's not surprising people think the world is ending. Vali knows the end is coming. He wants us to stop it, and if we can't, to be prepared to survive,' Elsa added.

Bianca turned sharply, furious, like a hawk about to pluck a mouse from the ground. 'As I was saying. He welcomes all to his fold, everyone willing to work together to save the world. It requires real dedication, there can be no tourists, however we acknowledge no one will fully commit, as Elsa and myself have, without having time to consider it, and having faith as we do.'

'Wow, it sounds so exciting.' Teresa's eyes were glazed and wide with awe.

'It makes so much sense, I've known for years we need to do more, but I had no one to guide me. It's so wonderful Vali wants us to be included in the movement,' Gemma said.

The spell Bianca used to influence people listening had a similar effect to Jacob's singing voice. She must be powerful to have such a potent effect on the two women without the intervention of the gods, as she and Dinah and Jacob had.

'You'll have to excuse me, I must speak to other attendees, but if you stay for the ceremony in a little while you'll be able to see what we do.' Bianca turned away from their group and they all exhaled as one. The spell was broken, and Freya let the resistance she had been holding drop with it.

'She's such an inspiration, isn't she?' Elsa said after a moment.

'I can see why she's the favourite. Did you say she's new to the community up here?' Freya asked.

'Bianca came to us in the last month, but she and Vali have an understanding; maybe they knew each other in a different life, or maybe they were spiritual companions in another realm, in any case, they spend a lot of time together in his study. I would love to be that important to him.' The look on Elsa's face could have been love.

'Do you spend any time with Vali one on one? He must struggle to get time with everyone if he's busy trying to save the world,' Jacob asked.

'I've been called into his office once or twice, although last time Bianca was there as well. Being in his presence can be really overwhelming; he's just so perfect.'

'Goodness, what a treat that would be.' Gemma's face had reverted to her normal expression although she was still grinning. 'I can't wait for the session later, I've never been to something like this in real life before, only online.'

'You'll have a wonderful time, but eat something, have some more tea.' Elsa looked to Bianca who was beckoning her. 'I'll be right back.'

Jacob glanced at the retreating woman in the mauve dress. 'I think I've left something in the car, do you want to come with me while I go check?'

'Sure.' Freya looked for Eva and Dinah who had moved on to a conversation with another of the groups of people in the main reception area, they had a woman in mauve with them, but didn't seem to have attracted the attention of Bianca.

'Sorry, that wasn't very subtle,' Jacob said when they were outside the house and walking towards the car.

'I don't think Gemma or Teresa will have noticed.'

'Did you feel the whammy Bianca tried to put on us?' Jacob's voice was a coarse whisper, trying to cover his agitation and keep his volume low.

'It nearly worked, even though I knew she was doing it.'

'It was intense. I mean, far out, no wonder the witches she left were worried. She'll fill Vali's cult on her own.' Jacob unlocked the boot of the car and made a show of flipping through the items in it.

'That's what he's good at, not a strong practitioner on his own, but charming and persuasive. If someone like Bianca believes in him, she'll do anything.'

'And does she believe they're trying to stop it?'

Freya paused. 'She believes what she's selling. Vali definitely doesn't. Fascinating that he's able to deceive someone as strong as her, but maybe it's more about what she wants to believe than the evidence in front of her.'

Jacob let his arms flop down to his sides.

'Were you actually looking for something?' she asked.

'No, I was acting. Good, wasn't it?' He turned to her and winked. She was so surprised she giggled. 'Let's get back in before Bianca sees we've left. She was suss, we might need to pretend to be enthralled next time she tries that trick.'

'Agreed.'

They walked back inside and found that Bianca waiting for them at the door. 'I thought you might have run off.'

'No, just went to get a pen and paper from the car, but we realised I had left it at home, so, here we are again.'

Jacob spread his empty hands out as if to prove they hadn't found anything in the car.

'You won't need to take notes.' There was a slight sizzle of power in the air.

'No, you're right,' Jacob replied. Even though they had just agreed to go along with her when she used her power, it felt wrong down to Freya's bones.

'The ceremony will be in one of the smaller chambers, we've set it up for ritual and other important works. Are you all okay to sit on cushions on the floor? I realise it's not ideal for some people, but it's best to connect with the earth and your fellows.' Bianca was addressing the room as a whole, making hard accusatory eye-contact with each person in turn. Freya tried to keep her expression as neutral as possible, looking interested every so often.

Bianca turned and walked from the room; she moved more like she was gliding along the floor than walking, her long purple robe hovered just above the boards, adding to the illusion by obscuring her feet. Her pace was deceptively quick, and Freya had to hurry to keep up. The corridor from the main reception room had dark oak wainscotting over the lower half of the walls, the upper half was covered with deep forest green embossed wallpaper; both had seen better days. The wallpaper had started to lift at the joins and peel down from the corners near the ceiling. It must have been a very grand house when it was built, although a couple of generations had let it run down. Heavy dark oak doors led off from the corridor on both sides, all closed except the one Bianca turned in to.

This room had had the Moroccan tent treatment; deep red, gold, and maroon fabrics draped from the ceiling, peaking above the lantern-like light fitting in the centre, and sweeping down to the walls. On the floors were dark, patterned rugs, on which had been laid a multitude of enormous, equally patterned, flat cushions. Freya wasn't sure why this style had been chosen, perhaps it hid a hole or stain in the walls or ceiling. The room had a mystical feeling, and although it was only three or four metres along each wall, felt cosy rather than claustrophobic.

'We'll sit in a circle.' Bianca had taken a place at the far end of the room near a particularly ornate cushion. She arranged herself in a cross-legged position, affecting a look of patience as the rest of the participants murmured and took seats around the edge of the room. With the women in mauve and all their potential new recruits there were twenty people in the room, Freya's knees brushed the woman beside her, and she and Jacob were almost in each other's laps.

'Take the hands of the person either side of you. We will start with chanting.' Bianca paused to allow the group to join hands. 'The purpose of the chant is to get us working in harmony. We are one voice. Try to continue without breath as long as possible, then break to breathe and start again. With so many people, each breathing at different times, we should be able to get one long continuous sound.' She ran her eyes over the group, as though daring someone to ask a question, but she was met with silence. 'We will be chanting the opening of the *Havamal: Gáttir allar, áðr gangi fram*[1] Just follow along, those who are more experienced will keep it going if you get lost.'

The room began to mumble along with Bianca who chanted clearly from her cushion at the front. The other followers in mauve dotted around the room were confident although not as loud or commanding as Bianca. A sleepiness started to creep into the room, the frisson of magic was small, but clearly Bianca was influencing them, lulling them, much as Jacob had done with his singing. Freya tried to keep up with the chant while keeping her mind on the white light that kept her slightly apart from the group while still being a part of it. If she hadn't been holding Jacob's hand, she wondered if she would have been able to resist, but the warmth of him on her right and the press of his leg against hers, kept her from being swept away in the tide of Bianca's magic. Time slowed down and sped up at the same time, her throat was dry and her jaw stiff by the time Bianca began to slow her chanting, and eventually ceased. The feeling in Freya's feet had disappeared, they must have been there for at least half an hour.

'Now we are all in tune with one another, and are working as one, we will do a small ritual.' Bianca uncoupled her hands from those next to her, and placed

---

[1] It sounds like 'goh-tirr allarr, oh-ther gang-i fram'.

their hands on her knees. 'We call on the spirits to look over the flock here gathered. We call upon the spirits to bless the work we do to protect this earth and all its inhabitants. We call on the flock here gathered to give of themselves to ensure the protection of this earth, our one true realm. We are the caretakers; we have been given the divine task of tending to the earth and we have failed in this task. We repent for our selfishness. We undertake to do better, to right the wrongs we have done. We promise this in the name of Vali, the powerful and beneficent leader of our group, may his guidance protect us and show us our true path.'

A hush fell over the room and those in the circle stared blankly ahead of them, eyes glazed, blinking slowly. Freya held her face slack, and slowly moved her gaze to Eva and Dinah. Eva seemed out of it, apparently staring at nothing, Dinah seemed sleepy, but still present, her eyes roamed the room slowly. Freya caught her eye and there was a flicker of a message in them, but it would have to wait until later.

She was desperate to stand up, her feet and legs were numb and the room had become stuffy with the heat and breath of so many people. More fabrics had been hung over the walls and there didn't appear to be any windows or doors other than the one she and the others had come in through. Just as she was sure she couldn't hold up the pretence any longer, some of the younger women in the group moved and stretched. The women in mauve were the first to stand, the rest followed with various grunting and stretching of limbs.

'We'll move into the library now so you can have another cup of tea, read some of Vali's works or chat with your fellows. We'll be able to spend some time with each of you and suggest work to be done at home, or with us here in the community.' Elsa said in her quiet voice before turning and walking out of the room.

The library was further down the corridor, away from the reception area. A large square room, the dark wainscotting continued around the walls, and mustard yellow and brown patterned wallpaper where the walls were not covered in floor to ceiling bookshelves. An immense bay window looked out over the deep green-grey eucalypt trees and the rolling fields outside. If it hadn't been the home of a doomsday cult trying to bring on Ragnarök, Freya would have very much liked to sit in the squat, overstuffed armchairs and read the old volumes on the walls. Someone had moved the urns and cups into this room—unless they had another set—although there were no more snacks.

Bianca didn't follow them into the library, instead she continued into another part of the house with two mauve-clad assistants. Elsa was left as the only representative of the Children of Vali in the library.

Dinah and Eva were mingling with some of the other guests, Freya took Jacob's elbow and steered him over to the bay window.

'I think Bianca is onto us. She hasn't looked at me straight since we met, and I don't like the fact she's run off.' Freya kept her voice low.

'You might be right. That session was exhausting, trying to keep my protection up and not get sucked in but still look like I was participating. I'll be glad as soon as this undercover thing is finished.'

'Any idea what we were chanting?'

'I know I've seen the *Havamal* referenced, but it's a story, one of the myths, I don't know it well enough to have memorised the words.'

'We were saying 'at every doorway, ere one enters,' which doesn't make much sense until you say the next bit which is that one should look around to make sure no one is lurking to kill you.'

Freya was startled by Dinah's voice behind her. 'How do you know that?'

'Elsa.'

'You got that out of her quickly,' Jacob said.

'I put my hand on her arm and read that off her. It was sort of floating around in her mind, like listening to the radio. She didn't notice, she's whammied from Bianca.'

'I'm astounded she's standing after using that much juice,' Freya said.

'You felt it too?' Dinah asked.

'We thought we should pretend to be under the influence even though we weren't. I'm not sure about Eva, she seemed out of it.'

'Yeah, she went under all the way, and was a bit annoyed with herself about it.'

Freya looked around; Eva was talking to Elsa in another part of the library. The three older women looked pale and tired, maybe preparing to make their excuses and leave. Of the other people who had come to check out the headquarters two of the female pairs looked mildly distressed, and unlikely to return, although the mother and daughter pair were almost bouncing with excitement.

'Can we go home now? We've established ourselves; I don't want to wait around to see whether Bianca comes back.' Jacob sighed.

'Let's give it ten minutes. Dinah, you stick around another five minutes and then follow us, yeah?'

'Roger.' She nodded her head and walked back to Eva who was staring glassy-eyed at Elsa who seemed to be explaining something in great detail.

'Look out,' Jacob said, flicking his eyes to the door. A tall, slim man with wavy blond shoulder-length hair walked into the room. His nose was thin and his deep brown eyes unsettling. The energy in the room shifted as he stepped over the threshold, a collective indrawn breath. Vali was a remarkable-looking man on video, but in person he was captivating. He moved with the liquid grace of a big cat stalking its prey, yet somehow retained the aloofness of a royal dignitary. His burgundy silk robe was in the style of the others, but much more elaborate.

Bianca glided behind him whispering into his ear. He nodded to Elsa who rushed to his side. The three muttered together for a moment before his cold eyes landed on her and Jacob.

'Shit,' she said. Freya grabbed Jacob's hand and took a slow breath to calm her nervous system which had kicked off a fight or flight response. As he came nearer, her mind filled with wave upon wave of intense visions. She wanted to focus on what they were showing but they were so thick and fast it was hard to retain anything. Through the haze of visions, she watched Vali approach—as if time had slowed down. She clenched her teeth and pushed the visions away.

'Bianca said I needed to meet you two, I'm Vali.' He held out his hand to shake hers, with all the force of will she could muster, Freya took his hand and tried to remain calm and steady. He clapped his other hand over hers in a gesture she hated even without magic transmitted by touch. The handshake lingered, she had no chance to read him, as all her effort was on keeping herself from being read.

'Freya,' she managed to say.

'What a beautiful name, well met, Freya, the goddess of love and sex and war.' He turned to Jacob, releasing her hand and taking his.

'I'm Jacob.'

'Biblical, very nice. Well met, Jacob.' The two men clasped hands, neither one speaking or moving for a long time, Freya found herself not daring to breathe until they had separated.

'It's wonderful to see people such as yourselves showing an interest in our group. We can find a role for many in the quest to recover the world and repair the damage we have wreaked up our mother nature. But . . .' he hesitated, staring into their eyes one at a time. 'I must agree with Bianca, you're not a good fit for our community. We must have people who bring harmony and work with us towards out common goal. Your intentions might be good, but you have chaotic energy. I can't risk the group with wild cards such as yourselves.'

Jacob opened his mouth, leaning his body forward as though to protest.

'No, don't say anything. My mind is made up. Jacob, you, for the most part, are benign and we would have been able to welcome you with open arms if you weren't so inextricably bonded to this woman.'

'I—' Freya began.

'We don't mean to offend. This work requires powerful dedication, you might be passionate, but you do not have the bearing of someone who will persevere and give your life to the cause. Thank you for coming. You are welcome to follow our work online, and to donate to the upkeep of the centre, of course, but we will thank you not to return to our home.'

The images that had been flashing through Freya's mind since Vali walked into the room became stronger in her inner eye—her anger and surprise at his pronouncement of them, her in particular, as unworthy had loosened her control. He retreated, his eyes locked on her for several steps before he turned away to speak with the other attendees.

Freya put her tea on the nearest tabletop, adjusted the handbag strap on her shoulder and marched from the room; down the long corridor, out through the now deserted reception room, and into the carpark. When the cooler, fresh air outside hit her cheeks she slowed her pace and looked around for Jacob.

'I was worried you were going to storm all the way home,' he said, his mouth raised in a half-smile.

'I've never been so angry in my life. I wanted to . . . to smite him right there. Reach out to the source, draw the whole lot into my body and crush him.' Freya opened her hands which had contracted into balls beside her.

'Breathe. I'm glad you didn't. I was not ready for the battle royale just yet.' Jacob clicked the button on the car key, and they climbed into the big silver four-wheel drive. Freya took the passenger seat, Jacob drove most of the time because of her eye, but this time she was too incensed to drive.

'I don't think I've ever seen you speechless with rage before.'

'I don't think I've been speechless with rage before.'

'I got a bad vibe from that handshake. It was like my skin was crawling with pinpricks.'

'He was trying to read you, but he's not much good at it, at least not magically. Bianca would have been keeping her eye on us while we were doing that ritual. I should have known it was a bad idea, but the ravens insisted.'

'We'll see if Eva and Dinah did any better. Maybe having you in the room was to distract Bianca, drawing her attention away from them.'

Freya opened her mouth to reply and then closed it. Jacob started the car and they drove back down the gravel driveway toward the main road. They remained quiet for twenty minutes until they were back on the freeway to Melbourne.

'Did you get any visions from him?' Jacob asked.

'Yes, but I'm not sure what to make of them. I've been trying to sort through everything. When he came towards me, my head was full of them—like in a movie and they try to show your life flashing before your eyes? It felt like I was seeing his whole life, everything he's ever done or thought or possibly will do, but all at once.'

'That sounds confusing.'

'Having no information is hard but having so much dumped on you is just as bad. Nothing is clear. It was like I was having every emotion at the same time. There was fear and anger and envy and . . . a lot of anger and maybe greed?' Freya tried to recall the images to her mind. 'I'll have to think about it, try to tease out some useful information. Maybe Dinah and I can do a mind meld and she can sort something out from the jumble. I don't think Bianca knew what we were up to—only that we were off.'

'Not as pliable as she hoped. She was using a lot of her power in there.'

Freya murmured something in agreement and stared out the window. Jacob turned the radio up as though he understood she needed time to think over what had happened before they talked more.

Chapter 13

The drive home seemed longer than the drive up to the compound. Jacob was quiet, and Freya was deep in her mind, mulling through the events of the afternoon and trying to tease any useful images out of the cacophony.

She yawned, her jaw cracking, as she mounted the stairs to their first-floor apartment, seeing the ravens perched on the railing was both welcome and irritating.

'Thanks for setting me up for that, boys.'

The ravens fluffed their feathers and squawked indignantly.

'I'm sure you had your orders, or reasons, but I'm still miffed to have gone all the way up there, in this ridiculous disguise,' she waved the long-haired wig at them, 'and for what? We got thrown out.'

'The birds weren't to know that Vali would do that.' Jacob put his hand on her shoulder.

'They were the whole reason I was there pretending not to be the empty woman with the scars.'

'They're on our side. I hope Eva and Dinah are in with the group and we can get on with the business of finding out when and where the ritual will be. You and I will be backup while they're the undercover in the field.'

Freya's bottom lip stuck out a pout. 'I wanted to be undercover.' She was being silly, but it was hard to deny her disappointment at being found out. The ravens clacked their beaks and made a chortling sound before flapping off into the darkening evening sky.

'Were they laughing at me?' Freya asked.

'They might be magical beings, but they're still just birds. I don't think they were laughing at you.'

Freya harrumphed before letting herself into the apartment. She flopped down on the couch and stared at the ceiling. 'Now what?'

'Wait for Eva and Dinah, debrief, then bed. All that driving and trying to keep Bianca out of my head has done me in.' He slouched on the seat beside her, resting his head on her shoulder.

It was nearly an hour before there was a knock at the door. Jacob got up to let his sister and Eva in. They looked as tired as Freya felt.

'What happened to you two?' Eva asked, bustling into the lounge room.

'One minute you were there, talking to Vali and Bianca and then you disappeared. And no text? Nothing?'

'Sorry.' Freya's cheeks heated. 'Jacob was driving, and I was preoccupied. We should have told you we left.' She checked her phone and saw several texts from Dinah.

'Bianca said we were "unsuitable" to be in the group,' Jacob said, returning to his spot on the couch. 'Our energies were too chaotic or something.'

Eva scoffed. 'Really? What a load of twaddle. Her energy was all over the place. It felt like she kept trying to get us to do or feel something. That ritual it was all over me. I kind of gave in to it, but I also kind of didn't.'

'I felt the prickle in the air, but because I don't hear like your do talking magic doesn't work as well on me.' Dinah gave a lopsided smile. 'I suppose that's one advantage.'

'I never thought about it like that, bonus,' Jacob said.

'We've been told never to return. Whatever Bianca felt from us, she has been in Vali's ear to ban us from the group. I dunno if she thought we were—'

'I can tell you,' Dinah interrupted. 'When they finished with you, they came straight over to us, I was getting barely anything off Bianca she was probably blocking me, but Vali isn't much good with magic, so I read the whole thing when he shook my hand.' She paused.

'And?' Freya prompted.

'Bianca said you weren't to be trusted, you seemed powerful but when she tried to probe or influence you, she got *nada*, and that was enough for her to say you were up to no good. It was Freya she spotted, I don't think she clocked you, bro.'

'Figures. She's the type to be more threatened by other women. And she wasn't concerned about you two?'

'Apparently not. We've been given homework and invited to the ritual next Saturday night.'

'What's happening on Saturday night?' Jacob asked, leaning forward in his seat.

'They were oblique, but I got the impression it was an initiation,' Eva said.

'Definitely not the big thing, it's at the house so no portal opening in fields yet,' Dinah added.

'Sounds promising but we need to be cautious. You two are in but they'll be keeping a close eye on newbies, be especially wary around Bianca, she's got a lot of juice.' Jacob leaned back again, but his left leg jiggled in agitation.

'Well done, both of you,' Freya said.

'You don't seem pleased,' Dinah said, her brows drawn together and down.

'I—' she stopped herself and started again. 'I'm annoyed at myself. I had always thought it was a bad idea to confront Vali directly, that he or one of his lackeys would read something in me to give me away. The only reason I went was because of the ravens.'

'But you said earlier if you hadn't been there maybe Dinah and Eva would have been under heavier scrutiny from the Children. As it was you were the only real threat, and now they have eliminated you they feel safe again.'

Freya folded her arms.

'I bet the ravens did it on purpose.' Dinah was smiling. 'The little shits, we were tricked by bird brains.'

'They're divine birds, so I think I should get a pass for falling for it.' Freya tried to make light of the situation, although she didn't feel it.

'I'm off. Let's have lunch this week, and I'll see you on Saturday night Dinah.' Eva stood, flicked her lustrous black her hair over her shoulder and stepped out the front door. She was always so graceful and erect; Freya envied her confidence after such a long day.

'I'm going to bed.' Dinah got up and went into the bathroom, still amused by Freya's agitation.

'I guess it's progress that I'm now the butt of a cosmic joke after being the worst person in the world,' she said.

'You're not the worst person in the world. I told you she'd need some time to get over suggesting she joined the dark side, but she found the raven's trick very amusing.' He pressed his lips together.

'You're not allowed to find it funny, mister.'

'I don't.' He laughed. 'Okay, I do. I love you, you're amazing. Let's go to bed, I'll be big spoon, how's that?'

She maintained her gaze a moment before smiling back at him. 'It's a good start.' It was hard to stay mad at him when he was being so cute. Freya remembered again how grateful she was to have Jacob in her life; keeping her grounded and saving the world with her.

*

Eva put off their lunch date until Thursday, saying she had lots of work to do. In the meantime, Freya and Jacob rewatched the Children of Vali videos, especially those since Bianca had arrived. Vali was the head of the group, but Bianca was the general—driving recruitment and rituals. She was powerful and had become careless in her use of magical power if their experience on the weekend was anything to go on.

'It's like she has no fear, y'know?' Freya said, slurping a mouthful of her soup. She had been craving the salty, noodley goodness of ramen lately, it was one of her comfort foods.

'I guess so. On the other hand, if you were at the head of a powerful religion, and they needed you to do everything you could to stop the end of the world, which is what Bianca thinks they're doing, why would you hold back?' Eva took a dainty bite of her sushi and looked intently into Freya's eyes, she had to look away. 'The main reason you don't use your power all the time is there's a chance you'll be punished. Each time you use it, it's possible an enemy will know, and you'll be in danger, but who are her enemies?'

Freya thought about this for a moment. 'I suppose so. Doesn't she get tired though? I feel like I've been hit by a truck if I use even half the magic she does.'

'You might be more powerful, but she's had more practice.'

'You could be right.'

'What are you going to do about your stamina? You can't go up against Bianca and hope to outlast her in your current state, given how much juice you said she used on the weekend, you'll tire first.'

'I'll have to use an enemy's strength against them, like in Judo.'

'You need to practice. We know the whole group will be distracted with this initiation whatever on Saturday night, it's a good time to do it.'

'I'll see if Jacob wants to try throwing stuff my way and I'll practice deflecting it. It feels like we're spending all our time on this; you're the only friend I've seen in ages.'

'It's hard, but we're trying to save the world. Not having time for some of your friends for a while is okay.'

'I can never tell anyone what I'm doing. I know it's the only thing we can do, but I get tired of having secrets.'

'The burden of being the chosen one.' Eva smiled and put her hand over Freya's. 'Once we sort out Vali, we can go back to a life of obscurity, free of magic.'

'I hope so.' Freya was not hopeful that this would be the last battle they would face. Now she knew about this other world she worried it would always be there, in the background, waiting to draw her back in.

She'd heard nothing from Theo and assumed it would be fruitless dropping in on him again. Her boss was getting annoyed by the number of long lunches she had been taking, and the last thing she needed was to be reprimanded at work on top of everything else.

*

On Saturday Jacob and Freya planned to head up to the shed, just the two of them once more.

'Let's stay there tonight. We can take the tent or camp in the back of the car; it might be a bit close, but perhaps more comfortable than the ground.'

Freya raised an eyebrow. 'I'm not a great fan of camping, but I know the drive there and back, especially after you've had a full day of magic training is difficult. We could make it fun.' She thought of exploring his body under the stars, not worrying about accidental sex magic because they were miles away from anyone, although perhaps after all their practice they'd be too exhausted to fool around.

'I think we can come up with something to keep us amused.' Jacob winked at her, and she giggled.

Traffic was heavier than usual; the weather was forecast to be fine and warm over the weekend and it seemed Melbournians were keen to get out of the city for a while. Freya had not managed to understand many of the jumble the images from Vali. They had about six weeks until the summer solstice, which seemed the best time for the portal ritual. Odd given they wanted make a portal into a frozen world, but perhaps Vali wasn't thinking that way. Bianca might have chosen it to fight Ragnarök, perhaps thinking to tap into the renewed energy of the world in the height of summer. She shook her head, trying to apply logic to magical ritual choices was never a good idea, even Hettie, the most sensible of the mystic writers she had come across made decisions that made little sense.

The shed was the same as always, although on such a warm day it would be sweltering inside. After parking Freya set about opening the rolling door to allow air flow into the large space.

'What's the plan? Are we going to spar?' Jacob said, resting one shoulder against the doorway, his body in silhouette against the bright day outside reminded her how hot he was.

'I thought we could try it. There are a few defence spells in the books, but we can just fool around, we need to build up stamina.'

'In the movie version of our lives, this will be the training montage.' He chuckled. Freya reached out to the source in her mind, the silver power flowing through her, and she imagined Jacob floating to her. To her great surprise he started to move towards her, immediately falling over as the support of the doorway was taken away.

'Hey! I wasn't ready. Also, who said you could move me with your mind?' A flicker of fear had crossed his face when he felt himself move.

'Sorry I thought it would be funny, but I guess not.'

'It would be funny if it wasn't terrifying.' From his hands and knees on the floor he stared at her, brows drawn together, and she felt a prickle in the air. No doubt he would retaliate in kind, so she planted her feet and made herself as heavy and immovable as possible.

Jacob's face was set in concentration, he moved his hands up and pushed them forward and thought she felt the force against her, she imagined roots down into the ground, which kept her steady. A moment later he dropped his hands and panted.

'How did you do that?' he asked.

'I told myself I wouldn't move, I knew it was what you would do, so I resisted. You try.' She drew down power and pushed her hands out in a move that should have pushed him back, but this time he hardly moved at all.

'Wow, that's pretty cool,' she said. 'What did you do?'

'I thought about your power flowing around me like a river, or a slipstream, but not really touching me. It seemed to mostly work.'

'Okay, try something else, don't tell me what you're going to do.'

He looked up around the room for a moment, as though searching for inspiration or recalling a particular spell. Jacob's arms were by his sides, his fingers splayed wide and straining. A greyness seemed to form in the air in front of her, not quite smoke as it didn't curl or cloud, more like the air became opaque. The first thing that popped into her mind was to sweep away the air between them, but what if the greyness wasn't the air, but perhaps some other element, or even an illusion that wasn't there at all.

In an instant, she decided to lift the greyness, whatever it was, by pushing her own clarity under it. She pulled at a thread from the source, put her arms by her sides, palms forward, and raised her arms. While she did this, she imagined clear vision, both literally and psychically. For a moment nothing happened, but slowly the air around the ground started showing once again—the haze was rising. As the space between them became visible, she saw that Jacob was sweating and straining.

'Let go,' she said. He let out an enormous grunt and the electrical prickle in the air subsided.

'I was trying to hold you off but you're really strong.'

'It wasn't easy, I felt like nothing was happening for a bit. What was that, smoke?'

'I dunno, it's one of Crowley's. You create a barrier between your enemy and the thing they want, it manifested as fog but I'm not sure it would happen that way every time.'

'It was an illusion?'

'I don't know. I think it was real, in the sense that any of this stuff is real. You do one.'

Freya took inspiration from Jacob's last attempt and decided to try to produce an illusion of darkness and binding of limbs. She imagined Jacob covered in a thick, black molasses-type liquid that would block out everything he could hear and see, and stop him from moving. In her mind she held the image firmly, the details of the slow-moving liquid were vivid to her. Jacob made a small squeaking sound, and she momentarily loosened her concentration. The moment of weakness was enough for him to break the illusion and she staggered back a step.

'Wow, that felt like a rubber band coming back to hit me,' she said, shaking her body to release some of the tingling magical energies that were crawling over her skin.

'Blackness that takes away vision, and hearing and movement, I wouldn't have thought you could be so cruel.' Jacob bent down, resting his hands on his knees. 'I need a break. I have to get that image out of my head.'

He walked outside where the sun was beginning to set without looking to see if she had followed. Part of her was ashamed that she had freaked him out, but another part was elated it had worked. It was the first time she'd tried anything like that, although it had been hinted at in one of the spell books.

'I'm sorry for overwhelming you. I'm not good at predicting how things are going to affect you, am I?' she said, approaching him slowly where he was perching on the bumper bar of the car, his face turned to the sun and eyes closed.

'I panicked. I don't know if I've ever told you I nearly drowned once as a child. I was down the coast near Torquay, and we were swimming in the ocean. Down there it gets rough, without the protection of the bay, and I was dumped by a wave. Before I could get above the surface, another wave, and another wave came over me. I couldn't work out where to swim to get out, even though the water was shallow. After what felt like an age, I was pushed into the sand at the bottom, and I knew that the other way was up. I surfaced and managed to make my way back to shore, but to this day I don't like surf beaches.'

'My God, that sounds horrible. What did you parents say?'

'My dad laughed and said I would have to get used to that if I wanted to go back in the surf. My mum said being afraid of water was childish. Really empathic.'

'How old were you?'

'Nine. It was a family holiday, Christmas. But being in that illusion, or whatever, brought all those feelings right back.' He shivered.

'Are you cold?' Freya asked.

'No. I'm okay.'

They sat listening to the birds chirping and warbling, as the sun dipped lower and lower.

'We should set up for sleeping before it gets too dark, or we're too tired.'

They worked without speaking to erect the tent and put an inflatable mattress inside. Freya regretted what she'd done but didn't know how to fix it. Jacob wanted quiet to think it over, but surely there was something she could do. Normally Eva and Dinah were her advisors if something went awry with Jacob, but they were both busy with the initiation.

'How do you think Dinah and Eva are going?' she asked.

'I don't know. We're so far away if something goes wrong. Should we have gone to a town nearby and stayed in a motel?'

'We wouldn't have been able to practise.'

'My sister could be in real danger, and you're worried about being able to practise?' he yelled, eyes flashing.

'I didn't mean it like that.'

'You never do. You can be really self-centred sometimes.'

Freya opened her mouth then pressed her lips together to give herself more time to think before she spoke. 'The safety of the four of us is the most important thing. Being able to practice my magic, and to practice defending against attacks, will help keep us safe when the shit hits the fan.' She paused. 'I'm worried about them too, but my presence may have put them in more danger.'

'You're infuriating.' He backed out of the tent and paced up and down the tussled grass. 'I'm helpless being so far away. And then you try to drown me and that reminds me of the last time I felt properly helpless and it's more than I can bear.'

She followed him out of the tent, took a step towards him, then stopped. She wanted more than anything to hold him, stroke his hair and tell him it would be alright, his sister would be safe, they would find a way to save the world, like they did last time, but it would be platitudes.

'What can I do?' Freya asked, her voice small.

'Nothing. I'm going for a walk to clear my head. I'll be back in a bit.' Jacob turned away and marched off towards the old orchards.

Freya took several calming breaths; her blood was pounding in her ears, and she worried she might collapse if she didn't rest soon. The magic she'd used through the day, and the adrenaline of their fight had caught up to her. She sat on the air mattress, crossed her legs and started to meditate. Long deep breaths in and out. She let her mind wander; thoughts floated by like clouds. Scenarios of what might be happening at the Children's initiation ceremony, flashes of images from her contact with Vali, her desk at work, her boss's face when she was late back from lunch again. With the exhale she imagined blowing the thoughts away, wafting them on like an irritating insect.

When her body had calmed down, and her breathing was slow, deep and steady, she tried to find Jacob, sending her mind around the farm looking for his energy. He was sitting with his back against an old, crooked apple tree, knees up, elbows resting on his knees, hands covering his face. He could have been sleeping, but his shoulders heaved and shook. Why did he think he needed to be alone to feel that? Why would he hide that from her? She released the image, letting him process in privacy. Her mind floated around the farm, meandering through the rows of trees when she felt a great pulse in the east, where the Children were performing their ritual. Freya's mind went to Elsa, the young girl in mauve from their visit last week. She would be there, perhaps Freya could just slip into her point of view and see what was happening. Maybe she wouldn't notice but before she could try it the cries of ravens outside the tent interrupted her.

'What are you two doing here?' she asked, sticking her head back out the flap into the twilight.

One of the ravens flapped and cawed urgently, while the other circled above them a few metres up.

'Has something happened? Or are you trying to tell me that getting into Elsa's head was a bad idea?' Freya held out her hand to the bird closest to her, running her fingers over its chest feathers.

A vision of Jacob came to her, he was still in the orchard, but had slumped over and looked like he'd passed out. 'What happened? Is he okay?'

In response the raven on the ground took flight and swooped around her.

'Am I following you? This is new,' she said mostly to herself. The ravens lead her to the spot where Jacob was, still lying on his side there the base of an apple tree.

'What's happened? Jacob, can you hear me?' She gently shook his shoulders. His eyes opened, they were bloodshot and dazed.

'Why am I lying down?' He pushed himself up. 'I was alone, then I felt all dizzy and now you're here.'

'The ravens came. I was trying to spy on the ceremony, and they interrupted. I felt a big like ripple of magic from their direction, maybe it affected you somehow.'

'I wish we could contact Deens. I have a bad feeling about this.'

'Let's text her. If she's okay, she'll reply. If they're still doing the ritual, she might have her phone off, so let's not panic if she doesn't get back to us straight away. I'll text Eva too.'

Checking in to see how the session is going. Felt some interesting ripples out this way. Big afternoon, will tell you about it tomorrow.

Freya sent the same text to both of them, hoping they would get a response before she and Jacob went to sleep, but suspecting strongly they wouldn't.

'Should we make some dinner?'

Jacob looked up; his face flat with fatigue. 'Sure.'

They had bought sausages, fresh bread and coleslaw in the supermarket in the last town before they got to the shed. Jacob had been a keen camper until Rhonda had dampened his enthusiasm. He'd kept the equipment and used it sometimes when his ex-partner was on her long stints interstate for work. It was one of the small rebellions he had through the relationship. He said he felt bad about the lies he'd told her. Looking at Jacob now, shoulders hunched, eyes on the ground, she knew he wouldn't be up for cooking.

'You'll have to set up the cooking whatsit for me. I'll be right once it's going.'

He nodded, and slowly stood up, she held out her hand to help him, but he didn't take it. She followed him to the car and waited while he set up the camp stove. The food took twenty minutes to prepare, Jacob had plonked himself in a folding chair with a beer in one hand and his eyes closed.

'Ready to eat, babe?' Freya said, holding the plate out to Jacob. He sighed but didn't stir, perhaps he was asleep. She prodded his foot.

'I'm up,' he said with a start.

'Food. Eat up, then we can crash.' Her plans of seducing him in the tent, or perhaps in the open under the stars were disappearing. She was tired, but not the same crushing inability to move she'd felt after previous experiences.

'Thanks, babe.'

They ate in the quiet of the country night, at least it was too early in the season for mosquitoes, but the night became cold quickly after sunset. Dishes could wait until they got home, Freya put everything in the back of the car to save it from scavengers, Jacob had crawled into the tent. Before she followed him, she checked for messages from Eva and Dinah, nothing so far.

'Are you okay?' she asked.

'Yeah . . . I feel like death. Hopefully I'll feel better in the morning.'

'Okay.' She kissed his forehead and snuggled into the blankets next to him, wishing she could do something more.

*

Freya woke alone, she checked her phone for any news from Dinah or Eva, there was nothing. It was early, the light or possibly the sound of Jacob leaving had woken her. Outside the tent, he was stretching.

'Morning.'

'Hey, I tried not to wake you,' he said

'It's fine. What are you up to?'

'Any word from Deens?'

'Not yet.'

'I'm going for a run, I'm full of anxious energy.'

She nodded, Jacob often woke early to run or workout, sometimes she joined him, sometimes she preferred go at night. 'If you show me how to turn on the burner, I'll make some coffee for when you get back.'

He set up the stove and showed her the ignition. He would be gone for at least half an hour, so Freya did some yoga poses to pass the time, before she put the water on to boil.

The early morning was still and cold, Freya considered whether she had the energy to do a couple more spell experiments before the coffee was ready. She closed her eyes, planted her feet firmly on the ground and sent her mind inwards. If the powers that be wanted to show her something she was open and ready. Given the reaction yesterday to trying to project into the Children of Vali's headquarters she wouldn't try that again.

A vision filled her mind of walking through an empty field towards the black, slick-looking portal on the ground. She squatted down, put her hand into the dark pool, and was transported to the freezing forest of

Jotunheim. Vali's smiling face flashed in front of her, then Vali and Bianca in bed, Freya was somewhat surprised Bianca would allow that, but it explained the hold he had over her. The vision faded and was replaced with Vali in bed with another woman, perhaps Elsa, although she couldn't quite see her face.

'Freya?' Jacob's voice cut through and she fluttered her eyes open.

'You're back.' She smiled, relaxing her stance and stumbling forward half a step as dizziness washed over her.

'Jeez, are you okay?' Jacob reached out to grab her arm, he smelled like fresh sweat and grass, and hot.

'I was having a vision. I must have been in there longer than I thought, the water's boiling and I haven't brewed the coffee.'

'Anything good in the vision?'

Freya poured hot water over fresh coffee grounds in the French press they'd brought from home, then waited a couple of minutes for it to steep.

'You've got a message,' Jacob said, waving her phone at her. She grabbed it and opened the messages.

'It's from Dinah "Yeah, it was a lot. More magic than expected. Will give deets at your place. Eva's fine too."'

'That's a relief. It was a big whammy if you felt it from here.'

'Mmm.'

'You wanna head home after coffee? I can't rest up here,' Jacob said.

They were home before eleven, having stopped briefly on the way for a drive through breakfast. Jacob was agitated; tapping his fingers on the steering wheel as he drove and now pacing around the living room.

'You know Dinah and Eva won't be here for a while yet. They probably wanted to have a proper breakfast and it would seem odd if they left before the other attendees. Try to relax.'

'I don't know how. Dinah went into this with her eyes open, but she's still a kid, and she's my sister. I have to look out for her. At least last time when we were doing this stuff the three of us were together, now I'm not even nearby in case anything happens.'

'Your sister is stronger than you think. I'm sure if she needed to, she could talk her way out of most things, and if that fails, she has some skills like the Jedi mind trick. Eva is there for backup.'

'I know she's your best friend, but she not gifted like we are. I wish she hadn't insisted on being part of the action, but if we forbade her, she would do it on her own, without us guiding her.'

Freya choked out a bitter laugh.

'What was that for?'

She shook her head. 'The idea of us being in the know. We may have more information than the average Joe Bloggs but half the time we have information we don't understand, the other half we know what we need to find out but can't. If there are rules for working with gods, I don't understand them. Why send the ravens if Odin could come down himself and tell us?'

'Maybe he can't—can't travel from Asgard anymore or can't appear directly to humans because he'll blow our minds. There's plenty of stories about why angels and other emissaries have to act as go-betweens.'

'Delicate little humans would explode in the presence of an actual god. Seems unlikely given the number of demi-gods the Greeks produced.'

'The Norse gods were less keen on fathering half-mortal children.'

'It's like I'm stumbling around in the dark all the time. I had visions of Vali in bed with at least two of his disciples. How does that help us?'

Jacob frowned. 'You didn't mention that.'

'You were running and when you got back were busy being anxious, I didn't think it was the time.'

'True. You could have told me anything this morning and I wouldn't have heard it. Anything else come to you?'

'More Jotunheim, Vali's sex-life. Maybe he has a magic dick.'

Jacob snorted. 'Never say that to Dinah. Good lord. We don't need to put any more sex magic into her head than is already there.'

'She's sixteen. I don't know about you, but I was well down the fooling-around path by that age.'

'So was I, but she's my sister.'

'I know. I wasn't suggesting we tell her about Vali's magic dick, but maybe we should. He's very charming, she's a young woman who probably thinks she knows what she's doing. We don't need her getting any ideas put into her head. She hasn't straight out told me, but I expect she's a virgin and having him as her first time would be a disaster, if not now, later when we have to destroy him.'

Jacob shut his eyes. 'I don't want to think about that . . . wait destroy Vali?'

'How else are we going to stop him? He's going to throw everything he has at us; Bianca and her groupies will try to stop us, it can only end that way. I just hope if we get rid of Vali all the people following him will be released from whatever spell they're under—'

'Assuming it's a spell. There have been plenty of cults where no magic was used.'

'That's heartening,' she said, slumping forward to put her head in her hands. Jacob sat next to her on the couch and rubbed his hand over her back. She remained still, worried he might stop if she looked up. His hand stilled and slipped down her back, the couch shifted as Jacob leaned back. Freya turned to him, his head was back, and eyes closed, and she lay her head in his lap.

Sharp knocking woke her with a start, they must have both fallen asleep. As she opened the door a tired-looking Eva and Dinah walked in and slumped onto the furniture.

'Are you alright? Shall I put the kettle on?'

'Yes. Coffee,' Dinah said.

Eva nodded.

She made herself tea, and coffee for the others, when she returned to the lounge, they were all waiting. Dinah seemed to have spread herself out so there was no more room on the couch, Freya found a cushion and sat on the floor at the coffee table, waiting for the story.

'You have no idea the sludge the Children tried to pass off as coffee earlier today. It's one thing joining a cult, but they're all vegan and can't taste anymore. It's beyond me how they end up like that.' Eva cradled her mug in front of her nose.

'It's little-by-little changes. First you give up your time, then maybe give up meat, then after you move in you have to wear the dumb linen robes and become vegan. Did you sleep well?' Jacob asked.

'No. The ceremony lasted ages, we didn't go to bed till after one, and then they were up clanging bells and making us help with breakfast by seven,' Dinah said.

'Sleep deprivation is great for getting people to make decisions they wouldn't otherwise,' Eva said.

Freya fidgeted in her seat. 'I'm dying to know details of what went down last night.'

'It was so much. Bianca did most of it, but Vali was there too,' Dinah started.

'There were six people from the open day, including us, which I thought was a pretty low conversion myself—but given they excluded you, Freya, maybe they told other people they weren't suitable. It's got to be a delicate balance inviting people into a cult,' Eva said.

'The mum and daughter were there, Helen and Meredith, and Gemma and Teresa who you were speaking to. Elsa was there, and five other mauve-robers whose names I don't remember. There was a kind of buzz when we got there, we were all hanging around in that reception area again, but there was no food out. Must have been at least half an hour before anyone from the centre greeted us, right?'

'At least. It felt like ages, like it was a test. Eventually Elsa came and took us down to the tent-room, we were supposed to get there at six, so we didn't eat, and then there were no nibbles so I was starting to feel annoyed and hangry by then,' Eva said.

'The tent-room looked the same as the other time, but there were like, a hundred candles in the middle, arranged in a shape that looked like two vees hugging and then a bigger upside-down vee over the top,' Dinah said. 'I think they were runes. I looked up the runic alphabet in the car, and the two vees together is like a J and the upside-down vee is like our V.'

'V for Vali, clearly but what's the J for?' Jacob asked.

'Jotunheim,' Freya replied, 'where he wants to go.'

Jacob nodded and looked back to the other two to continue.

'So, the candles are all in the middle, and we sit in a circle around the outside, same as last time, but with less people. Eva and me both have our pouches hanging under our shirts—which reminds me, if we ever need to change or wear those robes and take them off that could be awkward, maybe we need to have them on a waistband so they're not seen? Anyway, Vali says some deep nonsense at the start—'

'He was welcoming us and saying how important we all are, and that we're chosen star children,' Eva interrupted.

'But super flowery. He doesn't do much of the webcasts anymore, Bianca and the others do it. I dunno if he talks like that all the time, but I wouldn't let him do the videos if he was like that all the time. Puts you off.'

'Wait, you said there were five people in mauve, plus you six newbies and Bianca and Vali. That's thirteen, he's got his power number now,' Freya said.

'I wondered about that, he won't include himself in the final circle, he's not powerful enough, and it makes sense for the circle to be all women,' Eva said. 'After Vali finished waffling about our mission, avoiding giving out any actual information mind you, Bianca took over.'

'It was more like the stuff we've done in the past, she called on the spirits to open the circle, more formal than the chanting we did when you were up there. It felt a bit like her voice was inside my head, like she was talking with a megaphone directly into me. I didn't like it at all,' Dinah said.

'She was super-loud, but she didn't seem to be shouting, we were supposed to have our eyes closed but I snuck a look at the circle and no one else seemed to notice that she was blasting us,' Eva said.

'There was a bunch of her chanting at the start, not in English, maybe Norse, it was hard not to get sucked into it, she was seductive, like lulling you to half-sleep. It must have been another half an hour, although it's hard to keep track of time.'

'I found myself swaying in a kind of rhythm with her words. When she stopped the silence was profound. I could hear people breathing. Then she started giving us instructions.'

'She went around the circle asking for what we wanted to get out of joining the group. Thankfully me and Eva weren't first, so I got some ideas from the others, I think I said something like a deeper connection to the world, and a feeling of meaning in the grand scheme of the universe,' Dinah said.

'It was very convincing.' Eva turned to Dinah before continuing. 'I said something about finding myself, you know, eat-pray-love nonsense? Anyway, Bianca didn't seem to be worried. Vali and the other mauve-robers didn't say anything so she moved on to the next step which was pledging.'

'Bianca made us repeat a pledge to follow the teachings of the supreme leader and embodiment of the divine, Vali, and to promise to dedicate our lives to furthering his cause, and to protecting the Earth from the destruction of the human race, and a couple of other things. She stood up and made us hold out our hands, then she put a little smoky quartz crystal in them, and some ground herbs, and then tipped hot black wax over it. What did she say?'

'I don't exactly remember, something like you're now reborn as a child of Vali and will be blessed with his protection and guidance,' Eva said. 'I felt kind of tingly when she said that, like we'd signed a magical contract. I admit I was a bit freaked out by this stage, feeling a bit faint and tired and anxious because we were lying to her, you know?'

'Sounds intense. The tingling would be her using the source to bind you to Vali. I might need to do some reading about breaking spells, so you aren't stuck with some side effect when we try to take them all down.' Freya frowned and stared at the carpet for a moment.

'What do you mean side effect?' Eva asked.

'I don't know, but if she's used power to bind you, there will be a consequence for disobeying. If we can get rid of that before the big portal opening night, you won't be in quite so much danger trying to sabotage it.'

Eva's face was pale, she swallowed and licked her lips. 'Right.'

'After that more chanting, we all joined in that time, and then we each took one of the candles and said, "Blessed is the life and path of Vali," before blowing them out. Bianca ended the ritual, and we were able to leave the room,' Dinah said.

'When we got back to the reception room, the people in mauve came over and talked to us, and we all drank green tea, but still no food. It was after ten by now and my hunger had faded,' Eva said.

'Bianca and Vali came in after about ten minutes and presented us newbies with dusky pink robes. I guess we have to prove we're good enough for mauve, and no one except Bianca gets purple. Vali brought in some samosas, which he said were a welcoming treat for his children.'

'They were good samosas,' Eva said. 'We had to hang around in the reception space till after one, when Vali said we could all go to bed. They had set up bunk beds in one of the rooms that were closed off last time we were there; four to a room. I didn't sleep much, too much going on in my head. And then we told you already, they were back at seven to get us up.'

'We had to meditate for a while then we had some rice porridge or something for breakfast, then more hanging around talking, then we came back here.' Dinah sat back into the couch and sighed.

Freya shifted, stretching her legs out in front of her as her feet had started to fall asleep. 'Wow. I wonder what the tremor was that I felt.'

'What time was it?' Eva asked.

'I'm not sure, it wasn't properly dark yet, so maybe seven or seven thirty?'

'That would have been when Bianca started the ritual. It's funny I didn't notice it at the time.' Dinah yawned and shook her head. 'I'm normally more in tune when someone turns on their power, especially now we've been hanging out a bit more lately.'

'It's something to think about, but I'm more concerned about the fact that you're now bound to do what's best for Vali. We need to sort that out, I don't want anyone to twigging that you're betraying them because they have some alarm set up,' Jacob said. He looked at his sister, brows furrowed, and deep concern written on his face.

'Maybe it's something Theo can help with,' Eva suggested.

'Maybe.' Freya was suspicious of the old man in the bookshop, he might still be working his own angle somehow. No to mention she had been recognised in the shop and had put them all in danger. There was the woman at the magic supplies shop in the arcade too; she had seemed on their side in their past interactions, but Freya didn't even know her name, and it seemed unwise to trust someone she didn't know. 'I have meetings tomorrow around lunch time, but I'll go this week.'

'It's too bad we can't put him in a contract,' Jacob said.

'Why not? We know what Bianca did now, I'm sure I could recreate it,' Dinah said.

'You and Eva were willing participants, albeit not for the reasons they thought, I don't think it would work if he didn't consent. At least it wasn't a blood ritual, that would have been harder to break,' Freya replied.

'I'll bet the mauve robe ritual involved blood.'

Jacob rubbed his hand over his sister's shoulder.
'Let's get you home. Eva looks like she might fall asleep
any minute—not that you aren't welcome to sleep in the
chair but . . . it isn't very comfortable in my experience.

In spite of the hot drinks and debriefing they all
struggled to stay awake. Freya stood and tidied up the
cups, keeping her hands busy while she considered their
next move. All signs pointed to Eva and Dinah having
been accepted into the Children, part of her was worried
it had been too easy and there would be more to come to
prove their loyalty. They had a month before the solstice,
no doubt there would be more rituals to get them ready to
open the portal. How Vali was going to do it was still
unknown, from what she could gather about Bianca
causing the apocalypse didn't seem like something she
would do, but she was also the second in command to a
powerful and manipulative cult leader.

'I'm heading off,' Eva announced when Freya came
back into the loungeroom. Eva stood, and Freya hugged
her tightly.

'Thank you, I'm glad you were there with Dinah,' she
said in a low voice.

'I told you I'm in this with you, and I mean it,' Eva
replied, before raising her voice to be heard by the rest of
the room. 'We'll keep you updated with anything coming
from the Children. No doubt we'll be bombarded with
homework.'

'Thank you, Eva,' Jacob said from the couch, his arm
still around his sister.

Freya closed the door behind her friend and saw the two ravens were perched on the roof top not far from the apartment, she nodded to them before returning inside.

'Muninn and Huginn?' Dinah asked.

'Yep.' Freya took a seat in the now vacant armchair. Her body was weary, but her mind was whirring away. She closed her eyes and focused on her breath, hoping to sooth her spinning thoughts.

She must have fallen asleep, because she was woken by Jacob gently shaking her arm. 'Freya?'

'Mmmm?'

'I'm taking Deens back to Dad's. Do you wanna come for a ride?'

Freya glanced from her boyfriend to his sister, there was a pleading in their faces that made it hard for her to say no, although she would have been happy to stay in the chair. 'Sure.'

I wonder what that look means, she thought to herself.

'Jacob doesn't want to have to drive back alone. He's worried about me,' Dinah said, answering her unspoken question.

'Did you read my thoughts?' Freya asked.

'I read your face mostly. And don't you complain,' she said, turning to her brother. 'No matter how powerless you might feel with me in the cult and you outside of it, leaning on Freya for support will help. We're in this together, remember? The original three musketeers.'

'Plus D'Artagnan, now Eva's with us,' Jacob said, smiling. 'Let's go.'

'Can we get Maccas on the way?' Dinah asked.

'Every time. Yes okay, but don't tell Dad.'

*

Jacob and Freya stayed in the car, Dinah had told her dad she was staying with a friend.

'I hope she's keeping up with school,' Jacob said, watching her walk the half-block to her house.

'Why? Because she spends all her time running around with cults and researching magic instead of doing her homework?'

'Yes, because of that.' He pulled out from the curb and started the return drive.

'If she can get through the end of the year, she'll have exams but she's not in VCE yet so any failure will be recoverable, maybe. On the other hand, if we don't stop Vali there won't be any school next year…'

Jacob stared ahead. 'I hadn't thought of it that way.'

'It's not pleasant, but Dinah knows how to balance her schoolwork and her saving the world stuff. And if she doesn't, we'll fix it next year.' Freya put her hand over Jacob's where it rested on the gear stick.

Chapter 14

Freya left her office at lunchtime on Wednesday for a quick visit to Theo. If she could be back before one o'clock her boss wouldn't notice she'd taken a longer lunch.

Too bad I can't tell him I'm trying to save the world, Freya thought as she walked up the stairs into the occult bookshop. As soon as the door swung open Theo's head swivelled towards her, eyes wide and frightened like an animal caught in headlights, although he replaced this fear with a more neutral expression. Freya looked around for anyone she knew from the Children of Vali compound. Her natural, short-cropped black hair was visible as were the scars around her eye. No one looked familiar, there were only two other customers, both women in their twenties speaking in hushed tones by the tarot card decks.

'Hello, Theo,' she said.

He bobbed his head, managing to choke out 'Hi.'

'I have some questions for you.' Freya made no effort to soften her expression, if Theo was frightened in her presence, nothing she could do would change that. Perhaps it could prove to her advantage if he let slip something he hadn't intended to tell her. If she could touch him, she might be able to get a vision, or a read from him, but he was wary around her to have shielded himself from casual prying.

'It's lovely to see you, you're looking well,' Theo said, his long-fingered hands clasping each other.

Freya raised an eyebrow, but did not respond.

'There haven't been any further updates about people leaving their . . . groups, I would have told you if there had been.' He flicked his eyes over her shoulder, and she turned to see the two young women leave the shop—no purchases this time.

'Vali has his twelve disciples now. They're ready to do their ritual.'

Theo's eyes widened in alarm before he went back to his natural hooded look.

'You weren't aware of that progression. Bianca is at his right hand, she's running things.' She paused, but he showed no reaction, 'You knew that already. Dinah and my friend Eva were initiated into the Children on the weekend.'

Theo leaned forward slightly. 'I felt something on Saturday night. A ripple, it seemed important . . .were you also playing with your power then?'

Freya said nothing.

'It would have been a good time, while they were otherwise engaged. Anyway, they've been accepted into the group.'

She nodded. 'Bianca clocked me almost immediately and said I wasn't welcome in the group. My energy was too chaotic, she said, which meant she couldn't read me and didn't like it. At any rate, Dinah and Eva swore to serve Vali's interests as part of the initiation and I want to break whatever the spell is that will hold them to it.'

'Ah, yes.'

She waited for him to elaborate, but he didn't. 'I assume there will be something to warn if they've broken the pact, a consequence like pain, or an alarm that Bianca will notice. I don't know how magical vows work. But we need them to be free of that before they go back.' Freya had not intended to tell him quite so much, but her instinct told her he was afraid and his scheming had taken a back seat. When she had a feeling like this, it paid to follow it, even if the outcome was not what she had expected.

Theo stopped wringing his hands, and he looked off into middle distance, frowning, as though trying to bring something to mind. 'Might be tricky to do without Bianca knowing. Everything I've heard about her is that she's very skilful, and powerful for a person who has not been blessed by the gods.' He stepped out from behind the counter and went to the back bookshelves, eyes scanning the titles.

'Here it is.' He pulled out an old leatherbound volume that was more than a little worse for wear. 'This one is an old German book, the avatar Dinah made, as you and Jacob did, will have taken on the oath. She should be free to disobey or betray the group without consequences to her health or raising the alarm with Bianca. They have a bit in here about totem objects, which are similar but not quite the same, you see?' He pointed to a spot on the page, but the text was in German and Freya could only rely on her feeling he was being truthful.

'And what about Eva? She doesn't have an avatar, we gave her one of the protection pouches, to help hide her thoughts but since she has little power, it didn't seem necessary. . .'

'That is more difficult.' Theo ran his finger down the page, flipped to the next page, and did the same, then flipped back. 'Damn. It doesn't specify how to unbind yourself, only that in order to protect yourself when going undercover, as it were, you need the totem first.'

'There's nothing we can do?' Freya's voice rose in pitch.

'I didn't say that. But it does make it rather more difficult.' He fell silent, and remained so for several minutes. His eyes squinted and his mouth moved as though having an internal conversation with himself. Freya waited.

'One idea comes to mind.'

'Yes?' she prompted.

'I can't guarantee it will work, so you can't come after me when it fails.'

He said when it fails, not if, she thought. 'And?'

'The allegiance has been sworn to a human being, albeit a powerful one—since Bianca did the ritual, and she has nominated Vali as the leader to be followed, the magic will see the allegiance to her primarily, and him as a second . . . if Eva were to swear the same sort of oath to a god, and that god were to accept the pledge, I think that would override anything she swore to a human.'

'Right.' Freya paused for a moment, thinking the information through. 'It's easy enough to swear to Odin, as the source of our power and the driving force behind the whole affair, but having him accept the pledge, how do we know if it's worked?'

'I seem to remember you have two ravens following you. They would be able to act on your behalf. If they think it's a good idea, maybe you can take it as agreed?'

'You don't sound very certain.'

Theo chuckled. 'Dealing with gods is a murky business at the best of times. Even if he did accept the pledge, and that negated the vow to Vali, we won't know for sure until it comes time to betray him. At which point the consequences will be unavoidable.'

She nodded, not an insurmountable obstacle, but one that could be problematic for their little group. If Theo's solution worked, they would be able to sabotage the solstice ritual, but if not, perhaps Eva would not be on their side, or worse would alert Bianca to the plan. And they wouldn't know until the moment they tried it. Freya glanced at her watch, time to get back.

'Thanks for your help. Remember to let me know if you have any news,' she said.

'I will.' Theo bobbed his head once more, now his hands were free of the book he had begun wringing them again.

As she approached her office building, she saw a lone raven perched in one of the plane trees.

Hello, she thought in her mind. Unlikely she would get any answers or interaction this time, but she was glad to know they were keeping an eye on her. Walking under the tree the raven squawked and flew off. *Let's chat later*.

*

Freya came home that night to an empty apartment, odd since Jacob started and finished work before her. She kicked off her shoes and put on gym clothes, figuring she may as well go for a run while Jacob was out. No messages from him on her phone, perhaps he had a late client.

It was still light outside, the November sun set after eight o'clock, she put her headphones in and selected trancey electronic music. She was a couple of blocks away from the apartment down the shared bike track when she saw the two ravens hopping around on the grass beside the track.

'Hello, you two.' She slowed her pace and knelt near the birds. 'Something you need to tell me?'

It wasn't a good place to deliver a message, most often they would wait for her on the balcony, but as messengers of Odin, they played by their own rules.

One of the ravens, Muninn or Huginn, she still couldn't tell them apart, hopped closer to her outstretched hand. She stroked his silky breast feathers.

In her mind, she saw Jacob and Dinah sitting in Dinah's room. Their heads were bent over the girl's computer.

'Is that where Jacob is? Helping Dinah with something?'

The raven bobbed his head and clacked his beak. She took that as agreement. Her mind's eye cleared and another vision took shape, a seated circle of people in the tent-room at the Children's compound, the group were swaying, mouths moving in sync, although she couldn't hear their chanting. In the centre of the room, instead of candles were what looked like whips or weapons of torture, with a large chalice filled with an unknown substance. Bianca took one, a wooden handle with long leather straps attached to it and started to beat her own shoulders and upper back with it.

'Self-flagellation? That's a bit medieval,' she said aloud. The raven squawked and flapped as though to tell her to stay quiet. It was mad enough stroking ravens in a public park, let alone having one-sided conversations. 'Sorry.'

The final image was the four of them in a circle in the shed. Eva had cut her forearm and was adding blood to a cauldron in the centre of the circle.

Is this what we need to do? Have Eva swear a blood oath to Odin and break the bond with Bianca? Will it work? she asked in her thoughts.

The raven whose feathers she had been stroking fluttered and hopped away.

'Thank you,' she said softly, and then they were gone. Freya stood and resumed her jog, finishing the half hour circuit in good time. The apartment was still empty when she returned, so she made herself dinner.

Got some good info from Theo today and had a visit from the ravens. Where are you?

She texted Jacob while she ate, there was nothing good on T.V. and she was too indecisive to pick something else. When she'd washed up her dinner dishes there was still no response from Jacob. Whatever he was doing with Dinah had better be important, or she would be annoyed he'd worried her with his lack of communication.

The books Theo had given her those months ago had a section on binding oneself to the will of another. Crowley was unclear on the topic, but Star Eagle had some guidance on the ritual. As she'd seen in her vision, the strongest versions of the spell involved a blood sacrifice. *Better tell Eva.*

Freya picked up her phone to call and saw Jacob had replied.

Spending the evening with Deens, needs help with an English assignment. Might be back late, don't wait up. I meant this send it at four when I knocked off, oops. Just finishing up now.

'Dufus,' she said aloud.

Okay. See you soon.

Perhaps a little less warm than she would have liked, but with Jacob on his way home, she would only have

271

half an hour to tell Eva about the new plan before he got home and she would have to tell him the story again. Unless she told them both at the same time, when Jacob was home. It was after nine, and her best friend was not much of a night owl.

'Hey,' Eva said answering the phone.

'Hey.'

'Speak to Theo?'

'Yeah,' Freya said and went over what she had found out at the bookshop, from the ravens, and from her research.

'Jeez, a blood oath sounds intense. Are you sure that's the only way?'

'It's the best solution I can find so you'll be able to resist Vali. What if you try to go against Bianca and your ears start bleeding? Or you become paralysed or end up in another magical coma.'

'Don't even say that as a joke.' Eva's trauma from the last magical coma was still raw, but perhaps it would emphasise the seriousness of the situation.

'We don't know if you can even resist them at the moment. If she can force you to follow her orders then you might end up working against us or telling her our plan. You'll have to swear to Odin.'

Eva sighed. 'Okay. Let's do it soon. I got an email from the children with a long and confusing video from Bianca and Vali about how we need to show our dedication and that the time of testing our commitment is coming—'

'About that,' Freya interrupted. 'I may have left out the part where you all drink something and beat yourselves. You have to go through an ordeal, Crowley is super into that as a demonstration of your faith so you can become mauve. In my visions of the summer solstice, you're all wearing mauve, not the dusty pink numbers you got the other day.'

'Great.'

'And if you've sworn to Odin, no matter what else Bianca throws at you, you're protected by god-magic, and she only has human-magic, see?'

'I'm sceptical but in the absence of another plan.'

Keys scratched in the door, and Freya looked up to see Jacob's weary face. 'I better go, Jacob's home.'

'He's late,' Eva said.

'We'll do the thing on the weekend, talk soon.' She hung up, knowing that Eva had wanted to know why her boyfriend was home late, but deciding not to tell her.

'Hey babe, who was that?'

'Eva. Just filling her in. How's Dinah?'

Jacob sighed, sat down, slipped off his shoes and lay his head down on her lap where she was curled on the couch. 'Freaking out. Her schoolwork is piling up and she's convinced we're all gonna die or end up in Jotunheim freezing our tits off. I think the ritual on the weekend rattled her.'

'Understandable,' Freya said, stroking Jacob's thick salt and pepper hair.

'Tell me about your day?'

She told him what had happened with Theo, just as she had told Eva, and about the plan to swear allegiance to Odin.

'She wasn't enthused, and to be honest, I'm not either, any plan that can't be tested ahead of time should be avoided in my opinion, but there isn't any other plan.'

'The ravens haven't steered you wrong before.'

Freya scoffed. 'Unless you count sending me to meet Vali in my dodgy disguise. But then they intended for me to be made, so Eva and Dinah would be unnoticed.'

'You're still annoyed about that then.' It was a statement, not a question. Jacob sighed.

'Wouldn't you be in my position?'

'Probably.' He yawned. 'Let's get to bed. We'll have plenty of time to try this insane, untestable plan on the weekend. The ritual isn't till the solstice.'

'Five weeks might seem like a long time, but it'll go before we realise, which reminds me Christmas is coming, the idea of shopping for presents is just what I need on top of saving the world. And Mum will want to have us around for Christmas lunch.'

'This conversation will have to wait until I've got more brain cells. Come to bed with me.'

'Alright,' she looked down into his icy blue eyes and smiled. He was hot, even upside down with purple rings under his eyes.

*

As they had in the weekends before, the four musketeers took Jacob's car up to the shed on Saturday.

274

Dinah's soccer game hadn't finished until after lunch so it was late afternoon by the time they arrived, although there was still plenty of light. Freya had brought along her duffle bag filled with various ritual bits.

'All the reading I've done on these spells confirms what Bianca made you do. You cast the circle, swear an oath, and use some symbolic items held in the hand to seal the deal. For this I'm using wormwood for the herb, smoky quartz which I've cleansed, and black candles. Are we ready?'

The four were sitting inside a ring of salt in the middle of the shed, she just had to pour out a little more to close the circle and start the ritual.

'Are you sure it won't hurt? Will Bianca know?' Eva asked, for the third time since they had agreed on the plan.

'We won't know until we do it. There's very little in the books, or online about doing this.'

Eva sighed.

'It'll be okay. You've got us here, and when we go back to the compound, I'll be there with you. I'm pretty good at reading people's thoughts, so I'll know if Bianca suspects you, and if she does, we just turn around and leave,' Dinah said.

'And she'll be okay with that will she?' Eva laughed nervously.

'This isn't an easy path. You've chosen to walk it with us, but no one will think less of you if you choose to leave,' Jacob said, putting his broad hand on Eva's slim shoulder.

'No, it's okay. I'll do it.' She sat up straighter and pressed her mouth in a determined line.

Freya cast the circle and called on the spirits to start the ritual.

'Today we honour you, Odin, All-Father. Our friend Eva wishes to bind herself to your will, and in doing so, to be favoured with your protection. We have no right to ask this of you, and humbly offer our service in exchange.' Freya lit the black candles. 'I use this wormwood to repel the influence of Bianca and Vali and to send any harm they may cause us back to them. I use this wormwood to heal our sister, Eva, to remove the venomous promise extracted from her by your enemy. I use this wormwood to confuse the enemy's senses and to obscure our true intent.' Freya dropped the pale grey green leaves into Eva's hands.

'Repeat after me. I, Eva Chowdhury, take this pledge freely and with full knowledge of what it may require of me.'

'I, Eva Chowdhury, take this pledge freely and with full knowledge of what it may require of me.'

'I pledge myself to Odin, All-Father, the protector and holder of knowledge, that my skills, my energy, my time and my body might serve his purpose.'

Eva repeated the phrase.

'I will follow the path the All-Father shows me, I will honour him in my thoughts and my actions, and all other allegiances will be forsaken.'

Eva hesitated, looking up at Freya with wide fearful eyes. She nodded encouragement at her friend.

'I will follow the path the All-Father shows me, I will honour him in my thoughts and my actions, and all other allegiances will be forsaken.'

'Now, I'm going to put the crystal into your hands, roll it between your palms and bruise the wormwood.'

Eva pushed her hands together and rolled the herb and crystal together, a fragrance that reminded her of cooking rose from the crushed leaves.

'Now for the blood part.' Freya handed Eva a small, very sharp knife. Eva pushed the tip into her left inner forearm, enough so her blood would drip down over the herbs and crystal. Freya picked up the candle and held it above her friend's open palms.

'I do this in the name of Odin, All-Father, protector of us all. We are honoured by your protection and guidance in our task.' She tipped the candle and fat drops of wax fell onto the crystal, leaves, and blood. Freya held the candle high above her friend's hands so the wax would have time to cool before it hit her skin. She looked up expectantly, and saw that Jacob and Dinah were staring at Eva as well. 'Do you feel anything?'

'I don't know,' Eva said.

'I think that's it.' Freya thanked the spirits for their protection, blew out the candles and drew a line through the salt, opening the circle. As she did, a great gust of wind felt like it went past her, although nothing seemed to move.

'What was that?' Dinah asked.

'You felt that wind too?' Jacob said. Freya turned to Eva, whose eyes were glazed over and fixed on her hands.

'Eva? Are you alright?'

For a long moment, Eva didn't respond, until she gave a great shudder and seemed to come back to life. 'I was trapped in a freezing forest. I thought I was never going to get out, but then there was a great rush of wind and I was back here.'

'That's Jotunheim.' Dinah said. 'Freya sees it in her visions.'

'How do you know?'

'Mind-reader, remember?'

Eva smiled, at least she tried to, her lips seemed slow to respond. Jacob helped Eva to stand, her legs were unsteady, and her movements slow and disjointed. They may not have been able to test if the ritual had broken the bond to Bianca, but it had done something. The sound of birds calling came through the walls of the shed.

'Hello, friends,' Freya called to them as she stepped out into the fading sunshine through the tiny wicket gate. The ravens were perched on the car both fluffed up and ruffled-looking. 'Something wrong?'

The birds shifted their feet, turning their sleek black heads this way and that. After a moment Jacob, Dinah and Eva followed her out of the shed. One of the ravens cawed loudly, picked up a small pebble looking object and landed in front of Eva.

'Uh, who are these two?'

'Huginn and Muninn, they're Odin's messengers.'

The raven hopped towards her, Eva bent down and held out her hand. 'Nice to see you.'

Opening his beak, the bird dropped a small flat stone in Eva's hand before taking flight in a cacophony of squawking. The two birds circled up in the air calling to one another before setting off towards the road.

'What is it?' Dinah asked, pulling Eva's hand towards her.

'I dunno.'

'Cool, it's a rune.' Dinah held up the small stone. 'See, it's got Odin's initial on it. I guess you're in.'

On one flat surface of the stone a symbol had been carved; it looked like a square, rotated to sit on one corner, with two lines extending the square, or possibly it was cross with an upside-down V-shaped hat on, or a strange fish.

'That's an O in the runic alphabet,' Dinah continued.

'If there was ever a sign from the gods, a rock with an O on it is a good one,' Jacob said. 'Give Eva her stone back, she should keep it with her.'

Dinah gave the rune back and Eva sighed.

'Is it wrong I feel slightly left out?' Freya said.

'You got the ability to throw objects across the room with your mind, you're still Odin's favourite. All I got was a rock with some lines on it.' Eva smiled at her friend.

'That's true.'

'Now what?' Jacob asked. They looked at each other.

'Dinner at a pub or straight home are my suggestions,' Freya said.

'I vote pub,' Dinah replied, grinning.

'You're not getting any beer,' Jacob said.

Dinah pouted in mock sadness.

*

The next evening Freya was in the armchair scrolling through YouTube looking for something to watch while Jacob was reading a book in bed when she came across a new video from the Children of Vali.

'Babe?' she called.

'Yeah?' Jacob replied from the other room.

'There's a new Vali video, will you come watch it with me? I don't want to be alone if they start saying something terrible.'

A loud sigh came from the other room followed by bedclothes rustling and grunting as he got up from a comfortable position. 'Put it on the TV.'

Freya cast the video from her laptop to the big screen. Bianca and Elsa were in the thumbnail, sitting in front of the plain purple background the group favoured for official videos. She shifted to sit by Jacob on the couch and took his hand.

'I have a bad feeling about this,' she said, pressing play.

'Welcome friends, we have some very important events to report to you today.' Bianca was speaking, eyes staring into the lens in an unnerving way. 'Last night something terrible happened. A change, a ripple, in the magical fabric of Melbourne. Someone performed a powerful, dark ritual last night, one that, despite being shrouded in shielding magic, I felt from the safety of our communal home.'

Freya turned to Jacob. 'Does she mean us?'

'Shh.'

'This magic is a direct attack on the work Vali has been ordained to do. We are creating a powerful circle to respond to the threat posed by other rogue groups.

'We have reason to believe the woman with scars around her eye, the empty soul, performed this dark magic to undermine Vali. It is only through his divine care we are able to keep people like this Empty Woman from taking us down a path which leads to ruin and death.'

'It's like she doesn't know she's the one trying to bring on an apocalypse,' Jacob muttered.

'Last week we welcomed six new women into our inner circle. It is this inner circle who do the rituals which keep us safe. We have been blessed to find so many skilled practitioners dedicated to the mission in such a short time. It's clear the day of reckoning will be soon. There are more and more spikes in magical activity across the city as this Empty Woman, and those fool enough to follow her, prepare to make their move. But be warned, we know who you are. We know you are coming for us, and you will not deter us from our purpose.'

Freya shuddered.

'At the next new moon, we will initiate the new members as full disciples of the circle. The clock is ticking, and it is on us to make sure we are ready for what's coming. Our followers out in the world will be keen to hear a few words from our glorious leader Vali, he will bless us with his presence at another time. The signs are there, the time is nigh, and we need the prayers and meditations of the faithful to ensure we are successful. Elsa will now lead us in a chant.' Bianca sat back her eyes on the younger woman beside her. Elsa shifted forward, adjusting her robe nervously as she began to chant something in old Norse.

Freya paused the video. 'I hoped she wouldn't feel us. So much for that.'

'You used some heavy-duty stuff yesterday, Odin sent that rune and probably put out a ripple or two as well. It's fine, they knew we were working against them before. Nothing has really changed.' Jacob squeezed her hand.

'The new moon is in two weeks.'

'What's the hurry?'

'Crossing between worlds is easier at the solstices. It's a significant day in the magical calendar and Vali is impatient to destroy the world and become king.'

'What happens if we fail?'

'If Vali starts the apocalypse, I assume frost giants come through from Jotunheim, storm all over the Earth, destroying everyone except Vali's chosen few. And then he ends up king?'

'That doesn't sound right.' Jacob frowned. 'Wouldn't the frost giants take over here if they invaded and killed everyone? Why make Vali king?'

'Maybe he's got some deal with them. But there's nothing to say they wouldn't screw him over as soon as the portal is open.'

Jacob shook his head. 'We have to stop them.'

'Vali or the giants?'

'Both, I suppose. Preferably we manage to prevent them opening the portal, but if not, we have to close it and deal with anything that came through.'

Freya shivered again. The more she heard, the more impossible the odds became.

Chapter 15

As the days went on Freya worried more and more about the second initiation. She'd dreamed several times of the tent room where Bianca chanted, soundlessly, the twelve women around the circle were there without their leader. Perhaps this was women's business. In the dream last night, Bianca handed around a cup of liquid, and each woman drank from it. They chanted for a long time and the image in Freya's head became stranger and stranger. Despite being a dream, she was sure the cup held a hallucinogen.

As she watched the maroons, reds, and browns of the fabric covering the walls and ceilings moved and swirled, Freya felt sick and tried to look away but wherever she moved her eyes the patterns and colours spun and billowed.

Freya looked up to see Bianca give Dinah a long-tailed flogger and instruct her to beat herself. The young woman's eyes widened in surprise, and she shook her head, but Bianca was firm. Dinah hit herself in the upper back, flicking the tails of the whip over her shoulder. Bianca snatched the whip back and demonstrated on herself how hard the hits should be on herself. When Dinah tried a second time the impact was visible in the wince on her face and the shudder through her body.

The dream went on and on, Dinah hit herself over and over. All sense of time was distorted, whether by the vision or by the liquid they'd drunk. The flogger went around the circle, each woman who was to be initiated punishing herself in front of Bianca, to prove that she was worthy. Then it came to Eva, what if she refused? Dinah would be left alone in the group, without a friend to turn to when the time came to open the portal, what if she did something to expose herself, or worse, forget her mission and help.

'I've been having bad dreams,' she had said to Jacob.

'I'm sure it's just stress.'

'They're like the visions I used to get; it's what is going to happen. Dinah and Eva will have to whip themselves. Shouldn't we tell them?'

Jacob lay next to her in bed, staring at the ceiling. 'Dinah will be frightened, if they're taking drugs as well it might be enough to throw her off her game. It's no good for her to lose her confidence. And I don't know Eva, but I can't imagine being forewarned will help. Not to mention if Bianca knows that they know we might blow their cover.'

'But Dinah can read my mind. How do I stop her from seeing it?' Freya bit the corner of one of her nails, a habit she thought she had kicked.

Jacob was silent for a while, she told herself she wouldn't interrupt his thinking, it was something she often did when he was considering his answer. 'Can you put it into your avatar? Like we did with hiding the protection spells.'

'They didn't work that way, I had to put memories into the avatar and the rest was hidden but it never worked on Dinah, not properly.'

'Maybe you'll just have to stay away from her till after the initiation,' he snapped.

'Why are you angry?'

Jacob rolled over and made a sound between a growl and a sigh. 'Because I hate all of this. My sister there without me. Magic we can't control. I want it to be over. Can't we just, I dunno, kill Vali and have it done with?'

'And make him a martyr?' Freya laughed a bitter laugh, shaking her head. 'Bianca would never let his cause die. She loves him too much, enough to share him with every other member of the inner circle it seems.'

Jacob turned back to her. 'We should probably warn Dinah about that.'

'I'd say she already knows, what with her mind-reading and all that. If she got within a few metres of him, she'd get more than an eyeful.'

'That's true. I'd feel better if we checked though.'

Freya sighed and pulled out her phone.

Hey Deens, I've been having dreams about you and the initiation. Vali might try to seduce you, and the others. So far as I can tell, he's already sleeping with everyone in mauve. Be on the look out and try to avoid being alone with him. I don't want to find out

whether he would force you. PS: I've told Jacob, but not in detail so maybe don't say anything.

'Sent. Does that soothe you?' Freya waved her phone in Jacob's direction, not allowing him time to read the message.

'Thank you.' He blew out a heavy breath. 'I don't know if I'll be able to get to sleep, I'm all jangly.'

'Warm milk?'

'I'm not eighty.'

'It works. I think we've got some sleep tea around somewhere.'

Jacob moved towards her; the heat of his body pressed against hers was comforting. It had been a while since they'd been intimate, with all the stress and trips out of town they had got into a funk. Although it didn't seem the most appropriate time, Jacob started to run his jaw across her shoulder, nuzzling.

'I thought you were angry,' she said, unsure she was reading his signals right.

'I was, but now since we're awake anyway…'

'I cannot understand you sometimes.' She turned to face him and pressed her lips against his. His smell flooded her nostrils, and she didn't need much more encouragement. 'But you make a good argument.'

*

The new moon was two weeks away, Freya and Jacob kept in touch with Dinah and Eva by text, but they didn't get together the following weekend, and Freya thought they might have gotten away with avoiding a face to face until after the initiation ceremony.

Eva had texted the group on Thursday night, Freya woke to see the message and a cold chill of fear swept over her.

Should we all have lunch on Saturday? I'd feel better knowing we'd had a chance to go over final strategies before the big night.

'Babe, have you seen Eva's message from last night?'

'No, why?'

'She wants lunch on Saturday. I don't think we can say no without making it obvious we're hiding something. How can we see Dinah without her knowing what I know?' She was pulling on her clothes ready for work more brutally than usual. She sighed and sat on the edge of the bed to lace her shoes.

'That does pose rather a problem.' Jacob leaned on the doorway to the bedroom, a piece of toast in hand. 'If it's only an hour or two, could you use the cotton wool protection thing? It might keep Dinah out for long enough that we wouldn't need to tell her about the dreams.'

'Wouldn't she notice I was using it though? I would be unreadable, something that hasn't happened before.'

'We could say it's an experiment? Seeing if you can carry on a conversation while actively maintaining the protection spell.'

'What happens when she tries to breach the spell? You know that's the first thing she'll try.'

'I'm confident we can get her to leave it alone if we present it right—'

'And what about you? You know almost as much as I do.'

'Shit.' He chewed and swallowed the last of his toast before brushing his fingers against each other. 'I won't come, I'll say I have to work at the last minute. If you're there it'll be alright. I hope.'

'I guess I'd better reply.' *Great, I'll be alone with Dinah, trying to not act suspicious while also maintaining a spell against her reading my thoughts.*

Sounds good. Where should we meet?

Freya sent a message to the group and went about her morning routine. Jacob left before her, as usual, and his reply came through as she was on the train into the city.

I've been called in to cover a shift last minute. I'll have to hear about it from Freya.

At least it wasn't the first time Jacob had worked on a weekend, the hospital where he worked had a skeleton staff over the weekend for any urgent care needs, although occupational therapy wasn't usually an urgent need, they had a policy of having someone on site for a couple of hours on Saturday and Sunday just in case. Jacob used the time to catch up on paperwork and reading journals, and Freya suspected he watched videos on his phone as well.

She practised the protection spell a few times during the day at work, although no one there would have been able to tell whether she was doing it. It used a very small amount of power and didn't require her to call on the source at all. When she got home that night, she was tired and her jaw hurt from unconsciously clenching trying to maintain the spell.

Jacob raised his eyebrows in question and concern when she arrived home. 'You look wrecked. Is it a takeaway night?'

She nodded and snuggled into his arms. 'You're lucky you're so cute or I'd be annoyed you don't have to go tomorrow.'

Eva and Dinah were already waiting for Freya when she arrived in the little Italian restaurant in Collingwood. It had been Eva's choice, given she would be driving up to the Children of Vali compound after they were done.

'I need to have at least one good meal before we go, I don't like or trust their food,' Eva said.

'I think they do it on purpose to distract you, not feeding you.' Freya said. Her white fluffy light had been cast around her as she left her car so Dinah wouldn't get any snippets on her way in.

'The protection spell's working pretty well. I'm not getting anything except the avatar stuff. Good one.'

'Thanks, Deens, but if you could refrain from poking at it, that's not part of the experiment.'

'I know, I was just sussing it out.'

Freya sighed.

'What's that for?' Eva asked.

'Nothing.'

'I don't believe you.'

'I'm worried about this ritual, that's all. The last one was intense, and I can only imagine the mauve robe stage will be more so.'

'You haven't had any visions about it? Nothing to give us an idea what to expect?' Dinah asked.

'Nothing clear, no. Other than the sex thing, which I've warned you about.'

'What sex thing?' Eva interrupted.

'Oh, I didn't tell you yet. Vali likes to sleep with all his disciples. I've seen more than I wanted on that front. You're a grown woman, so I trust you'll be able to decline him without too much trouble . . . unless you don't want to, but he seems like a dud.'

Eva sipped her coffee and regarded Freya over her cup. 'You dirty perve you've been watching Vali and his various women and said nothing.'

'I didn't ask for these visions. I'm sure I would have got the basic idea without having the graphic details projected straight into my brain.' She shook her head to dispel the images which had crept back into her mind's eye, after which she was careful to re-wrap herself in white fluffy light, that had slipped when she thought of Vali's conquests.

'Sorry, I didn't mean to upset you.'

'I hate having everyone's ideas in my head all the time, I can kind of turn it down, and when I sleep, I'm just asleep. I can't imagine having my dreams taken over by some creep,' Dinah said.

'You can't turn them off at all?' Eva asked.

'Not really. I can force them, like I can do them on purpose sometimes, but if they're not coming from me, they just come whenever they feel like. Mostly when I'm asleep.'

'It's a wonder you sleep at all.'

Freya closed her eyes for a moment, 'sometimes I don't, it was really bad with Victor and the Withering. But a person has to sleep eventually.'

The three around the café table were silent for a moment. Freya stared at her hands, her fork forgotten, hovered over her plate.

'How's it all going?' the waiter asked, the sudden interjection shook her from her stupor.

She looked up and forced her face into a polite smile. 'It's lovely, thank-you.'

The others murmured their agreement. As the waiter wandered away, buzzing from table to table in the busy way good hospitality staff had, Freya renewed her concentration on the white light protecting her, it had lessened when she considered the burden of her visions. She put her cutlery together on the plate, appetite gone.

'I don't have premonitions like you do, but I get a bad feeling about tonight. I wish you and Jacob could be there to back us up,' Eva said, her eyes glistened as though she were fighting back tears.

'You've got this. You're so strong and capable, just take everything in your stride, except perhaps sleeping with cult leaders, I advise against that.' Freya smiled, and

Eva pulled one side of her mouth up in an effort to be comforted.

'I've been wondering if we could, like, call you and Jake and put the phone in our pocket, so you can hear what's happening,' Dinah said.

'They didn't confiscate your phones last time?'

'Yeah . . . but I reckon I could fake it, maybe Eva could cough or something when I put mine in and I could pull it back out. You'd have to mute your end, so no one heard anything.'

Freya glanced at Eva, who looked back searching for the same information.

'I don't know if it's worth the risk. If she finds the phone, and sees you've called someone they'll know you're traitors, and you could be hurt before Jacob and I can get there, even if we're just down the road.'

Dinah's face fell and she looked away.

'On the other hand, if it makes you feel safer to have us on call, I'll support you. Eva?'

She chewed slowly, taking time to form her response. 'I think it's worth the risk.'

Freya nodded. 'Right. How big is your phone Deens?'

Dinah held up her smart phone, which was large and would not easily fit behind her hand or in her pocket. 'Should we get one of those little cheap ones?'

'Yeah. They have them in the supermarkets. We can grab one on the way up and you can send Freya and Jacob the number. At least that way no one will accidentally call you, and you can put your other phone in the collection. Winning all round.' Eva grinned.

Despite her misgivings, Freya was glad she'd be able to hear what was going on. She and Jacob would drive up and park somewhere along the road near the compound, ready to provide back-up. 'I will only come busting in if there's a genuine emergency. We have to do everything we can to keep up your covers.'

'Agreed. What about a code word? Something innocuous but that we wouldn't have cause to say in an ordinary situation?' Eva said.

'Any ideas?' Freya asked.

'What about "did we remember to lock the house when we left?"' Dinah said.

'Sounds perfect.' Freya looked at her watch, they'd been there over an hour and her ability to hold up her protection spill was starting to fail. 'I'd better get going. You'll be fine. I'll text you to say we're having dinner at my mum's as the signal we're in place. Just remember not to let anyone see the second phone.' She pushed out her chair and started to gather her stuff to leave.

'Thanks, Freya, you're the best.' Dinah and Eva both stood to hug her goodbye. In an extra effort of will, Freya held the protection spell strong as she had physical contact with Dinah.

Back in her car she sighed and let go of the spell. She'd had two coffees but they had no effect on the wave of fatigue flooding over her. Freya sat breathing slowly as she meditated to recover a little from the effort of her spell.

I hope Jacob thinks the phone idea is a good one, she thought as she started the engine and headed home.

*

'This is a disaster waiting to happen,' Jacob said as they pulled over ten minutes away from Vali's compound.

'You said that already. We can't contact them now, and I really think Dinah might have called it off if she hadn't had us sitting out here waiting to rescue her. The big silver four-wheel drive was sitting on the shoulder of a gravel side road.

'If I'd been at lunch, we might have been able to convince her it was a terrible idea.'

'I don't know about you but having ears on the ceremony makes me feel safer, and if they have a brain cell between them, they got the smallest phone they could find.'

'Sound quality will probably be terrible.'

'Yeah.' Freya watched Jacob's hands on the steering wheel of the idle car, listening to the clicks of the engine cooling and the silence of the country settled around them.

We're at mum's about to sit down to dinner. Have a good night!

Freya texted Dinah the code phrase but didn't expect anything back. A few minutes later her phone showed the message had been read.

'They know we're here. We'll get a call sometime, I guess we just wait.'

'Great.' Jacob shifted in his seat; he hadn't unbuckled his seatbelt. Freya released hers and turned to her partner.

Jacob couldn't sit still. He turned the radio on, then off again, he pulled out his phone and started scrolling through his social media before sighing and putting it down again.

'Did we bring a charger cable? In case the battery runs low,' he asked, reaching over into the glove box to rifle around inside.

'Yes, if you move your arm, I'll get it out.' Freya had put a charger into her handbag before they left. The last thing they needed was to be part-way through the call and have the battery die. 'I hope the phone Deens has is fully charged.'

She put the cable on the console between them, no need to plug it in yet, but Jacob was anxious and anything she could do to reassure him was a good idea.

The sky was a dull blue heading to grey as the sun set behind them. Previous rituals hadn't started until after dark. Freya tried to calm her thoughts, breathing through her nose, but Jacob's constant shifting, and tapping and sighing crept into her consciousness.

'Meditate with me,' she said without opening her eyes.

'I can't.'

'Try? Breathe, in for four, and out for four.'

There was a flurry of rustling as he settled himself into a comfortable position. He started to breathe more slowly, she matched his rhythm, they were in sync. She was starting to relax when her phone rang.

'Shit.' She opened her eyes and scrambled to answer, immediately putting their side of the call on mute.

All they heard for a while was rustling, perhaps fabric brushing over the microphone as Dinah put the phone in her pocket, or in her bra, so they could listen.

'Now you've had some refreshments and changed into your robes, which look wonderful, we will be starting the ceremony shortly. I'll collect your phones so we don't have any unexpected disturbances.' Bianca's voice was muffled, but audible.

'Refreshments?' Jacob asked.

'Maybe they put the drugs in the tea, not in the cup in my vision.'

'It's a good half an hour if you take stuff through food, but in a tea, maybe half that? I bet they wouldn't want anything to kick in before they were in the tent room, that would ruin the vibe.'

Some more rustling and mumbled words followed by the clunk of phones being put into the plastic tub.

'Follow me, Elsa will make sure we're all in.'

More scratching and muffled conversation; Jacob and Freya didn't speak. She strained to hear any scraps in the low murmuring and shuffling, and then there was quiet on the line.

'This ritual will signify your ascension to full members to the group. As Children of Vali, we must do everything we can to protect his legacy, his divinity, his goals. This is not to be taken lightly, and while we have done our utmost to ensure you are the right people to join the group, I will ask now, if anyone wants to leave? You must be here of your own free will.'

A long pause followed, Freya imagined Bianca was glaring at each person, or possibly walking around the circle daring someone to leave.

'Since you have all decided to stay, I will cast the circle and start.' Bianca used the same words to begin the ritual as she did previously, calling on the spirits of the compass points and the gods to watch over and bless their working.

'We will start with chanting a powerful mantra and you may start to feel strange. This is normal, accept the feelings and focus on repeating the words.' Bianca started the chant; and the group joined in. The words sounded Norse but Freya didn't recognise them.

'Do you know what they're saying?' she asked.

'No. It's too distorted to get a good idea of the words, even if I understood the language.'

The droning voices were soothing, Freya found herself becoming sleepy, docile. The repetition of the sound was like white noise, and although Bianca would no doubt be using her talent to influence the people in the room, the magic wouldn't work over the phone line.

The chanting went on and on, Freya looked at the time, it must have been at least half an hour. 'They'll be well and truly in the thick of whatever they took by now, not to mention the fact chanting like that makes you high.'

Jacob nodded, and a few minutes later the chanting died away.

'Your chanting had brought the blessings of the gods and the spirits upon us. To be joined with Vali and become one of his children, to be a part of the family and enjoy the everlasting life that his divinity promises, we put new initiates through a test of will.'

A blinding flash of light flared behind Freya's eyes and she found herself in the tent room with Bianca and the Children. She hadn't intended it, but the vision was intense. Bianca in her deep purple robe stood, walked to the centre of the circle and picked up the long whip. She began to flog herself, crying out a little with each strike.

'What the hell is that?' Jacob asked at the sound of the leather hitting flesh came through the phone.

'Bianca . . . flogging herself.' Freya's words were slurred, it was hard to make her brain send the signal to her mouth. Frowning, she added, 'vision.'

Jacob made an agreement sound, and Freya fell back into the unfolding scenario in her mind. Bianca hit herself thirteen times, then she held the whip out to the first woman in a pink robe.

'She's asking another woman to do it,' Freya said aloud.

The woman frowned and shook her head, but when Bianca didn't move, the woman took the flogger, stood, and repeated what her instructor had done. Freya counted thirteen strikes and the woman looked to Bianca for approval but received only an icy frown. She struck herself over and over until Freya lost count before the older woman held up her hand. The woman holding the flogger was weeping and shaking. She let the whip fall from her fingers and Bianca handed it on to the next woman in the line. One by one each of them flogged themselves.

'Eva is next.' Freya's throat was tight, she wasn't sure whose perspective she was in, but the colours and trails when someone moved showed they had taken whatever was in the tea. Eva had been watching the whip pass from one woman to the next and had set her mouth in a firm line. Barely a sound escaped her.

'Why is she taking so long?' Jacob asked.

'Bianca isn't stopping her. Maybe it's about suffering, or being broken down, and Eva is being stubborn. If only she showed her pain.'

Bianca put up her hand to stop Eva and passed the whip on to Dinah. In her mind, Freya saw the young woman stand unsteadily, take a deep breath, and start to hit herself. The sounds of pain that came through the phone was so much louder than any before, hidden in the folds of Dinah's clothing it picked up her voice clearly.

'That's Dinah, isn't it?' Jacob asked.

Freya nodded and bit her lip; in her mind's eye and in her ears, she heard the anguish of each strike. She counted thirteen and dreaded to hope they would be enough for Bianca.

'That is enough. Thank you, you are the last to be brought into the fold.' The sound of the whip thumping onto the floor came over the phone audio, along with Dinah's laboured breathing.

The vision in Freya's mind cleared and she was back in the car. She glanced over at Jacob; his face was tight with worry.

'My vision faded, maybe the worst is over.'

Tapping the face of the phone, she checked the time elapsed on the call, it was well over an hour. Her nerves were rattled, her head throbbed from worry and the aftermath of her vision.

'You have proven yourselves worthy of Vali's love. In the tradition of generations of witches before you the ordeal you have undertaken provides an initiate with grounding and experience before they join a group. You may find your mind and body feel the effects of this night for a while after we reopen the circle—perhaps hours, perhaps days. It's normal, we will provide you with blankets and some simple stew and tea to help you through the next few hours.'

The phone started to crackle and break up, buzzing and squeaking.

'What's happening?' Freya asked.

'Dunno. Maybe the battery is going, maybe the reception is dodgy—'

As he spoke the phone line cut out.

'Battery, I guess.' She looked at Jacob's face, his angular nose a slightly darker shade of grey against the navy sky. The silence stretched out, the sounds of the bush started to come to Freya's attention; a rustling of leaves, and then a thud on the bonnet of the car. They both jumped, before she recognised the sleek black shape of a raven.

'Hey, buddy. What's happening?' she said aloud. 'Can you turn the car on so I can wind down the window?'

Jacob turned the key in the ignition, the lights on the dash illuminated and the radio came back on splintering the peace. He stabbed at the radio power switch and shut it off as suddenly as it had come on. Freya pressed window down button and the raven, perhaps Huginn, hopped across the bonnet and landed on the window ledge, croaking softly.

'Is something up?' Jacob asked.

The bird tipped its head from one side to the other, clacking his beak together.

'Just visiting, are you?' Freya put out her hand to stroke the raven's breast, he was so warm and soft, it always surprised her. No more visions came, just a feeling of calm.

'What's he saying?'

'Nothing. I don't think there's a message. He just came to check up on us maybe.'

'Right.'

Freya continued to stroke Huginn's feathers in a sort of dreamy haze. Jacob was fidgeting behind her; she could feel him shifting and tapping.

Can you give him some of the calm? She asked the raven in her mind. He cocked his head and hopped away from her hand.

'Coming in, are you?'

The raven bobbed across the dash and settled himself in front of Jacob.

'He wants you to give him a pat too,' Freya said when Jacob did nothing.

'Uh, why?'

'Maybe there's a message for you?'

He turned to look at her, tension and apprehension written across his features, she tried to smile reassuringly and looked back to the bird. Jacob held out his hand, hesitating just before the breast, then made contact. The breath he must have been holding sighed from him and his shoulders dropped. They stayed in that position for what felt like a long time, Huginn pleased to accept the attention and Jacob transfixed, in another world.

Then the raven fluffed up his feathers and inelegantly exited throw the open window.

'Bye,' Freya said at the retreating black shape against the navy sky. 'You alright?'

Her partner didn't say anything for a while, swallowing a couple of times before getting anything out. 'He showed me the ceremony. I think Deens is okay. They're all like, passed out in the dorms now.'

'That's good.'

He had never really had the visions, it wasn't part of his talent, but if he hadn't calmed down and been reassured everything had gone to plan, he might have charged into the compound and ruined their chances.

'Do we go home then?' she asked. It was after eleven, they were out in the middle of nowhere and hadn't brought their camp gear.

'I don't think I can drive home . . . I might be made of jelly.' Jacob's face was blank, relaxed and his eyes were hooded.

'I'll drive us home. I don't fancy getting a motel, even if there were any open.'

The drive home was subdued, Jacob fell asleep almost as soon as they were on the highway and snored the whole way home. It wouldn't have surprised her if he gave himself a headache from the angle his neck was at.

*

Despite getting home after one o'clock in the morning, Freya was awake at first light the next morning. There were no texts yet from Dinah or Eva, perhaps it meant they were still sleeping. She was too restless to stay in bed and got up to try to read on the couch. But she was too anxious for that too. Everything in her body was on alert, and even though she was so tired as though her eyelids were covered in sandpaper, she slipped on her running shoes and went out for a walk.

Summer was only a few days away, but the mornings were still cool. The neighbourhood was busy with joggers and cyclists early on Sunday morning. The coffee shop where she brunched opened at seven, so she took the long way there, hoping to grab a coffee and maybe a pastry on the way back. She strolled around Fitzroy North, the wide streets with their central grassed areas and overhanging trees, brick workers' cottages dominated, but every so often there would be an apartment development.

Her mind was too turbulent for a podcast, so she listened to a playlist of nineties hits; songs she knew the words to but couldn't tell you how she had learned them.

'You're up early, or have you not been home?' the barista said when she arrived at the café at five past seven.

'Couldn't sleep.'

The barista winked, but Freya had the feeling he assumed she was still up from the night before.

I must look rough, she thought as he steamed milk for her latte.

Back home, her coffee cup and the paper bag which had held an apricot Danish empty, Freya crept in quietly so as not to wake Jacob. She needn't have bothered, his deep breathing came from the bedroom, every so often punctuated with a low rumble of snoring.

She opened the Alistair Crowley book, Jacob had read it in detail, but she had avoided it. He was so vulgar she found it unpleasant to read, but perhaps there was wisdom in there she was missing out on. He was famous for a reason, she supposed.

'Was it that interesting?' a deep, gravelly voice asked from above her. She startled and jerked upwards, the book slid from its position on her chest and onto the floor.

'I must have fallen asleep. What time is it?'

'Half-nine. I'll make coffee.'

So much for getting some research done this morning, she thought.

Checking her phone she saw there were several messages in the group chat from Dinah and Eva.

Survived the night. Lots to tell you. I'll have to come up with a story to explain the marks on my back if Dad sees. Fark, you didn't warn me there would be whips.

Eva had replied.

That was wild. If you knew about any of that beforehand and didn't tell us, you're a better bloody liar than I give you credit for Freya Gordon.

I'm so sorry! I had visions of the whole thing but I didn't dare tell you in case it put you off. I knew you would be okay. The ravens were very clear about this being the next necessary step.

Freya was terrible at keeping things from her friends and having it out in the open felt a weight lifted from her.

I knew there was something you were hiding from us! I told Eva but she said you were a terrible liar and I must be paranoid. You're brilliant at that shielding though, I tried to get whatever it was out of your head, and nothing. We're heading back now.

Freya wasn't sure if she should be flattered. They had been accepted as mauve members and were safe from any more tests or ordeals, for now.

Chapter 16

Eva and Dinah were both pale, their eyelids drooping, when they arrived at the apartment an hour and a half later. Dinah immediately flopped onto the couch, unheeding of her brother who was already sitting there. Freya vacated the comfy chair so Eva could rest; she would be exhausted after the ordeal and the drive.

'You survived?' Freya said.

'Barely,' Eva replied.

'I'm glad you were driving home,' Dinah mumbled from her position reclined on her brother's lap.

'How are your backs?' Jacob asked.

'I don't want to talk about it. Did you hear all that down the phone line?' Eva asked.

Freya nodded. 'I saw it in my mind too. I could have done without that.'

'We must have been so high, it seemed like a reasonable thing to do, but now every time I move, I'm reminded of the thudding, stinging pain.' Dinah flinched and shifted. The silence drew out between them.

Freya had slept poorly, but she was also tired of fighting, of being the saviour. She would have given it all back, her powers, her insights, to have her normal, two-eyed life back.

'Nothing else much planned till the solstice,' Dinah said, raising her head a little. 'I couldn't get much out of

Bianca, she's well-shielded, but some of the younger ones were easier to read. Elsa had the solstice in her head a lot—that seems to be the important day.'

'We've got a week and a bit between then and now, time to recoup, plan, and prepare ourselves for the last stand. We have to stop the portal to Jotunheim.' Freya chewed her lower lip for a moment. 'Victor managed to have the portal open for ages, but his didn't allow physical beings to pass through, it was only magical energy. Vali wants to create an actual doorway into the other world, something that he can pass through, and if he does that, there's nothing to stop creatures from Jotunheim from coming here. I don't want frost giants or anything else stepping into our world and trying to kill us, or feast on us, or whatever else they might do.'

'Agreed, Victor was an easy target compared to Vali. On a scale from one to evil genius, Vali's right up there.' Dinah laid her head back down and closed her eyes.

'Do you think he'd hurt us? I mean, would he kill us to get what he wants?' Eva asked.

'We don't know how far he'll take it. And I wouldn't put it past Bianca,' Jacob said.

'For someone who has recently joined, she's become radical quickly. Maybe she had been waiting for a messiah already, and now she had one. One that sometimes has sex with her as well.' Freya shook her head; Vali was very attractive, but he was insane, how could Bianca not see it?

'Some women are blinded by a sexy man paying attention to them,' Eva said, oblivious to the irony of her last few boyfriends. Freya nursed her second coffee, seated cross-legged on the floor it wasn't very comfortable and she started to get restless.

Meditation would help, she thought to herself, but there was no way to know how long Eva wanted to stick around, and they had to get Dinah back home before dinner. Freya shuffled over to the wall, leaning her back against it, her legs stretched out in front of her, and closed her eyes.

Focussing on her breathing, she tried to keep her mind blank and hoped no visions would interrupt her attempt to restore calm to her jittery brain. For a while, all she thought of was the sensation of the air flowing in and out of her nostrils. There were plenty of techniques to centre the mind, but this one felt right today. Sounds around her calmed, the mumble of the TV in the background, Dinah's heavy breathing, perhaps she'd fallen asleep, and were replaced with a sort of empty hum. A sound that was like silence but felt more like cotton wool. She braced herself for a vision.

Snatches and fragments of things she'd already seen flashed through her mind, painting the backs of her eyelids in dancing technicolour. Dinah and Jacob were sitting in the lounge, much as they were in the real world, but their eyes were darting back and forth under their lids as though they were asleep but they weren't.

The next moment she was in the field where the ritual would occur, only it was daytime. She was alone, walking through the long grass, following a goat track or something, until she realised it was freezing and she approached a massive, grey, hole in the world. All the hope drained from her, looking into the grey, frigid void, she was afraid, and then an enormous grey fist pushed out from the portal and grabbed her.

She opened her eyes with a gasp, whether it was a dream or a vision she couldn't tell. The others had no idea, busy inside their calm, sleepy bubbles. Freya stood and checked the time; it was after two o'clock. 'We'd better get you back to your dad,' she said, rather louder than she had expected. All three jumped at her voice as though coming out of a sort of trance, before blinking and agreeing.

*

Driving back to Fitzroy North in Jacob's four-wheel-drive, Freya stared out the window. Dinah had forgiven her, and Eva was okay with the small deception, but it still bothered her. She had lied to her friends; hidden something big from them.

'It was the only thing we could have done,' Jacob said, as though reading her thoughts.

'What?'

'You're silent and broody, I assume you're berating yourself for hiding stuff from Deens and Eva. But you shouldn't.'

'If I was them, I'd be pissed.'

'They probably are pissed, but they understand it was for the best. Vali is planning to destroy the world, being a little bit flexible with the truth is the least of our worries.'

'I—' she stopped herself. 'It's a slippery slope.'

'First, slippery slope arguments are bullshit, I've never known someone who tried marijuana one time who has inevitably ended up a full-blown crack addict who would sell their own mother for a hit. It doesn't work like that. There are some things we can compromise, like a little five-finger discount, but it doesn't follow that we'll become mass murderers. We each have our limits, and I don't believe for one minute your limit has changed because you left out a piece of information.'

Freya sighed. 'Why do I feel like such an arsehole?'

'Because you're a kind, empathic person, and it goes against your nature to lie to people.'

She pressed her lips together into a line.

'Ha! No come back to that, I must be right.' He put his hand on her knee, flicking a glance toward her before turning back to the road.

'Thank you.'

*

The next day back at work, Freya was sorting through her emails and preparing her to-do list for the week ahead. Her mind wouldn't focus, thoughts of the solstice and the ritual kept intruding. The air around her fizzed as though something was about to happen, like the smell of rain just before a thunderstorm, but it was not a smell. It followed her; walking to the station she looked up at the sky, searching for clouds; it lingered in the train and in her office. There were no goosebumps along her arms, but it wouldn't have surprised her if there had been.

'It's like I need to pop my ears, you know like in a plane, but I can't. The world isn't sitting quite right,' Jacob said on Monday when she asked him about it.

Eva said she felt weird but couldn't give any more details, Dinah was the same.

By Thursday, it was so distracting she decided to risk a visit to Theo. His eyes widened as she stepped into the little shop at the top of the stairs. Since her visit was during her lunchbreak, as usual, a few other customers were dotted around the cramped bookshelves.

'You shouldn't have come,' Theo whispered to her, his voice uncharacteristically harsh.

She was having none of his theatrical terror today. 'Do you feel it? It's driving me crazy, I can't do any work, my head is full of like, ants or static.'

'I haven't felt anything this—portentous since before the comas a couple of years ago. The energies are aligning for a big event. Whatever you were supposed to stop is about to happen and anyone with magical sensitivity can feel it approaching. Not everyone will know what it signifies.'

Freya folded her arms. 'I know all that.'

'What do you want me to tell you?' he asked, his voice cracking a little.

'What do I do?'

'Nothing. There's nothing you can do until the right time. This is a build-up, the energy is collecting, this is the intention of hundreds of people all concentrating on one thing for an extended period.'

Freya's focus softened and she stared over Theo's head.

The creatures in Jotunheim will be gearing up for the ritual too. I hadn't thought about their expectations bleeding into our world.

'I have to go,' she said, turning on her heel and dashing down the stairs back to her desk. Her mind spun with the idea that the portal could be opened from both sides, and somehow the inhabitants of Jotunheim would help. She couldn't tell Theo, he'd proven he couldn't keep information to himself, whether he slipped up on purpose or by accident.

Back at her desk, her emails had multiplied; everything was going too fast and too slow at once. There was no way she would be able to stop this ritual; they were the last line of defence in a battle only a few knew was happening.

Freya's skin prickled, goosebumps rose along her arms, and she felt lightheaded. She dashed into the bathroom, locked herself in a stall took some deep, controlled breaths. In her mind, she wrapped the pink cotton wool of protection around her, a bubble where she was safe and where the world wasn't ending.

'Freya? Are you in here?' a woman's voice called.

'Yeah, I'll just be a minute.' Freya looked at the time, already ten minutes late for a meeting she'd totally forgotten about.

'Graham and the team are waiting for you in the boardroom.'

'Thanks.' This was just what she needed on top of a panic attack, a six-monthly review meeting with her boss and the rest of the team. It had been in her diary for a month at least, but with everything going on she'd almost forgotten about it, and hadn't prepared as well as she would have liked to.

Freya texted the others in the group chat, then stood up and went to her meeting.

I've just had a really terrifying thought. Can we have a group call later tonight to talk about it?

It went fine, if a little dull, and was enough to take her mind off the impending solstice ritual. When she got home that evening, Jacob was in the kitchen chopping vegetables for a salad; the big salad bowl sat on the bench next to the chopping board and he was piling in everything they had in the fridge.

'Are you stress-salad-making?' she said, running her hand over Jacob's broad, hunched shoulders. He jumped at her touch, turning on her as though he hadn't heard her come in.

'It's you.'

'Sorry, I didn't mean to sneak up on you.'

Jacob mumbled something inaudible.

'You must have been really focused on those veggies.' Freya looked over his shoulder into the overflowing bowl. 'We might have enough now.'

Jacob straightened, rolled his shoulders back and looked to the bowl.

'I've may have gone overboard.' He ran the back of his wrist across his brow, pushing a rogue lick of hair out of his eyes. 'Next time you have a terrifying thought, can you leave that part out and ask for a chat instead? I've been trying to work out what the thought is, obviously something you don't want to discuss over text, otherwise you would have said it.'

'Sorry I freaked you out. I . . . had a freakout myself this afternoon and didn't think through how it would be to receive that text.'

'It's okay. What were you freaking out about?'

'Nothing, everything. It's hard to explain.'

'I'm making steak and salad.' He waved his hand over the bowl. 'As you see here, we have the salad portion under control. I'll put the meat on now you're home.' He smiled, but his eyes remained tight and sad, a smile to comfort her.

They ate without talking, Freya tried not to read into Jacob's silence, no doubt he was dying to ask her what she wanted to discuss but didn't want to make her go over it twice, they had a call scheduled for half past seven.

'I'll clean up,' Freya said, once they'd finished their meal.

Jacob nodded. 'Thanks.'

The kitchen was a mess, Jacob looked as though he had used every bowl and plate they had to create the meal, unlike his usual tidy style. Keeping her hands busy helped to calm her mind, but Freya still felt a sense of impending doom deep in her belly, the delicious meal was sitting in a ball right on top of it.

'You ready to call Eva and Deens?' Jacob asked from the living room; half an hour slipped away without her noticing, but at least the kitchen looked tidy.

They sat side-by-side on the couch, Jacob held his mobile phone in front of him, and started the group video call.

'Hey,' Dinah's voice came through, but she had no video yet.

'Hey, we can't see you.'

'Oh, hold on.' Some rustling came down the line as Dinah adjusted something on her end. 'How about now?'

'There you are,' Jacob said as her face came up on the tiny mobile screen, as she did so, Eva's face popped up. He turned the phone to hold it horizontally so they could see both at once. Eva's lips were moving but no sound came through.

'You're on mute,' Freya said.

'Can you hear me now?' Eva asked.

'Yep.'

'So, come on, tell us your terrifying thought.'

Freya took a deep breath. 'I had a small freakout at work. I went to see Theo about the . . . feeling in the air.

He said it was a cumulation of people's expectations something big and important was about to happen, and it occurred to me, what about the other side? What if their expectations and intentions are adding to the feeling? What if they're able to do a ritual on the Jotunheim side of the portal to open it? What if we can't stop them, and they pour through and destroy the world and it's all our fault?'

'Slowdown. That's a lot of what ifs.' Jacob put his free hand on her knee, adjusting his grip on the phone. 'We've prepared for this, we're much more ready to face this than we were last time, running down to the beach never having battle-tested our magic. And if we can't stop them, then we work on resealing the portal, just like we did with Victor.'

Eva's brows were drawn together, her deep chocolate eyes were shining with concern 'We can only do our best,' she said. 'If that isn't good enough then, maybe Odin will step in and give us a boost? I dunno, babe, but stressing about stuff we can't control isn't helping.'.

Freya looked at her hands, if she'd kept her concerns to herself, the other three wouldn't have to calm her down. If the world opened up and swallowed her now, she wouldn't have to worry about the ritual, or the embarrassment of this conversation.

'It's hard work being the chosen ones.' Dinah's voice was thicker than usual, as though she was crying, Freya looked up and saw her face covered in tears.

'Oh, Deens, I didn't mean to upset you.'

'It's alright, when you're upset you don't shield as well and wow, I didn't realise how much you've been keeping to yourself. You're having so many emotions and I'm can feel all of them.'

Freya wished she could hug her, but she was at home in her own bedroom. Instead, she concentrated on sending an emotional hug, given Dinah was tapped into her energy, she hoped it would help relieve some of the distress. Jacob put his hand on her knee, the warmth and weight were reassuring. Freya took a few breaths to calm her spiralling thoughts.

'I feel like an idiot,' she said after a long silence.

'You're not. I've been where you are, a couple of times.' Eva stared off to the side. 'Still, I'm glad I get to be one of the team, such as I am. Not like last time when I was trapped on the sidelines of my own brain.' She shivered at the memory.

'I'm glad you're here too,' Freya said. There was a short, exhausted silence.

'I gotta go, thanks for the call,' Eva said, waving a hand at the camera.

'Thanks, it was good to see your face.' Freya waved back, and then Eva was gone.

'Is she alright?' Dinah asked.

'I'm not sure,' Freya replied.

'She'll be okay. Just give her some space,' Jacob said. 'Speaking of which, we should let you go, Deens, you must have homework or something.'

'It's nearly the end of the year, so not much. But yeah, I should do some. Love you guys.' Dinah waved.

'Love you too,' Freya and Jacob said in unison before she hung up the call.

'Anything else bothering you?' Jacob asked, his voice low and gravelly.

'Other than saving the world? No. I wish it was over.'

'I feel the same. Let's go to bed, maybe read a book or something if you're not tired. Anything that's not research.' Jacob's eyes darted to the Crowley book on the coffee table.

'He's not invited into the bedroom, perve.' Freya smiled.

He smiled back and squeezed her hand.

Chapter 17

The day of the summer solstice, a Saturday, dawned cloudy and muggy. For Freya, it was a bad omen. She hadn't been sleeping well, in part because of the oppressive weather. Summer in Melbourne could be strange; she had memories of Christmas days past, where it had been raining and cold enough to wear a jumper, and others where they had all nearly melted in the stifling heat. This year she'd ignored Christmas, telling herself if they lived through the ritual and the world hadn't ended, she would brave the last-minute shopping to get her gifts and count herself lucky.

Eva was due to arrive at twelve, Dinah was in the spare room, still snoozing, and Jacob slept beside Freya. He wasn't having the same problem sleeping as she was; it was light outside but not even six o'clock yet.

Freya wanted to kick her feet in frustration. Today was the big day and she had only a few hours of disrupted sleep. The feeling of sandpaper under her eyelids was a constant companion these days. Sneaking out of bed, she tiptoed to the kitchen, a lot of coffee would be needed before this day was over. Their identities had remained safe from Vali and his cult for the final week, unlike the last time she was set to battle an evil wizard to save the world—they didn't know what was coming.

Taking the cup of fresh coffee into the lounge, Freya sat and tried to calm her mind. She wrapped herself in white healing energy and took several slow, calm breaths.

We're ready, we've done all the preparation. I can throw someone across the room if I need to, I have my three favourite people backing me up. Muninn and Huginn will be hanging around so if everything goes sideways maybe Odin will do something.

Inside her bubble of white light, Freya went through the moves she would need to make to stop Vali, rehearsing how each spell worked, how to call on the energy of the source, to protect herself, to shield herself from attack. By the time she'd finished going over everything in her mind, her coffee was cold and sounds of stirring came from both bedrooms.

A quick spin in the microwave resolved the cold coffee situation, by which time Jacob had shuffled out of the bedroom, stopping in the bathroom, before coming to stand with her in the kitchen.

'You been up long?' he asked.

'A while.' She glanced at the time. 'A couple of hours. I couldn't sleep.'

Jacob made a sound of agreement.

'I made coffee but it's cold now. I'll do a new pot for you and Dinah.'

He kissed her cheek and shuffled back to the lounge. It seemed to take a disproportionate amount of time for

Jacob to wake up in the morning, especially on a weekend.

'Have you put the location of the ritual into the map on your phone yet?' she asked, putting the fresh coffee in front of a more awake-looking Jacob.

'Yeah, I had a look last night, it's not far from the compound. It will be a trick trying to get close enough without them seeing us, it's all paddocks, but in the dark we should be alright. Dinah and Eva will be in the ritual already.' He ran his hand along his jaw before taking a sip of coffee, closing his eyes in enjoyment.

'I've been over it and over it in my mind. Once the ritual is started, they'll be distracted but it will also mean we are on the clock.'

'We could hide in the back of Eva's car,' Jacob said.

'I considered that. It could be hours and I think we'd get found out.'

'I was kidding.'

'I know. But my brain is in overdrive.'

Jacob put his hand out to rest on hers. 'How much coffee have you had?'

'This is my first. I tipped out the old one when I made more for you. I don't need coffee to be this paranoid. It's natural.' She smiled, but it was only for show. Her belly felt full of rocks and butterflies, fighting to make sure she knew something important was happening today.

Her brain bubbled with the knowledge today was the day, the test of her mettle as the chosen one. There were contingencies, but it would be so much easier if they could stop Vali before he let the beings of Jotunheim through into their world.

'We'll have to go on foot. Eva can drop us off somewhere under cover on the way in and we'll have to sneak up.' Jacob's knee started to bounce up and down.

'In the movies there's always a way to hide your approach, we need an invisibility cloak, or a hiding spell to get us up close before they see us,' she said.

'Crowley will be no help, he's not much for sneaking or being unseen.'

Freya stood and wandered over to the pile of spell books on the credenza, holding her hands over them and closing her eyes in case she felt one calling her. Nothing happened. She opened her eyes and shuffled the books around, trying to feel her way to the spell she needed, sure that Odin, or whoever was guiding her would point the way.

Her hand stopped on the dark brown leather cover of Hettie's spell book. 'Huh,' she said.

'You got something?'

'I'm not sure. Hettie's book felt right, so now I just have to find the right page and the right spell, and we're set.'

It wouldn't be that easy, nothing ever was. Returning to the couch she sat with her legs entangled with Jacob, they had often found themselves in that position in the last six months, researching, or reading a passage aloud to the other if it was pertinent or ridiculous, or sometimes both. Her fingers shuffled over the fore edge of the handwritten spell book, waiting for the little tug when something was right. After ten minutes of stroking the edge unsuccessfully, she flipped it opened and rifled the pages, eyes skimming the names of each.

On hiding in plain sight

A practitioner may have need to slip by an enemy, or a friend, unnoticed. Seidhr is a seeing magic, but one can twist it to be unseeing with a few small tweaks.

Bind each wrist with white and purple ribbons. White for purity and affinity to the moon, the hidden light giver, purple for power and hidden knowledge.

While tying the ribbons repeat the phrase below three times:

I am unseen in my journey, I am unhindered in my tasks, I am revealed only to those I choose.

Once you have said the words add a couple of drops of black wax to each wrist where the ribbons are tied to hold the spell in place until you're ready to be seen.

She showed the spell to Jacob who read it, frowning, before looking up. 'It can't be that easy.'

'Haven't we learned how much of this is channelling the power we already have into a shape that gives us what we want? This should do the trick, it's symbolic and straightforward enough to work, at least until we get close enough to blast the group.'

'Is that the plan, to blast them like you did with the water bottles?'

Freya hesitated. 'I hadn't thought about that part. Vali and Bianca are the two we need to deal with, the others are following them. Of those two, Bianca has the power. Whatever they're doing to open the portal we have to stop them. Destroy their magical ingredients or scare away the people in the circle. Once we do that, we have to stop them hurting us.'

'I think shock and awe will be the way to scare off the underlings, a lightning strike would be sick, and almost all of them would run. Probably would also destroy their paraphernalia too.'

'You seem to be confusing me with Thor, I can't call down lightning.'

Jacob grinned. 'Have you tried? Maybe you can. If not, I'm sure knocking them all out of the circle like water bottles will have a similar effect on morale.'

'Mmm hmm.' Despite herself she felt a little better after the absurd conversation, and the obscuring spell would help.

*

Eva, Freya, Jacob and Dinah left the apartment just before three that afternoon. They travelled in a little hatchback she'd hired, Vali's followers might have recognised Jacob's big silver four-wheel-drive. They had very little gear this time, no tent or esky full of food; if they came out the other side alive, they would spring for a motel room and takeaways.

The drive was quiet, Freya sat behind Jacob, who was in the passenger seat. Dinah sat behind Eva, who drove.

'I can feel the tension in all of you, even with the shielding,' Dinah said.

'Sorry,' Jacob said.

'I don't know what we can do about it. We're all pretty amped up.' Freya turned to Dinah. The young girl's eyes were narrowed as though in pain, it must have been brutal having to feel their anxiety on top of her own.

'I wish I could turn it off.'

'Maybe one of your meditations?' Jacob suggested. 'Eva can do one later, meditating while driving is not a great idea.'

Freya laughed, a small, choked sound. 'Need to keep your eyes on the road.'

'I'll do a mindfulness or something,' Eva said. Dinah grabbed Freya's and Jacob's hands, her palms were damp with sweat, perhaps they weren't the only ones who were feeling anxious.

'Close your eyes.'

Freya obeyed, focusing on the darkness behind her eyelids. This was often the time when visions would flood her mind, the same images over and over; the field, purple robes, wind, but this time all she saw was a warm red of the sun filtering through the delicate skin.

A clear bell-like voice sounded in her mind, it was Dinah's mind voice, all the muddiness and peculiarities of her speaking were removed in her mind, as though she wasn't using language at all but communicating in concepts.

We are strong. We are united. We will prevail against the enemy who wants to take power that is not his.

She repeated this mantra over and over in Freya's mind, and Freya started to repeat the words herself. She heard Jacob's inner voice joining in too. From the outside they would have been totally silent.

'Hey, guys?' Eva's voice broke into the trance-like state, and Freya fluttered her eyes open, dropping Dinah's and Jacob's hands.

'What's up?'

'We're about to turn onto the dirt track.' The car slowed to turn onto the unsealed trail and came to a stop. 'Jacob, jump in the back, and try to stay out of sight. When I get closer, I'll stop and let you out.'

With Dinah in the front, and the other two hunkered down in the back seat, Eva drove slowly along the trail.

'It's a bit potholed, sorry.'

She wasn't kidding, several times in the next ten minutes the bottom of the car scraped along the ground as they dipped into holes Freya couldn't see from her crouched position.

'Let them out here,' Dinah said. 'I can feel the others' minds.'

'We'll be there when the ritual starts, don't look for us. We don't want anyone to have reason to be suspicious of you,' Freya said. 'Are you ready?'

Eva turned in her seat and looked her in the eye. 'Not at all. But I'll do it anyway.'

'That's the way,' Jacob said, patting her shoulder before slipping out of the car. Freya squeezed the shoulders of both women in the front and followed him, closing the door quietly, in case anyone was in hearing distance.

Jacob headed into the wooded area beside the trail, his feet crunching through the fallen leaves, sticks and twisted barks lengths. He stepped carefully, as though to reduce his sound, and she did the same, but it still sounded loud to her ears.

They're going to hear us, she thought, the sound of her own breath was like a snoring bison.

'Let's stop up here behind this brush, I think we're far enough from the track no one will see us.' Jacob pointed to a clump of dense scrub just ahead.

'Okay,' Freya whispered back.

'Everything sounds loud because there's not much background noise, our voices won't travel that far.' He looked over his shoulder to smile at her.

'I feel like a heffalump clumping through cracking twigs and what not.'

'When we're in position, it will be okay, and we'll do that spell before we move towards them. Vali has no idea we're coming, he seems vain and idiotic.'

'Him maybe, but I wouldn't say the same of Bianca. She knows someone might try to stop her. She pushed me out of that open-day thing quick smart.'

Jacob made a non-committal grunting sound and forged on. No doubt he was trying to be encouraging and reassuring, but even after the meditation and all the preparations, Freya's mind was full of what could go wrong.

Sitting among the sticks and leaves waiting for the sun to go down was the longest couple of hours Freya could remember. The ground was damp, her bum was cold, and her legs kept falling asleep.

'I would make a terrible sentry,' she said as dusk settled, darkening the sky to a deep violet.

'You're a bit of a fidget. We can start moving soon.'

'How can you sit so still?'

'I don't know. Talented I guess.' He put his hand on her knee, and she was reminded how much she loved him. Here they were preparing to save the world, again. Before all the light faded, she pulled out the white and purple ribbons from her pocket and wrapped them around Jacob's wrists and then her own. He helped her to apply the black wax to seal them in place.

They joined hands and she drew on a tiny thread of power before speaking the words of the ritual over them three times: 'I am unseen in my journey, I am unhindered in my tasks, I am revealed only to those I choose.'

'Do you feel any different?' he asked.

'Not really, you?'

'I felt the juice you used, so something happened.' He let go over her hands and a shiver ran over her skin.

'I felt that.' She rubbed her hands up and down her jean-clad thighs, her fingers tingled slightly. 'We better get going.'

They stood, dusted themselves off and started walking back toward the track. Freya pulled the sleeves of her black long-sleeved T-shirt down over the binding to blend into the darkness better. They walked beside the trail, hidden still by the bush, until they found the edge of the clearing, from here they would have to rely on the cover of the spell to get from the trail to the Children's circle to stop them.

At the tree line they paused to take in the scene. Across the field a dozen or so cars were parked in an uneven semi-circle. Beyond them, silhouetted figures stood in clumps around a large fire, she could hear conversation but was unable to distinguish and words.

'They haven't started,' Jacob whispered.

Freya stole a glance at her watch, it was after ten o'clock. 'In the hours just before and after midnight the barrier between the worlds is thinnest. Depending on how much pomp and ceremony Bianca wants to put into it, they might start soon.'

'When they call the circle to order we make a move, yeah?'

She nodded and moved back half a step behind a straggly-looking stringy bark tree. It was impossible to see much of what was happening with the light from the fire turning the people she could see into silhouettes. The chattering and milling around continued for another half an hour, before Bianca's voice cut across the clearing.

'We all know why we're here.' Bianca's words reached her clearly, power was being used to amplify it.

'But before we start the formalities, Vali would like to speak to you all.'

The crowd cheered and whooped as their leader came forward to address them. His deep, sonorous voice rumbled across the meadow toward her, but she couldn't make out the words.

'Too bad he can't magically amplify his voice so we can hear him too,' Jacob muttered. She patted his shoulder in agreement. Vali's speech was longer than she expected, no doubt he was working them up into the right mind set, feeding them the story about creating a pathway to a better world, or whatever it was that he had told them to justify punching a portal to Jotunheim. When he finished there was more applause and whooping, the group were ready to spring into action.

'Thank you, Vali. Your words are an inspiration, as always,' Bianca said. 'We will form the circle now, if you'll all take your places.'

'This is it,' Freya whispered. There was less than an hour until midnight. From where they were she couldn't make out Dinah and Eva, but hoped they weren't too close together, their counter measures would work better if they were spread around the circle. Although Eva's powers were weak compared to the other three, every little bit helped.

A hush fell over the group, and they joined hands. Bianca chanted in old Norse, after a few repetitions the rest of the circle joined in, although Freya didn't believe they knew what they were saying. Under the cover of the droning voices, Freya and Jacob inched away from the shelter of the tree line.

The chanting grew and fell as they approached, sometimes coming up to a shout, other times fading to not much more than a whisper. Freya felt something in her chest start to flutter and vibrate, as though responding to the sound.

'Do you feel that?' she said, as loud as she dared.

'I have a bad feeling about it.'

They had reached the line of cars and took a moment to hide in the shadows. The circle was fifteen people, it seemed they had added a few to their number since the last ritual. Vali, Bianca and a couple of others wearing deep purple robes were in the northern part of the circle, flowing from their left and right were the mauve robed people, Eva was three people from Bianca, while Dinah was on the other side, four away from Vali. After the mauve there were four in the dusty pink robes of novices.

They've brought in people who don't even know what is about to happen.

All those in the circle had their faces raised to the clear sky and stars above them.

'We'll have to rush them from here before they get too much further into the ritual.'

Freya put her hand on Jacob's arm, she wanted to do one thing before they revealed themselves. With so many novices in the group, a show of strength at the start might be enough to get some of them to scatter, out of harm's way, and reduce Vali's numbers in one sweep. In her mind, she pulled a thread of silver from the source, curling it around and around itself to form vortex. She imagined it was a wind, coming down over them, blasting out the fire and pushing the members of the circle back. With a downward motion of her hands, she released her intention and loosed the vortex over the group. It was even better than she expected, the fire was flattened, its light reduced to glowing coals, while the vortex spread it lost some of its power but was still enough to force most people to take a step back, and two of the pink robes to fall onto their backsides.

She stepped out from behind the cars, striding towards the circle, Jacob followed her. She couldn't quite make out everyone in the dark but Bianca turned to her, fury written all over her scowling face.

'You have angered the gods. I am the chosen emissary of Odin,' Freya spoke, her voice filled with trickles of power, booming across the clearing. 'Stop this ritual at once or face the wrath of the All-Father.'

'Your cause is unjust. Your leader is a liar and a fraud. Leave now and we will not pursue you. Those who remain will be punished in the name of Odin.' Jacob's voice rang with a different power, the influence he exerted over people was thick in the air. The pink-robed members were closest to them as they approached and had naked terror in their eyes. After a moment of staring, the four pink-robed women, and three of the mauves fled on foot.

'Who are you to speak on behalf of the All-Father?' Bianca drew herself up to her full height, pushing all her power into her words and for a moment Freya doubted herself.

'I am Freya. I was chosen to stop you. The veil between the worlds must stay intact and I will destroy you all to ensure it does.' Freya wasn't sure where the words were coming from, her voice was strong, clear, resonant. Two more of the members wearing mauve looked around, fear written on their faces. Eva and Dinah were putting on a show of confusion.

Bianca took a deep breath in and brought her hands up in front of her, Freya knew the time for talking had finished, and she imagined herself in a bubble to block whatever Bianca was sending her. Jacob put up his hands and pushed towards Bianca and Vali, who were not quick enough to block his blows and went flying backwards. Dinah and Eva were now facing the other robed members, who were stunned and still trying to follow what was happening.

'You have no right to be here, we're doing the gods' work. Vali has shown us the true path,' one of the shouted.

'Why are you so afraid?' Dinah asked. 'You should leave while you still can.'

Around them, a wind had started up. Freya wasn't sure if it was a natural or supernatural wind, but her short hair stood on end, and the Children of Vali's robes whipped around their ankles, as they had in her vision.

'Your tricks don't scare me. I'm righteous and I will be protected,' Bianca shouted over the wind, having fought her way back to standing. Freya held her hand out to Jacob and he took it. She drew his strength into her, just a little, but it would be enough to double her power. This time in her mind she pictured the people in the circle being flipped and tossed across the meadow, creating an arc with her free hand she released the power. For a brief moment the world pulsed black, and she felt as though she might vomit, but then everything righted itself.

'Where's Vali?' Eva asked. Freya looked around and couldn't see him among the sprawled bodies.

'I don't see him.'

'He's run off. Slunk away like a coward,' Dinah said.

Bianca was back on her feet, only one other purple-robed woman tried to stand with her. Bianca grabbed her hand, dragging her towards the fire. 'You will not stop us.'

Freya looked up, the sky above them had clouded over, and the winds were increasing.

I'm not doing that, and I don't think Bianca is either.

Still holding the other woman's hand, Bianca screamed a few words in old Norse and flung her hand towards her and Jacob. It wasn't so much by thought, as by instinct, Freya threw out her first toward Bianca, and a blinding light spilled from her arm. A winding scribbly path was burned into her eyes when the flash faded and Freya saw Bianca lying flat on her back on the opposite side of the fire. The woman whose hand she'd been holding was beside her, their robes smoking.

They were the only two Children left in the dark, windy paddock now. All the other disciples had fled during the melee. Freya exhaled sharply, dropped Jacob's hand and ran towards Bianca. By the time she got there, Dinah was already kneeling beside them, her fingers on Bianca's throat looking for a pulse.

'She's dead.'

'Shit.' Freya looked down, the woman's eyes were open, staring unseeing at the cloudy sky. The wind had died away, and she was able to look at the body; a large black charred mark took up most of Bianca's torso.

'Did you throw lightning?' Eva asked.

'I . . . don't think I meant to.' Freya felt unsteady on her feet, and knelt beside the two prone women. Dinah moved to check the neck of the other woman.

'She's still alive.'

Freya fell forward onto her hands, her mind reeling and her vision dancing. She had killed a person, someone who thought she was doing the right thing.

'She wasn't going to let us stop her without fighting till the last.' Jacob's hand moved in small, comforting circles on her back.

'She didn't have to die.'

How could this have been the plan?

'We need to reverse the ritual. Something funky is going on in this field.' Dinah said.

'And find Vali, and get this one to a hospital,' Jacob added.

Eva was hovering near the remains of the fire; she rocked forward on her toes as though about to say something.

'You okay?' Freya asked her.

'Not really. If you put the injured woman in my car I'll head to the hospital, although what I'm going to tell them I haven't worked out yet.'

'You could say a lightning strike,' Jacob suggested. 'Give me a hand.'

Eva and Jacob lifted the purple-robed woman between them, she flopped limply as they carried her to the back of Eva's car.

'How will we get back?' Dinah asked.

'We could wait till some of the others come back for their cars and get a ride?' Jacob said.

'Gee, I'm sure they'll be really keen on that.'

'I need both of you to reverse whatever Bianca did before we . . . interrupted her.'

Freya, Dinah and Jacob linked hands in the middle of the field, now empty of all other living people. They stood beside the fire pit, Freya stood at the north of the circle, so she didn't have to look at Bianca's body. She saw the ravens above her, circling. Perhaps they had been there the whole time.

'We call on Odin, All-Father, and Freyja, the giver. We call on the spirits of the North, South, East and West to watch over us as we do our work.' She didn't cast a circle, as Bianca had already drawn one which hadn't yet been opened.

Freya closed her eyes and imagined a huge black room, so black it was impossible to see where the walls or ceiling were, as though the field where that stood had all its features removed and only the magical plane remained. Inside the room, she felt for trickles or remnants of power. At first, she saw nothing, then the blackness lightened a little to her left, about where the fire pit stood. Black lightened and a navy sliver began to resolve itself.

Do you see that too? she asked the others in her mind.

I see something. Not sure what yet. Dinah's voice responded.

Freya drew the energies of the other two into herself, making them a single being, and reached out again. The navy patch lightened through purple and mauve to a hot orange the colour of the embers. The light was glowing like fire, but coldness came off the place in waves—the gateway to Jotunheim.

'I call on the power of Odin, All-Father, to heal this rift. I repair the wounds to Yggdrasil, the sacred tree which holds the nine realms in their place. The power that opened this wound is defeated; their mission abandoned. We make whole again that which was torn.'

Freya said last sentence over and over as she imagined the orange patch getting smaller and smaller. It was more difficult than she had imagined it would be, much harder than the portal on the beach the last time.

Squeezing Dinah and Jacob's hands, she drew on their power as well as her own to continue the spell.

'We make whole again that which was torn.' All three of them were chanting now, and in her mind silver threads started to form across the gap in the worlds. It bulged and pulsed as the silver threads pulled the edges together, like a balloon covered in wool. She wasn't sure how long it took, the colours went back from orange, through the purples, navy and finally only a silver thread where the edges had met. Freya exhaled heavily, and she heard the other two do the same.

Fluttering open her eyes, she continued.

'I thank the spirits of the North, South, East and West for watching over us as we did our work. I thank Odin, All-Father, and Freyja, the giver, for watching over us as we did our work. The circle is now open, but never broken.' She released the hands of Dinah and Jacob. 'Do you know where Bianca's circle is to open it?'

'I saw her putting salt around the fire, I'll have a look,' Dinah said, her voice heavy with fatigue. A few moments later, she toed the ground and Freya felt power in the field release, like popping her ears. All at once, her legs were not strong enough to hold her up and she crumpled on the ground. Jacob sat next to her, not quite collapsing and Dinah joined them.

'Is it over?' she asked.

'Vali is still out there. The members of the circle are around here somewhere. Without Bianca they won't be able to cast the ritual again, but we need to find Vali before he can regather followers.' Jacob rested his head in his hands.

Freya wanted to lie down, the embers of the fire were warm and inviting, and the night was chilly despite it being summer. They rested in silence for a while, she wasn't sure how long before Jacob's head jerked up.

'What was that?'

'Maybe someone's coming back?' Freya looked around, her eyes had adjusted a little to the dark while they'd been sitting, and she saw movement to her right, over near the cars.

'She's terrified. We should tell her it's over,' Dinah said.

'It's okay,' Freya called out. 'We've finished fighting.'

The figure froze, perhaps deciding whether to continue forward, or hoping that if she was still, she would be unseen.

'What happened?' she asked finally.

'You were trying to cause an apocalypse, we were sent to stop you,' Freya replied.

'What's your name?' Jacob asked.

'Gemma.'

'I remember you from the open house a couple of months ago. I didn't think you'd joined up.' Freya tried to see the woman dressed in a dusty pink robe.

'I didn't at first, but then I changed my mind. It might have been a mistake.'

Jacob grunted.

'Come sit with us. We're waiting to see if anyone else slinks back now the magic is dissipating.'

'You were so powerful. I felt you working even from where I was in the trees.'

'That must be why I feel like a wet paper bag,' Dinah said.

'Do you know what that ritual was for?' Freya asked as Gemma sat a couple of metres away, not sure whether they were safe or not.

'Bianca and Vali were vague. It was about fixing a wrong, and getting power that was rightfully his, and saving the world. I didn't know what I was walking in to . . . but when the chanting started, I felt prickly and sick, like it wasn't natural.'

'Interesting.'

Prickly would have been the power Bianca was drawing, but I don't feel sick until afterwards.

'Do you think many others will come back?' Jacob asked, after a long pause.

Freya looked at the time, twisting her watch to catch enough light from the fire. 'It's after three. They drove here, if they come back, they'll be alright. We're not that far from town. Which is your car, Gemma? We need a ride.'

*

The trip back to Melbourne was long and silent. Gemma drove, Jacob sat in the front passenger seat beside her, Dinah and Freya in the back.

Freya sent a message to Eva struggling to hold her eyes open.

Did you get the woman to hospital?

The horizon was lightening as they approached the city. Freya asked Gemma to drop them off a few streets away from the apartment in Fitzroy North, just in case. Neither Jacob nor Dinah said anything until they were inside the house.

'I just left a woman dead in a field,' Freya said.

'What else could we have done? She was struck by lightning at some sort of party held by a cult. We weren't there. Gemma gave Dinah a ride home. The others we don't know anything about. Now isn't the time to figure this out, I need to sleep for a week then we'll sort out the aftermath of saving the world. Again.'

'I didn't intend to kill her. I didn't even mean to throw lightning, or call the storm. I don't know how that happened. She was my enemy, but she didn't deserve to die.' Freya slumped on the couch, her hands covering her face as she tried to keep the tears of exhaustion, rage, confusion and grief inside.

'Vali is the person to blame. He set this whole mess into motion. He found followers, he was prepared to bring on an end of the world level event, just to boost his ego, and give him magical power he believed he was entitled to. Vali twisted Bianca's mind to follow him and in doing that, she made herself his instrument. To stop him, we had to stop his followers opening the portal to Jotunheim.'

343

'I didn't want her to die,' Freya sobbed.

'I know, babe. None of us did.' Jacob sat beside her. 'We were there as emissaries of the gods, maybe they knew the only way to stop Bianca was to kill her, and Odin cast the lightning through you.'

'Or it was just an unintended consequence. They were dealing in big magic, and we used big magic to fight them. Sometimes the weapons we chose do more damage that we intended.' Dinah's words did little to comfort Freya, her guilt mixed with all the other emotions she felt at having stopped the ritual but not finished her task. She could feel her access to the source still there, last time when they were finished, her power had left her.

'I'm going to bed. And after that, we have to find Vali.'

Chapter 18

Freya slept through what remained of Sunday, waking for an hour or so to eat some toast and have a shower. Monday morning was Christmas Eve; neither Jacob nor Freya had to work, Dinah was still there in the spare room.

At midday she felt well enough to come out of the bedroom and assess what had happened after the ritual. Sitting in the armchair, she opened her laptop, and scrolled through the local news and police reports. Bianca's body had been recovered; the event was reported as a freak storm accident. It seemed given the people involved were linked to a known cult the authorities weren't interested in further investigation.

One woman was in hospital recovering from burns and a blow to the head from being thrown back, and one or two others had been released after an assessment cleared them of any serious injury.

At least I won't have the police coming after me.

Her belly rumbled and she looked up, seeing Dinah's pale blue eyes staring back.

'Morning.'

'Morning,' Dinah replied. 'I'm glad no one else was hurt.'

'You can read me? Is the avatar not working?'

'No, you're still mostly shielded, but your face is still easy to read.'

'Ah, the old non-psychic reading.'

'Breakfast?'

'I dunno what we have.'

'Oh.' Dinah flopped back onto the pillows, groaning.

If she gets hungry enough, she'll go and look herself, Freya thought, turning back to the screen. After a bit of searching in the weeks leading up to the ritual, they'd found the right Joseph Barrow, Vali's real name, who had worked in telemarketing and multi-level marketing schemes before starting the Children, according to his LinkedIn profile.

Now with his followers injured or otherwise scattered, would he be trying to regroup, or would he cut his losses and flee somewhere? The Children owned the house in the country where the group had been staying, and there was nothing in the news reports to say the property had been seized or their assets frozen pending investigation.

Dinah grumbled and levered herself off the couch to shuffled to the kitchen. 'There's nothing here. Can we get something delivered?'

Freya sighed. 'Sure. Use my phone to order something. Get something for me and Jacob too.'

Dinah rushed back into the lounge and grabbed Freya's phone from the table, tapping in the passcode which she had clearly picked up sometime during their time together.

Now we're ordering breakfast she has energy. Freya managed not to shake her head.

'Are we getting breakfast delivered?' Jacob emerged from the bedroom, his skin held a grey undertone of weariness, but otherwise he looked well.

'Yeah, Freya's paying.'

'I'll have lobster thermidor then.' Jacob winked in her direction. 'What you working on?'

'Looking for Vali, and for Joe who might have popped up again now everything's gone sideways. And to see whether the cops are after us. Looks like they're going with misadventure.'

'No surprise there, unless they admit magic is real, lightning is the only thing that could . . . uh do that.' Jacob clamped his mouth shut, no doubt regretting bringing up the death.

Freya went back to trying to find any other address details for Joe or Vali that they might be able to use to track him down.

'Old mate has an Instagram account,' Dinah said, waving her phone in their direction.

'Did you order food?' Jacob asked.

'Yes, I've done that and moved on. He has some photos of him down in Black Rock, with a woman who might be his sister. She works in this little café.' Dinah turned the phone in Freya's direction briefly.

'Show me.' Freya took her phone back, flicking away the text notification to say their breakfast was on the way, and went back to the Instagram feed. 'Here he is at

347

the launch of the café, his sister Jenny is the owner . . . wait that was three years ago. I suppose she might own it.'

'It's our only lead. Maybe Deens can go in and check it out. Your power is still working right?'

'Yeah, I can still hear everyone's thoughts.'

'Right, we'll find out if his sister is still there and whether she's seen him. If he's lost all his followers and friends, he might go back to family.' Jacob frowned.

Freya was worried too.

*

They ate breakfast and drove to investigate the café in Black Rock on the way to take Dinah home to her father. The two ravens were perched on the railing outside the apartment door when they exited.

'Hello, my friends. We didn't see you much after Saturday, thought you might have gone back to your master.' Freya reached out to stroke their glossy feathers.

'If they're still hanging around there's more work to be done,' Jacob said.

'We know that, do you think they have anything else to add?'

'You getting any vibes?' Jacob asked.

'Nope, maybe just moral support.' As she said it, Freya's mind's eye was filled with the image of a huddled figure on a windy beach. He sat on the sea wall gazing out to see in a defeated posture, but it was clearly the man who called himself Vali. And then the vision was gone. 'He's at the beach, moping. Thank you, friends.'

'Must be staying with his sister while he sulks. I can't believe he's run off without a thought to the chaos he's left behind,' Jacob said.

'He never cared about them. Cult leaders are in it for the glory and the power, they don't give a shit who their followers are, or what happens to them after it all falls apart.' Dinah's jaw was set, her arms folded across her chest.

'We'd better get going, the mission isn't over until we sort this twit out.' Freya dipped her head in thanks to the ravens who took off into the early afternoon sunlight.

The café, called Jenny's, was nestled in a strip of shops on the main road leading to Black Rock beach. The exterior walls were painted black, and large plate-glass windows took up most of the front. According to the sign, they closed at three, and the last few customers were sipping a late latte inside, two young singles with laptops, and one older fellow with a newspaper.

Dinah was the first in the door, head sweeping from side to side as she took in the surroundings.

'Are you still making coffees?' Freya asked.

'Yes, what can I get you?' the woman behind the counter had the same long thin nose as Joe, the same full lips and deep brown eyes, but none of the emptiness. Freya ordered three coffees to take away, Jacob and Freya chatted with Jenny while she made up their order, Dinah stayed quiet, her eyes narrowed in concentration.

It wasn't until they were all back in Jacob's four-wheel-drive that any of them spoke.

'What did you pick up?' Jacob asked.

'She's full of him, just under the surface. He's moved in with her, given her a sob story she doesn't believe a word of, claiming to have lost his job—'

'That part is true if leading an apocalyptic cult a job.' Jacob stared straight ahead through the windscreen.

'Anything with a beach? Do you think he'd be there now?' Freya asked.

'It was mainly complaining. We may as well go down there and wander for a bit. He might be sitting there like in your vision.'

Freya shrugged. 'It's not the worst plan in the world.'

'I would recognise his thoughts if he was close enough. Maybe we can cruise along the beach and see if I feel him?'

Jacob drove, Freya sat in the back with Dinah, sipping her coffee while Dinah held her other hand so the young girl could tap into Freya's power to amplify her own. There was no reason to hide now, Joe had no followers and very little power of his own.

'Left or right?' Jacob asked over his shoulder when they came to a T-intersection.

'Right.' Dinah's eyes were closed.

Jacob dawdled along the beach road at well below the speed limit. Thankfully there weren't too many other cars.

'There!' Dinah flicked open her eyes and pointed left, along the foreshore to a small parking lot. 'I can feel him in there.'

Jacob turned in and parked. Freya's hand tingled with the aftereffects of power Dinah has used, she supressed her urge to grin at the warmth of it. Vali, Joe, was the last obstacle in their way; the last thread to tie up, but she wasn't sure what she was supposed to do with him.

A sandy path lead over and through a small grass covered dune into the beach. A chill wind blew straight through Freya's T-shirt, she crossed her arms and squinted to look along the gritty, shell-covered beach. 'Nice day for it,' she said.

Dinah hurried off along the beach, Jacob and Freya following a little way behind. 'What happens when we find him?' he asked.

'I don't know. Victor managed to take himself out of the picture last time, but this fellow, he's slimier. Do we turn him over to the police for defrauding the cult members?'

'As if they'll be able to make anything stick.'

Dinah had stopped a little up the beach. 'He's up there, sitting on the sea wall, see?' She pointed to the black-clad figure hunched over about fifty metres from them.

'What's he thinking? Has he clocked us?' Jacob asked, his voice hushed.

'No, it's all woe is me, my plan dashed, what am I gonna do now, blah blah blah.'

Freya looked up and saw the ravens circling high above them, the other two followed her gaze. 'I wish I knew what I was supposed to do.'

As they approached, Joe didn't look up, too wrapped up in his thoughts. When Freya was about three feet from him, she cleared her throat, no response.

'Hello, Joe,' she said. He remained still. 'Vali?'

He turned his head toward her. 'Why are you calling me that?'

'It's what you called yourself, until a couple of days ago, you thought you were a god,' Dinah said.

'You seem familiar, were you one of my followers?'

'I was a mole in your operation. I was there when Freya killed Bianca and fucked up your plan to bring the frost giants here and take over the world. Which I don't fully get, wouldn't you be their bitch as soon as you let them in?'

'I had an understanding with their leaders.'

'The rest of humanity would be at their mercy, but you made a deal to save yourself. They were going to honour that, were they?' Jacob laughed.

'They would have made me a king.'

'Even you don't believe that,' Freya replied.

'What do you want?'

'You have to be punished for what you did.'

'And you have the authority to deal out those punishments, do you?' Joe swung his legs around off the sea wall and stood.

'We're Odin's chosen emissaries.' Freya flicked her eyes up to the two ravens, still circling.

'I'm not going with you. You can't make me.'

Freya drew her brows together, pulling a tiny thread of silver power from the source to bind him. He stood with his arms pinned to his sides, legs together, wriggling. Overhead, the grey overcast skies began to congeal and swirl. The bitter wind whipped their clothing around them.

'Let me go. You have no right. I am Vali, Odin is my father, I am vengeance you cannot stop me.'

'Come on, we're taking you to the cops and they can sort out what happens to you now,' Freya said, relaxing her grip on his legs and taking him by the shoulder to steer him. As soon as her hand touched Joe's shoulder a flash of bright white light surrounded them and deafening boom rolled over them. When her vision cleared, and the white-out started to recede, she saw Joe lying on the ground, his eyes open and glazed, blood slowly leaking from his eyes and ears.

'No, no, no, no, no—I didn't mean to.' Freya's voice was like an echo in her mind of when she'd said the same about Bianca.

'You might not have wanted him dead, but someone did. I guess when you're the emissary of the gods, they make things happen through you.' Jacob's voice was hollow, as though he didn't quite believe what had happened either.

'That's one way to ensure he doesn't hurt anyone else,' Dinah said. 'We'd better get out of here, being at the scene of a death by lightning once is probably okay, but twice, that's a whole other thing.'

Joe Barrow lay flat on his back, unseeing eyes towards the sky, on the concrete path next to the foreshore as Freya, Dinah and Jacob turned and hurried back the way they had come.

Epilogue

Jacob and Freya dropped off Dinah at her father's house without saying much. At the apartment later Freya found the contents of the cauldrons which held their avatars had completely burned up in their absence.

For days she avoided thinking about what had happened on the beach and in the field, before deciding to test her abilities. She had no access to the silvery source of power which was a relief and a disappointment in equal measure.

Dinah told them at dinner a couple of weeks later she'd stopped hearing people's thoughts as soon as Joe had been struck down. Jacob and Freya went back to their old lives as well as they could, although she spent a lot of time trawling through news websites for any updates on the cases around the two deaths, and about the Children of Vali, but there wasn't much.

Joe's sister Jenny wrote a short obituary for the newspaper; beloved brother and son, there was no mention of his other names, the things he did as Vali, or of the manner of his death. Freya was sure she hadn't cast the lightning herself, had been merely an instrument for an angry god, but ruminated on the two deaths and whether she could have somehow avoided them.

Going back to her job in the city seemed dull, but after all the excitement of saving the world twice, Freya was glad to only worry about whether her spreadsheet formulas behaved.

Every so often she would try to touch the source, just in case she was needed again, and every time she failed, she smiled. The world was right again, at least for the moment.